I0635892

Prospecting for Love

By Barbara Baldwin

Books We Love
A quality publisher of genre fiction.
Airdrie Alberta

Digital ISBNs
EPUB 9781771457484
Kindle 9781771457491
WEB 9781771457507

Amazon Print ISBN 9781771457514

Prologue

Peavine, Nevada Territory -- July 4, 1870

"You must undo the disaster that happened." A gravelly voice scraped against the dark cave walls, echoing in the frigid air.

Zeke literally shook in his boots, searching the gloom to locate the body that should have accompanied the voice. He could feel shivers shoot up and down his spine. Glancing at Lucky, he could see him, but he couldn't really see him. His brother shimmered against the dark walls of the mine, his scruffy beard and wrinkled face casting a glow such as it never had in real life.

Real life. That was the stickler, they had recently found out. Zeke and his twin brother, Lucky, had spent sixty years on this earth. Now it 'peared they both run plum out of any kind of luck. Else ways, why would they be shimmering in the dark hole of a mine, speaking to a body they couldn't see and having visions of the devil hisself rising up to take them to hell?

"Are we dead, Zeke?" Lucky always was slow on the uptake.

"Of course, we're dead. You think you glow like that 'cuz you took a bath last Saturday night?" Zeke growled at his brother.

"It doesn't appear to have sunk into your thick skulls just exactly what has happened." The voice came again, a blast of cold air against the old miners. Their worn flannel shirts did little to deflect the chill.

"We're dead, so I guess something pretty bad happened." Zeke figured if he was dead, he couldn't get no deader, so he might as well have his say.

"Your situation can be changed, if you decide to undo the disaster that occurred."

"What's he talking about, Zeke?"

"Jesse Cole's dead." Zeke didn't know how Lucky could forget that.

"We didn't mean for that to happen," Lucky said, tears springing to his eyes, for he had always been the emotional one. "It were an accident, pure and simple."

"I know," replied Zeke, "but we was his friends and we should've been watching his back." Nobody could feel worse about Jesse's death than Zeke, but he didn't see how nobody could change the facts.

"Jesse Cole is dead, and he shouldn't be. It wasn't his time, and plans had been made for him." The voice continued, gloomy as a hanging judge. "When something like this happens, it upsets the entire master plan, as well as the individual scheme of things. Numerous other incidents will occur which shouldn't, and those in turn cause other accidents, which in turn . . . You see what I mean."

Zeke wasn't sure he did, but agreed anyway.

"So you will just have to go back and fix it." The voice, now hard and unrelenting, grated on Zeke's nerves.

"How we going to do that?" Lucky questioned.

"Your current state of being allows you certain, shall we say, knowledge, and you'll know when and where."

"Oh, boy." Zeke didn't think he liked the sound of that.

"There's just one thing you must remember. You can't tell anyone in Peavine what actually happened."

"Now, how we going to manage that? Won't Jesse know he ain't dead no more?" Silence answered Lucky's question.

Zeke looked madly around. While he tried to find the source of the voice, at the same time, he almost hoped he couldn't.

"Hello?" Lucky's voice quaked.

More silence.

Zeke looked at Lucky, who stared back at him. Shrugging their shoulders in unison, they turned and trudged toward daylight at the end of the tunnel.

Chapter 1

Present Day -- northwest of Reno, Nevada

"Come back, damn it!" The girl kicked up dirt. "Curse your hide, you lousy --" she continued to shout and shake her fist at the cloud of dust until it drifted away at the end of the road leading from town.

She then curled her arms over her head in an angry gesture, turning in a circle. She continued to rant and rave, but Zeke knew she didn't yell at him or Lucky, since she couldn't possibly know they were there. After all, Peavine was a ghost town, and nobody lived there.

Zeke and Lucky glanced at each other, then back at the girl. "Boy, she's got a mouth on her, don't she?" Lucky asked.

The girl spun around and stared right at them, eyes wide and mouth open. Zeke hoped she didn't start hollering. Other times, people had come to Peavine and Lucky had decided, on a lark, to spook them. Most times, Lucky was the one that got spooked, but sometimes the women would cut loose with screams like banshees.

Lucky jerked his arm, but Zeke didn't even notice how hard he pulled. He was staring at the girl.

"Do you see what I see?" Lucky jerked again and this time Zeke did feel it. He pulled away.

"Yeah, I see, but I don't think--"

"Why not? The voice said we'd know what to do when the time come, and I think over a hundred years is 'bout time enough."

"Let's get a closer look." Zeke took a step forward.

"I'll be danged and hog-tied." Zeke whistled through his teeth as he came face to face with the girl. The wind blew her blonde hair around an oval shaped face. He could see more hair, tied back with a scarf, though it weren't as long as Elizabeth's.

Well, a girl could cut her hair, couldn't she? Even as he thought it, he knew Elizabeth would never do that. She was always primping and patting her curls.

As they watched, the girl lifted slim-fingered hands to her narrow hips, scrunched up her eyes and turned slowly around. When she stopped, her gaze sliced right through the two brothers to survey one dilapidated old building after another.

"It's kinda fun when they can't see us, ain't it, Zeke?" Lucky chuckled as he stepped behind the girl and poked her in the ribs. She swiveled around, quick as a wink, her eyes growing wide.

"Look at them brown eyes. She's the spitting image of Elizabeth."

"I know," Zeke breathed softly. Finally, after more'n a hundred forty years floating around Peavine, watching it slowly fade to dust as the mines petered out and people moved on to other ventures, it 'peared the time had come. The voice had said they'd know what to do, and lord knows they'd already had plenty long enough to figure it out.

This here girl looked just like Jesse's fiancée, Elizabeth Calhoun. He and Lucky'd had many a discussion 'bout the explosion that killed Jesse back in '70, and they came to the conclusion Elizabeth must have had something to do with it. Proving that might be like holding a lit stick of dynamite, but prospects looked a mite better right about now. Even so, he hesitated.

"'Pears she ain't going nowhere, so let's just keep an eye on her for a spell."

"What for? Let's just take her and run. I'm mighty tired of living like this. I've a hankering for a good game of poker and a bottle of whiskey."

Zeke turned to his brother. "She might look just like Elizabeth, but she sure don't sound like her now, do she? S'pose we take her back and Jesse finds out real fast that she ain't the real thing -- what then?"

Ellie's gaze rebounded wildly from one end of the old ghost town to the other. There was something spooky going on here. After that jerk of a guide had taken off with her camera, purse and cell phone, she had been just plain mad. Now, fear edged its way into her consciousness. She swore she heard voices a few minutes ago. And just as certainly, she thought she felt hands on her as she stood in the middle of the street. Perhaps it was the wind. She prayed it was the wind.

She dug in her jeans' pocket for her cigarettes. Thank goodness those had been in her pocket instead of her purse. As she lit the slightly bent cigarette, her gaze flickered from ruin to ruin, stopping only when she thought she saw a shadow against the wall of the building across the dusty street. "Calhoun's Bank and Trust," she said the name out loud. "Doesn't sound like a mining name at all."

She sniffed and shrugged her shoulders. The joke was on her. Before she started this assignment, she knew nothing about mining towns. Even now, her research had barely scratched the surface. She had told Hartman, her editor, she didn't want to know anything about the old west, but that hadn't gotten her out of the assignment.

"I want a story on ghost towns and old mines," he had insisted that day in the offices of Hartman Publishing, whose specialty was in travel magazines. "You get paid to write stories. What's the problem?"

"Why the old west? The closest I've ever come is liking the Eagles' song, Desperado," Ellie had replied. "You've always sent me to the eastern seaboard and on European tours. Why do you want to bury me under things old and dusty?"

"You know Jake is covering Civil War reenactments and Becky Sue is on maternity leave. That only leaves you."

Becky Sue and Jake -- now those were names that belonged in the west, Ellie had thought miserably as her boss droned on.

"Our largest client, Gold Mine Casino, wants a bigger draw, but most tourists don't go to Reno just to gamble any more. They want other things to do during the day. So, I figure we focus on hiking around nearby ghost towns, mines, panning for gold -- you know. Now, get a ticket and go west, young . . .woman."

So Ellie had spent days researching and digging around other old ruins in the hot, dry desert after landing in Reno a week ago. Last night, the cool, dark interior of the casino had beckoned, and she had spent most of the night playing Black Jack. Perhaps if she hadn't, she would have noticed the shifty eyes of the new guide who had been out front bright and early to pick her up. The casino had made the arrangements, and boy, would she let them have it when she got back.

Ellie sighed as she surveyed the old buildings. Regardless of whether she had wanted this assignment, she was still a professional and had done her background research. Peavine didn't look much different than Hunter's Station and Crystal Peak, two ghost towns she'd already visited.

She got up from the splintery boardwalk and sauntered around the buildings. She could almost visualize how it would have looked in 1870. Her gaze followed the line of old timber as she ticked off the buildings in her mind -- mercantile, hotel, bank, church. Unlike refurbished Belmont and Steamboat Springs, today's Peavine was totally deserted.

In her meandering, Ellie came to a creek that ran along the back edge of town. Her research hadn't uncovered much information about the creek, but this would make her story even better. She reached down and scooped some crystal clear water into her hands. Not only could people dig through the rubble for artifacts, but they could pan for gold in the creek. Very touristy.

She snorted as she stood, ready to head back to the buildings and look for a way into town. "Hell, the only thing Peavine needs is a couple of grizzled, old miners."

* * *

"Howdy, little lady." Zeke decided to make his presence known, figuring there was no other way they could get the girl's cooperation. When she whirled around at the sound of his voice, her eyes wide with fright and screeching like a polecat, he changed his mind but it was too late. Knowing that becoming invisible again would only make a bigger problem, he gritted his teeth and continued.

"I heared you hollering and yelling and wondered if I could help?" As he spoke, she scooted back, slipping on loose gravel along the creek bed, but she didn't go down.

"Who are you?" She whispered. Her voice sounded much better than when she shrieked, but Zeke wasn't a'tall sure she sounded like Elizabeth.

He stood still, hands at his sides, as she gave him the once over, staring at him so hard he almost blushed.

"Where did you come from? How come I didn't see you before?" The girl managed to keep her distance, one hand up in the air as though to ward off danger. Zeke could tell she was a mite curious and more'n a mite scared.

"Well, I live here."

She glanced around wildly. "Nobody lives here. It's a ghost town."

"Looky, Miss, I ain't gonna hurt you. I was up in the hills 'til I heared you." He figured it'd take a few minutes for her to decide he meant no harm.

The girl continued to stare, then slowly allowed her gaze to shift side to side. Zeke figured she was looking for someone else to jump out and grab her. He just hoped Lucky didn't show up yet.

She about made Zeke jump out of his skin when she sprung right up at him. "You have a car! You can get me back to Reno!" The girl was awful excited all of a sudden, waving her arms in his face.

"A wh … what?" Not seeing too many real people in the last century, the girl's closeness and excitement caused Zeke to stammer.

9

"A vehicle -- jeep, car, motorcycle -- I don't care as long as it can get me back to town."

"Well, we ain't got one."

"You don't -- you have to. How could anyone live out here without a car?" She was hollering again, and Zeke scrunched his head into his shoulders.

"What sense do it make to have something that we can't work?" Zeke shrugged and turned. He had seen contraptions like the girl mentioned whenever tourists had come to the ghost town. But the few times people had wandered off to the creek and he and Lucky had tried to work the horseless wagons, they couldn't get them to move. "Heckfire, we don't even got a mule no more. Come on."

The girl sized him up once more. Zeke guessed since he was old as the hills and shorter than her, she figured she could outrun him if'n he tried anything.

She followed him to the porch of Murphy's. Zeke watched her light a cigarette. He sniffed appreciatively at the wisp of smoke. He couldn't remember the last time he'd had tobacco, though he usually chewed. He was just about to ask her if she had a plug when he saw Lucky running up from the direction of the mine. Zeke could tell by his shimmer that Lucky hadn't solidified hisself.

"'Cuse me, Miss," Zeke said hurriedly and jerked his head at Lucky as he scooted back into Murphy's, hoping his brother would follow.

"You talked to her." Lucky accused, poking Zeke hard in the belly with a bony finger. "You showed yourself."

"How else we going to get her to help us?"

Lucky didn't have an answer for that, and hung his head.

Zeke knew how to make Lucky feel better. "Make yourself visible, Lucky."

Together they moved back outside. Night had fallen and for a minute Zeke panicked, not able to locate the girl. When the flicker of a fire caught his eye, he breathed easier.

They hurried passed the alley to the hotel, where the girl sat huddled on the boardwalk, her knees hugged tightly to her chest. She glanced up as Zeke drew near, eyes widening at the sight of Lucky. She grabbed a piece of wood from the edge of the fire and swung it at them.

"Who's he?"

Zeke thought he heard a note of fear in her question, but at least she didn't scream again.

Before he could answer, she chuckled and shrugged, dropping the wood back into the blaze. "Hell, I asked for two grizzled old miners, so what do I expect?" She looked from one to the other, an eyebrow raised. "You are miners, aren't you, or is this some incredibly sick joke of Hartman's?"

"'Course we're miners -- the best." Lucky boosted, then his face fell and shoulders sagged. "Well, we used to be, a'fore the accident back in seventy--"

"Who's Hartman?" Zeke interrupted, poking Lucky in the ribs before he could spill the beans.

"Never mind. I really doubt you two would know him." The girl shrugged off his question. She tossed more wood on the fire, the flames now jumping and sparking several feet in the air.

"You trying to burn the town down?" Lucky demanded.

That brought a snicker. "Like it would make any difference?"

"'Course it would. Peavine's one of the richest gold towns in the territory."

The girl looked around. "Excuse me if I'm missing something here, but there's nobody in this town. Who's going to care?" Although Lucky was dense at times, the girl's sarcasm wasn't lost on Zeke.

Lucky continued as though she hadn't spoken. "In 1870, why, there was over two hundred people living in this town. This here hotel you're hell bent on burning down had real leather seats inside." He turned and pointed across the street. "Calhoun's bank backed more'n one mining venture. There was even a church and post office called Poeville and a ten stamp mill."

"Well, la-tee-da." The girl didn't act at all impressed.

11

Zeke had a feeling she was all bluster to cover up her fright.

"This here's Lucky, my brother." Zeke felt maybe knowing their names would help set her heart to rest. "I'm Zeke."

She looked from Lucky to him, back to Lucky then to the fire, ignoring them both. How would they get her to help them if she wouldn't even talk to them?

Lucky didn't take no offense and began chattering away. "We don't get us many visitors here. Why'd you come? What's your name?"

"It doesn't matter. I just want to get back to town."

"That'd be a feat, for sure, seeing as how we got no way to get you there."

Silence met his statement.

Finally, with an audible sigh, she said, "Ellie."

Lucky's face fell. "Your name ain't Elizabeth?"

The girl made a face. "God, no, although that would be better than Eleanor. That's why I go by Ellie."

"But can we call you Elizabeth -- since you don't 'pear to like your own name?" Lucky asked hopefully and Zeke got the feeling he was pushing way too hard.

Ellie's forehead scrunched up. "What is your problem? Why would I want to be called that?"

Zeke piped up when he saw Lucky's face scrunch into a frown. "I'll explain to Miss Ellie."

"Why can't I explain?" Lucky argued.

"'Cuz I'm the oldest, that's why."

"You always say that and it ain't fair. We're twins."

"Yeah, but I come out first."

"P-l-ea-se." The girl interrupted them, then proceeded to cuss. Lucky's eyes opened in shock and Zeke had an awful feeling even if they convinced this girl to help, it would only get them in more trouble.

Zeke turned to the girl and tried to explain. After all, the voice didn't say outsiders couldn't know. But, how could he explain that their friend, Jesse, was dead and they had to make him undead?

"Look, we can try to get you back to town, but could you maybe help us out first?" He took her silence for a good sign and continued. "We got us a friend named Jesse Cole that's in trouble. The only way to fix it is to keep something else bad from happening."

"I'm sorry about your friend, but I did lose a lot of equipment, not to mention my purse and ride back to Reno," Miss Ellie replied, waving a hand off to the west, even though Zeke knew Reno laid to the south. "The sooner I get back and report it, the better chance they'll have of finding the guy. Besides, what's your friend got to do with me?"

"You look just like Jesse's fiancée, Elizabeth, so we was thinking you could take her place 'til we find out who killed . . .uh . . .tried to hurt him." Zeke waited for that idea to soak in.

"Now wait a minute. I'm not doing any kinky sex games."

Zeke could feel his face flame. He cleared his voice. "No, no. Lucky and me think Miss Elizabeth had something to do with what happened. If you was to take her place, then we'd figure it out for sure this time."

"You want me to play undercover cop? How's that going to get my equipment back?" She raised a brow in question, looking just the same as Miss Elizabeth did whenever she had quizzed Zeke about Jesse's whereabouts.

Zeke hoped God would forgive him for lying. It just seemed to him a man's life was worth more'n a couple pieces of equipment. "We'll get your stuff back, Miss, but first we gotta take you back to Peavine with us and make sure things go right this time."

"Back to Peavine? This is Peavine, and there's nothing here. What exactly do you mean?" Now she not only looked like Elizabeth, but sounded like her too -- always questioning him.

Before he could come up with a likely excuse, Lucky jumped right smack into the middle of things.

"If'n we take her back to Peavine, how we going to tell her apart from the real Elizabeth?" He asked.

13

Zeke thought, then said, "It's got to be something visible."

The girl held both arms in front of her, elbows bent, her fingers straight and close together. She widened her stance and braced her feet and Zeke thought she might try to hit them. She didn't look the least ladylike, and he began to doubt she'd be much help a'tall. Still, they had to try. He took a step toward her, and she raised a hand threateningly.

"Get away from me, damnit! I don't trust either of you and I don't believe your story."

"She has ear bobs," Lucky said, having ignored everything else since his earlier concern. "I'm dead sure Miss Elizabeth don't, cuz it just might hurt to have a hole poked in your ear."

"That might work," Zeke agreed, "but we gotta do something 'bout her swearing. Miss Elizabeth would never say words like that and how we gonna make sure this one don't?"

"I'm not going anywhere with you so what difference does it make?" The girl hissed at him through clinched teeth.

In the next instant, Zeke knew they were in trouble. His brother started shimmering and glowing 'til Zeke could hardly see him. One look at the girl's face told him she was having the same trouble. Lucky sometimes forgot to concentrate on being solid.

Zeke might have been able to explain the shimmer, but Lucky reached out to grab the girl's arm and his hand went right through her.

Zeke began to count. "One, two, three, four, five--" The girl fell forward in a dead faint and Zeke caught her under the arms. "Well, she lasted longer than most."

Lucky shrugged his shoulders. "I didn't mean to scare her."

"Might be the best thing you ever done." Zeke grunted as he turned the girl over. "Now concentrate and grab her legs." When Lucky caught hold, together they carried their burden to the mine.

"I guess we can worry 'bout her swearing once we get her back to Peavine." Zeke shook his head and sighed. He only hoped he'd be rewarded for his patience, for the Lord knows he was gonna need lots of it.

In the distance, where the mine shaft intersected with another tunnel, Zeke could see a bluish glow off to the right – the same light that had vanished the day Jesse Cole died.

"Come on." He motioned to his brother and grabbed the unconscious girl. They scurried towards the glow, never slowing down as the light became brighter and brighter until it appeared to swallow them right up.

Zeke dropped his burden when he felt himself falling, empty space all around as he tumbled head over heels. He couldn't shout, couldn't feel nothing as the brightness swirled around him. He only hoped his brother and the girl were following him through the spiraling emptiness.

Chapter 2

Ellie landed with a thunk in front of an old cabin. She rolled to her hands and knees, trying to catch her breath. A few minutes later, a man dropped to his knees beside her.

"Elizabeth, I glanced out the window and saw you sitting here in the dirt." There was a pause in which all Ellie could hear were her own frantic gasps for breath. "Where's the buckboard? Are you all right?"

Ellie couldn't think, and the man's questions confused her. She looked around wildly, her gaze finally focusing on the two old coots from the ghost town.

They pointed a finger at her and the man, then patted themselves on the back as though they couldn't believe they were really standing there. They somehow looked different, too, but it took too much energy for Ellie to stay focused on them. She closed her eyes to stop the dizziness and tried to recall exactly what had happened.

They had asked for her help and she said no, she was sure of that. She scrunched her forehead, looking around, but all she could see were trees edging a small clearing. At the back sat a cabin. Where had the ghost town gone?

She shook a finger at the two men, sucking in a breath to yell, and immediately began to cough. The man patted her none too gently on the back, which didn't help at all.

"Elizabeth, where's the buckboard?" He asked again.

"Who?"

Zeke hurried up. "Jesse wants to know where the wagon is, Elizabeth." He stressed the names and Ellie realized that regardless of her wishes, these two crazy old men had managed to take her to their friend's home.

Exactly where that was, she had no idea, but she didn't have to like it.

In anger, she pushed herself back on her haunches, turning to the man they called Jesse, ready to malign him for having such idiotic friends. The words died in her throat.

Plaid flannel covered incredibly broad shoulders, and while she couldn't tell his height because he squatted beside her, there was entirely too much of him to be short.

Stormy blue eyes scrutinized her to see if she was hurt. Even as she watched, their color lightened and crinkle lines appeared as he grinned. A scruffy growth of beard and tousled black hair framed his face and yet he looked great. Definitely not GQ, but he had a rugged appearance that ignited Ellie's basic instincts.

Perhaps she could manage a few hours as this man's fiancée. After all, she didn't have a ride back to town yet.

"Elizabeth, are you hurt?" The words came out deep and throaty. "How did you get here?"

Never one to be taken in by a man, Ellie now found herself mesmerized by his voice. But his eyes questioned her, and she suddenly realized she had no idea what he had said. On top of that, she didn't know how to respond because she wasn't Elizabeth.

Lucky rushed to her aid. "Maybe she decided to ride out here?"

Jesse chuckled. "Ride? A horse? This is Elizabeth, Lucky. She'd just as soon eat rattlesnake as ride a horse." He turned to her with a grin, apparently pleased with himself for defending her. "Isn't that right, Elizabeth?"

Ellie had finally caught her breath and could utter more than one word at a time, and now she was so mad she sputtered. She had never ridden a horse and had absolutely no desire to do so. However, she detested the smug expression on this man's face and his words that implied she wasn't at all capable.

She glanced around but could see no horse. Regardless, she jutted her chin out and lied defiantly. "As a matter of fact, I did ride out here, but the horse--"

17

"--got spooked and throwed her," finished Zeke.

Jesse scowled and looked at the three of them. Ellie doubted he believed them. She wouldn't believe a story like that. Then he shrugged, standing and extending a hand to help her up. "Perhaps that explains your clothes, then."

Ellie glanced down. What was wrong with Levi's and boots? Not much different from what he wore, except his sleeves were rolled up to show very muscular forearms, and the denim hugged his hips and crotch in an almost indecent manner.

"For a woman who's always lecturing me on upbringing and manners, you've displayed a little uncivilized behavior yourself today." Jesse's eyes twinkled as he spoke, and though Ellie thought he teased, she began to think she didn't like him very much.

She dug in her pocket for her cigarettes. "Look, I only came here because--"

Zeke grabbed her hand before she could withdraw it, interrupting her in the process. "That fall musta jarred your brain." To Jesse he added, "I'm sure Miss Elizabeth could use a cup of coffee."

"You're right. I'm sorry, Elizabeth. My manners do sometimes desert me. Come along." He reached for her hand.

Again, Zeke stepped forward. "Just go on in and get it, Jesse. I'll dust Miss Elizabeth off and bring her to the porch."

Jesse arched a brow but then shrugged and turned toward the cabin.

"Damn it, Zeke, what's going on?" Ellie turned on the old prospector the minute Jesse disappeared into the cabin. "And don't you dare touch me," she added when it appeared he would swat her butt with his hat.

"Quit that swearing, Missy." Zeke growled at her, then muttered to himself, "Darn it all. This is gonna be a lot harder than we thought."

Ellie couldn't believe her ears. "You cart me off to Podunk City, or wherever the hell we are, and you think you have it rough? I told you I wouldn't help." Ellie was still searching her brain for some illusive thread of time she had lost in the process of getting from Peavine to here. "Besides, how can I act like this Elizabeth person when I know nothing about this. . . this man you have me attached to."

"Now, you're not attached, 'xactly. Miss Elizabeth hadn't started making marriage plans or nothing like that. 'Sides after what happened, I doubt Jesse'd marry her, anyway."

"Just 'xactly what did happen?" Ellie mimicked, but her sarcasm was lost on him. Zeke's face scrunched up in thought and Ellie sighed in exasperation. Lately, nothing in her life had been easy. "Out with it, Zeke."

"Well, seeing as how we're back now, and Jesse ain't dead--"

"Dead?" Ellie definitely didn't understand.

"Ah, dead on his feet from working," Zeke added hurriedly. "Maybe it don't matter no more. What day is it, anyhow?"

"How would I know? It was Saturday when my gear got stolen, but why do I get the impression I've lost some time along with my belongings?" Ellie couldn't shake the feeling that something wasn't right. She looked around, trying to find a familiar landmark, but because of her lack of knowledge of the region, everything looked foreign.

"Say, where's Lucky?" She realized the other old timer had disappeared again.

"I sent him to get rid of the real Elizabeth."

"He's going to kill her?" She couldn't believe two old prospectors could be so callous.

"No, just get her out of the way so as our plan will work."

"If you have this Elizabeth person out of the way, she can't get Jesse into any more trouble. So why do you still need me? Just take me back to town."

"There's more to the problem than that." Zeke looked decidedly uncomfortable. "Look, just watch what you say. I'll explain the plan . . .later."

19

Somehow, Ellie doubted it. A churning started in her stomach. In agitation, she reached for her cigarettes. Zeke tried to grab them away, but Ellie was faster. However, seeing his crestfallen face, she stuffed them back into her pocket instead of lighting up. She looked at him as he nervously shuffled from foot to foot. "You don't have a plan, do you?"

Zeke's silence was incriminating.

"Damn your hide, and Lucky's too," she hissed just as Jesse came out on the porch with two steaming mugs of coffee.

"Elizabeth, are you coming?"

"Elizabeth?"

Zeke poked her in the ribs and whispered urgently, "That's your name."

Ellie narrowed her gaze, hoping to thoroughly mortify him with her anger, and to make him worry what she might do. Then, quick as a wink, she pasted on a sweet smile and turned back toward the cabin. "Coming."

She heard Zeke's frantic whisper behind her. "Remember, no swearing, no smoking, and your name is--"

"Ellie," she stated loud enough for both men to hear.

Jesse looked at her in surprise, then more thoroughly as she sat on the step and took the coffee he offered. A slow grin spread across his handsome features. "I tried to call you that from the time you wore pigtails, but you always said Elizabeth sounded more grown-up."

"Well, perhaps the fall from that horse did some good after all," Ellie replied, wondering if he already saw through their ruse. She began to feel guilty. While she hadn't wanted to help Zeke and Lucky -- she had only wanted to get her assignment done and get back to town -- neither was she a vengeful person. She wouldn't deliberately hurt another human being.

How would Jesse feel if he found out they were lying to him; that she wasn't who he thought she was? Zeke had said it was to keep him from getting hurt. Ellie didn't know what to believe. She did know that at the first opportunity

20

she had some serious questions that Zeke better be able to answer.

* * *

Jesse invited Zeke and her to remain for supper. While she would rather get on with whatever plan Zeke had concocted, she couldn't very well say no to her supposed fiancée. He took a pot from over an open fireplace, bringing it to the table along with a loaf of bread and a wicked looking knife. He dished up the meat stew and fresh bread and poured them some water in crockery style mugs.

Ellie traced a crack in the mug with a fingernail. Ellie Weaver, connoisseur of fine wines served in the best crystal all over Europe, sat in a rustic cabin in the woods drinking water from a broken cup. There was definitely something ironic here. Yet the man called Jesse didn't look the least out of place in the one room cabin.

Ellie savored the rich broth of the stew and thought perhaps this guy had some talents -- like cooking -- that she could admire. Especially since she came from a family of microwave dinner gourmets. As she ate, even asking for seconds, she looked around the cabin.

It was definitely old, with a fireplace on one wall, a bed on the other, and the table in-between. Two shelves by the bed held a few books. Figuring this guy probably only spent weekends here and then returned to a nine-to-five job, she wasn't surprised. She thought she might like a peek at his reading material, though, to see what he liked. With a shrug of indifference, she guessed financial manuals or e-commerce.

She ignored the men's talk as she continued to assess the cabin. Pegs on the wall by the door held clothes, and some roughly made shelves and a counter supported foodstuffs and a pitcher and basin.

Her brow crinkled as she took a second look. She didn't see a coffee pot, toaster oven, or a ceiling fan. A single lantern sat at one end of the table.

How odd, she thought. Even modern rustic cabins had electricity. Another lesson learned about the wild west for her travel article -- leave your curling iron at home.

Thinking back on her reason for being in Peavine, she still didn't understand how she ended up at this cabin of Jesse's. The last thing she remembered was being on the hotel steps in the ghost town. She recalled Zeke saying he lived in the hills, and assumed this cabin also sat in the hills near the ghost town. Zeke and Lucky must have carried her here. The why of it evaded her.

She would rather they had left her in Peavine, just in case the sheriff came looking for her. Regardless of what the two miners had said about helping, all she wanted to do was get back to Reno in time to catch her plane.

After dinner, Jesse poured more coffee from a battered old pot and Ellie thought how nice it was to be waited on. She listened to them talk about mining, of all things. She supposed she should listen more closely for background material for her article.

Instead, she tried unobtrusively to study Jesse. The combination of black hair, blue eyes and ready smile made him devastatingly handsome. But more than his looks, she sensed a gentleness about him. Most of the men of her acquaintance were too busy being macho to be tender. In Jesse, his sweet smile didn't detract from his masculinity but rather enhanced it.

His voice was somewhat cultured and Ellie wondered how he had ended up in a cabin in Nevada, even for the weekend. Momentarily forgetting her role, Ellie spoke up during a lull in the conversation. "So, what do you do when you're not playing woodsman?"

Jesse cocked a brow at her question.

Zeke jumped in. "Miss Elizabeth, maybe we'd best get you home to rest a spell. You know Jesse's a miner; he don't got no other job."

Ellie shook her head. She'd done enough research to know there were few active mines left, certainly not near Peavine, Nevada, and definitely not any that were privately owned. "The mines have petered out--"

Lucky came bursting through the door just at that moment, breathing hard as though he'd run all the way. Zeke cleared his throat shaking his head vigorously at Ellie when Jesse turned towards Lucky.

"Lucky, where'd you run off to?" Jesse questioned, and Lucky's face immediately turned even brighter red.

"I, uh," he stuttered, then shrugged. "I had me an errand to run." He pulled a plug of tobacco from his pocket and bit off a chew, grinning at his brother.

Ellie hid a grin behind her hand, seeing the agitated look on Zeke's face. Lucky, who always seemed to take orders from Zeke, had apparently stopped somewhere along the way to get himself a treat. Seeing it, though, made Ellie want a cigarette, but knew she couldn't smoke in front of Jesse. Zeke had said so.

She only hoped a Quick-Trip was somewhere close because her pack was almost empty. Then she remembered she didn't have any money on her, and they were too far from town anyway, so it was all academic.

"I suppose we should be walking Miss Elizabeth back to town," Zeke said, scooting back his chair to stand.

"Town? You can walk me to town?" Ellie sprang up, instantly angry. Did Zeke mean the ghost town of Peavine or back to Reno?

Jesse touched her arm, his warm hand causing tingles to shoot across her skin. "Elizabeth?" At her annoyed look, he started again. "What is wrong? You've acted strange all day."

Ellie stood, hands on hips, glaring at the three men. Little did she realize her posture so exactly mirrored Elizabeth's that any charade they were trying to perpetrate was instantly cemented. If that hadn't done the trick, her words did. "What's wrong? These two old coots lied to me, that's what."

Ellie saw Zeke standing behind Jesse waving his arms and shaking his head, but that didn't stop her. She was mad. "They said you were in trouble and needed help. They forced me to come out here."

"Forced you? You mean you wouldn't come and see me on your own?" The hurt was unmistakable in Jesse's voice.

"Well . . .that is . . .I had things to do," Ellie tried to backpedal.

"I see. Then perhaps we should get you back to town so you can do them."

Ellie looked outside. "It's dark." She didn't like the dark.

"Yes, it usually does that at night." Jesse's sarcasm gave Ellie pause. Was he so tenderhearted that her one comment had punctured his entire male ego? Then she saw his grin.

"I'm sorry." She stated simply.

In answer he extended his arm and Zeke and Lucky rushed to open the door, all the while arguing over the plug of tobacco Lucky kept in his possession.

Ellie allowed Jesse to lead her down the path. When they got to a creek, he led her to where flat rocks had formed natural stepping-stones to the other side.

Disappointed, she realized that this was probably the same creek she had seen earlier in the day. That meant they weren't very far from Peavine ghost town, but were too far from Reno to walk -- in the dark. At the moment, she thought she might prefer to stay at Jesse's cabin.

As soon as Jesse hopped the last rock, she clutched his arm again as he walked unerringly forward. She tried to keep from thinking of the blackness surrounding her and the very long dark night ahead in the ghost town. She searched her mind, instead, for anything to discuss so there was noise.

"I understand there are several Fravel mines in the area," she stated, and instantly Jesse's arm tightened beneath her hand.

"Elizabeth, you know I won't discuss anything having to do with Clayton Scott or his mines. Why would you bring it up?" His angry reaction was so startling, Ellie couldn't think of a response. "Is that the 'something you had to do' -- visit with Clayton Scott?" Jesse pulled away from her and stomped off ahead.

Ellie could hear Zeke and Lucky "uh-oh-ing" behind her, but she didn't know what she had said wrong.

"Wait," she called out to him. This was like performing in a play when everyone knew the script except her. She hurried to catch up with Jesse, turning to face him and walking backward since he didn't stop when she stepped in front of him. Trying to imagine how the unknown Elizabeth would handle this, and hoping to gain insight into the situation, she smiled sweetly and said, "Jesse, please don't be mad. I keep forgetting--"

"How can you forget Scott owns most of the rights to Fravel's mines on this side of the ridge? Did you also conveniently forget he runs your father's bank, which holds notes to most of those same mines?"

"He does?" Ellie questioned without thinking.

That stopped him. In fact, he stopped so abruptly that Zeke and Lucky just about collided trying to keep from bumping into him. Even in the dark, Ellie could see the questions in Jesse's eyes.

Think fast, she told herself. Being an independent, freethinking woman, she hated what she was about to do.

"Of course he does," she twittered, waving a hand aimlessly. She giggled, hoping she wasn't spreading it on too thick. "You know I have no head for business. Father would always handle that."

"Yeah, well, I wish he were still here to do it. I don't trust Clayton Scott any further than I can throw him." Jesse's tone indicated he was pacified, and as Ellie moved to his side, she shot evil looks at Zeke and Lucky. Boy, did they have a lot of explaining to do.

They broke through a line of trees and suddenly there were lights from town. Ellie blinked and shook her head, an unsettled feeling gnawing at her stomach. Her feet slowed. Soft glows came from several windows, as though fireplaces were lit or candles used instead of iridescent light bulbs.

Ellie's gaze swiveled from side to side; her stomach plummeted and her chest heaved. She stumbled, a flash of realization screaming through her brain. If Jesse hadn't grabbed her, she would have fallen face first in the dirt.

"El, what's wrong?" It was a question Jesse had kept repeating all day, it seemed, but Ellie sure didn't know how to answer him.

Buildings swirled in crazy patterns before her eyes. She hugged herself, squeezed her eyes shut, then reopened them, trying to focus on something solid. Newly painted signs hung over several buildings -- Calhoun's Bank and Trust, Murphy's Mercantile and Feed Store. Slowly, as she walked further down the street, she tried to make sense of what her eyes saw but her emotions refused to acknowledge.

The buildings on the main street were the same structures as she had seen earlier that day when her guide had left her stranded in Peavine -- with one major difference. These buildings were new; long years of wind and rain hadn't damaged their fixtures.

She struggled for breath, knowing she had to get away from the ghostly shapes that seemed to jump out at her in the dark. She didn't want her mind to shuffle the fragments into a solid thought. All she wanted to do was get back to Reno, and home. This was definitely not what she had bargained for when she took this assignment.

Apparently Jesse noticed her pallor, for he hurried her along, turning down a side street to the second house. He led her up the two steps onto a wide covered porch.

Ellie looked from the door to Jesse. Why had he stopped here?

"You're home." Almost as though he read her mind, he turned the handle and the door opened beneath his grasp, squeaking slightly.

Didn't people lock their doors around here, Ellie wondered idly? She looked into the dark interior. If she ventured across the threshold, would she be permanently tied here; would she never escape and get back to where she belonged?

26

Panicking, she turned around, looking past Jesse to where Zeke and Lucky stood. Lucky appeared quite pleased with the arrangement, but Zeke's face was still apprehensive. At that moment, Ellie hated them both because they were the cause of her distress.

If not for them, she wouldn't be in this predicament. For that exact reason, she had to depend on them, because they were the only ones who knew how she came to be here. And how to get her back to where she belonged. Conflicting emotions caused her to lash out in anger.

"You two, inside, now." Ellie pointed as she barked the command.

"What?" All three men clamored at once.

Ellie gritted her teeth and squeezed her eyes shut. She breathed deeply and counted silently to ten. She had to get past her fear and talk to Zeke and Lucky alone. She didn't know Jesse at all, so she couldn't predict what his reaction would be if she exploded in front of him. He might have her hauled off to jail or something; some place Ellie couldn't escape from.

"Excuse me. Might I have a word with Zeke and Lucky, please?" She tried to sugar coat her words, but almost gagged on the effort.

"Why?" Jesse pushed his hat to the back of his head and a curl of black hair fell across his forehead.

Lord, he was a handsome guy, Ellie thought. But he's not yours, her other side countered. She reminded herself she didn't even want to be here -- especially now that she had a vague idea of where here might be.

"Why? Well, let's just say they did me a mighty big favor earlier today, and I want to see they're properly rewarded." She hoped her gaze flashed fire at the two old prospectors.

"Shucks, Miss Elizabeth, it can wait for another day." Zeke replied, and Ellie figured he had caught her drift right away.

"What do you mean, wait?" Lucky asked, clearly confused. "Why can't we get our reward now?"

Ellie liked Lucky, for he was gullible enough to play right into her hands. "He's right, you do deserve something very special for what you did."

Jesse didn't seem inclined to linger. "Then the boys will see you in, Elizabeth." He nodded his head and touched the brim of his hat.

"Ellie," she reminded him, but he'd already turned away.

"Zeke, you and Lucky don't keep Elizabeth up too late, and get yourselves some shut eye. We've got a long day tomorrow and the two of you look a hundred years old."

The minute Jesse stepped off the porch and into the night, Ellie herded the other two inside, swinging the door shut behind her. Again, it creaked, making her think of ghosts and haunted houses. She had to find some light. Her fear of the dark overshadowed everything, even her anger.

Making out the outline of a lamp on a nearby table, her shaky hands managed to strike a match and light the wick. Immediately upon the lamp catching, she swung on the two men.

"What the hell have you gotten me into?" She shouted and instantly got a hand clamped against her mouth.

"Missy, you just gotta quit talking that way." Zeke pleaded, his shadowy gaze becoming more distinct as Lucky moved the lamp on the table closer.

She clawed until he let go.

"Look, I'll talk any da...damn way I want." Lucky's crestfallen face did nothing to abate her anger. "When you asked me to help -- and I distinctly remember saying no -- there were a few things you forgot to mention. What am I supposed to do now? Take me back this instant." Ellie stepped forward, hand on the doorknob. She would rather stay in the ghost town, in the dark, than here where she didn't understand what was happening.

Zeke blocked her path and they stood nose to nose. "You can't leave."

"And why not?" She could do as she pleased.

Zeke ducked his head to the side, shifting his gaze away from her. "'Cuz we don't know how to get you back."

"You don't know . . .that's ridiculous. There's got to be a way." Ellie's heart was pounding with anxiety. She wiped her sweaty palms on her jeans, trying to make sense of all this.

"OK, calm down," she muttered to herself. She lifted her hands, palms up, in a placating gesture, even though she seemed to be the only one upset. She closed her eyes for a moment and took a breath. "You said you had to keep Jesse from getting into any more trouble. How long is this trouble expected to last?"

Zeke shrugged. "I don't 'xactly know what part of the month it is."

She raised a brow and glared at him. "Do you even know what year it is, Zeke?" She knew her sarcasm hit home when he scrunched his shoulders and looked anywhere but at her.

"1870," he whispered.

She had made the comment mockingly, not ever believing what her eyes had seen. She just knew there had to be another explanation. Now, shock rippled through her. She shook her head, trying to clear it, clutching the back of a chair for support.

It was impossible to fathom that two old miners had somehow taken her back in time. And yet everything she saw, from the houses to the lanterns to the lack of any type of vehicle, assured her it was true. If it had been daylight, she would have walked right out of there and headed -- where? Without her maps or any money, how far would she get?

"How long do I have?" The question made it sound like Ellie was terminally ill, but at the moment, that was exactly how his news impacted her.

"Maybe a month, give or take a few weeks."

"A month?" She squeaked. Earlier today she had thought it might be a lark to be Jesse's fiancée for a few hours, but she definitely didn't want to be here a month. Not in 1870. She thought of the lack of electricity and modern conveniences. "I don't know how to live here."

"Do what ladies do." Zeke said, smiling slightly as though trying to make light of the situation. Ellie wasn't amused.

"Yeah, you know -- sew, visit, cook," Lucky added, trying to be helpful.

"I can't. I don't know how," Ellie moaned.

"Well, what can you do?"

"Play golf and racquetball; drive a car." She leered at them just to make Lucky sputter.

"Well, you can't do none of that, whatever it is, so you'd best learn some womanly things," Lucky replied, sounding out of patience.

They left her then, totally alone with no TV or satellite news, no fridge full of ready to eat food. She found a candle in a drawer and lit it, then another and another, grabbing every lamp and candlestick in the house and lighting them, too. Once, she had thought candles were romantic -- used to set the stage for a sensual evening. Now, she wanted light to keep the ghosts at bay.

She wandered through the house, vaguely aware that it was really well made. Wood trimmed all the doorways and windows, glass on the windows revealed what little moonlight there was. Well, what did she expect -- rags over open holes and drafts through chinks in log walls?

She didn't know what to expect. That was exactly the trouble.

* * *

Jesse pondered Elizabeth's strange behavior as he silently walked back to his cabin by the Nightingale Mine. Something out of the ordinary had happened, but for the life of him, he couldn't quite put his finger on it.

He had known Elizabeth over half his life. Their fathers had been friends, moving to Peavine when copper and gold had been discovered in '63. He'd watched her grow from a gangly, long-legged girl into a beautiful woman. As a girl, she had told him that she would marry him when she grew up and when he struck it rich, and Jesse

30

had always smiled and teased and asked her what if he didn't want to wait until she grew up.

As the years went by, Elizabeth had talked less of marriage. Then her mother had sent her back east to finishing school and she had changed. She hadn't even come home when her mother had died. If that wasn't enough to break her father's heart, when she did arrive eight months ago she'd been somewhat of a pain in the posterior.

She had brought home some highfalutin ideas from her schooling. Jesse didn't agree with a one of them, but he couldn't deny she had become a beautiful, if spoiled, young woman. He still intended to marry her, but she wouldn't give him a definitive answer until he had more in his pockets than a few ounces of gold dust.

Normally, he wasn't obsessed with Elizabeth. She was part of his life and he just got used to her being around, he supposed. Today, however, he noticed different little things about her. She had cut her hair, for example, and she seemed fidgety for some reason. He knew Clayton Scott had been visiting her quite often since her father's death, and now he wondered if it had been about more than business.

Her unusual comments didn't really bother him for he attributed them to her schooling. All her years back east only seemed to have instilled in her a sense of flightiness, instead of anything useful. It was a good thing her father had left the bank in trusteeship, for he doubted Elizabeth had any idea what to do with the business.

Why was it too much to hope that her education had broadened her horizons? And why was he spending so much time thinking about her?

Perhaps one of the reasons he now contemplated Elizabeth so intently was that all afternoon he had found himself staring at her. It wasn't her hair or her nervousness. It was her eyes. There had been a sparkle in their brown depths he didn't recall seeing before.

When she had looked at him, her gaze spoke of anger and independence; but he had also glimpsed fire and passion.

31

Passion. For the first time in their acquaintance, Jesse's loins had tightened in response to her nearness. That had been the real surprise. He had always felt comfortable around Elizabeth -- comfortable and somewhat complacent. Tonight she had ignited feelings in him that were anything but indifferent.

Chapter 3

Ellie paced through every room in the house, trying to figure a way out of this predicament. Seeing none, she tried to convince herself that she could survive a month. At times when she had gone to Europe, she had stayed in out-of-the-way, rustic places. Though most had electricity and phone service, she supposed she could endure without it.

She'd just pretend the airport and civilization lay on the other side of the mountain. Actually, no matter what she saw here, she couldn't imagine that they didn't. It was inconceivable that she could be in any time other than her own.

But if by some chance she had managed to traverse time from the present to Peavine in 1870, she could damn well reverse it and get back home. Zeke and Lucky knew the way and if she had to kidnap them, she would.

She sat on a bed in what she could only assume was Elizabeth's room. Frills and lace covered everything from the curtains to the bedspread and canopy. Carefully, she placed one lit candle on the small table beside her. It sputtered in its holder and she knew she would soon have to blow it out, because as much as she hated the dark, she was afraid of starting a fire even more.

Her fear of the dark was unreasonable, or so the doctors kept telling her. Being locked in a closet for hours when she was seven by a mean baby sitter shouldn't regulate the rest of her life, even to the point that at twenty-four years of age she still needed a night light. Regardless of what the experts said, however, her fear had never fully abated. There had even been times in college when she refused to go outside after dark.

Now, her hand shook as she pinched out the flame. Only the tiniest bit of moonlight came in through the open window, and she could only hope the moon was waxing instead of waning. Despondent, she sat in a huddle staring into the shadowed darkness until her eyes blurred.

Somewhere close to dawn, she collapsed from exhaustion. As she drifted off to sleep, she wondered how Elizabeth's father had gotten such fine furnishings across the mountains.

* * *

"Hey, you gonna sleep the day away?"

Ellie squinted against the bright light coming through the window, groaning as she rolled over to bury her head under the pillow. She didn't want to put a name to that voice. Something prodded her in the arm and she swatted at it, but her hand met empty space.

"Zeke told me to come see how you are."

Oh, God, it was true. Ellie had hoped -- prayed even -- that the whole Peavine episode was only a dream. Though she had never before dreamed of ghosts and dropping through holes in history, or about a handsome miner named Jesse--

"Enough!" She tossed her hair out of her eyes and abruptly sat up on the edge of the bed when Lucky continued poking her arm. Leveling her meanest look at the unfortunate man, she reached for her cigarettes only to remember she had smoked the last one in the dark last night.

"Go away." Ellie wasn't a morning person, and used that as an excuse -- one of many -- for not marrying. She didn't want anyone to see her first thing in the morning; not before she'd had coffee and a shower.

"Can't do that. Zeke told me to keep a close eye on you." Lucky squinted one eye as he spoke, staring at her with the other. "You sleep in your clothes?"

Ellie glanced down at her wrinkled attire and decided his question didn't need an answer. "Do you know how to make coffee?"

"'Course, I do. Any fool can make coffee."

34

Ellie smiled, despite the early morning hour. She doubted Lucky even realized what he said. "Good. Make me some while I go take a shower."

"Go where? You can't leave the house. Not a'fore Zeke gets here." Lucky shook his head and held his hands up to keep her on the bed. "Zeke says you'll just get yourself in trouble."

Ellie couldn't debate even with Lucky this early and without a cup of coffee first; no matter how absurd his comments. "Where's the bathroom?"

"The what?"

Ellie sighed. Why was everything so difficult for him to understand? "I need to...brush my teeth and wash." She refused to tell even this man some things.

"Where you come from, you got a whole room to do that sort of thing?" Lucky said in awe.

"Lucky!" Her tone held a warning which even he was able to grasp.

"There's a chamber pot under the bed and a wash basin right over there. And," he glanced around wildly, probably afraid she'd go after him if he couldn't give her what she needed. "I'm 'fraid you gotta take a bath in the kitchen. There's where the water can be pumped and heated and where the tub is." Before Ellie could yell at him again, he disappeared through the door.

No shower? Ellie glanced skyward and wondered just how she was to survive any time at all, much less a month, without a shower. If this was a trial of virtue or some such thing to test her strength, she would fail miserably.

Ellie's morning routine was sharply curtailed without the necessary facilities, but she managed the best she could. She had stripped to her underwear to wash, but when she picked up her jeans to put them back on, decided they were beyond wearing.

A quick search of the room found a closet full of clothes, but no jeans. While Ellie had no aversion to wearing a dress, and did so quite often to attend the opera or opening night events in New York, she certainly didn't feel inclined to wear a dress for Lucky.

The dressing table drawers were full of frills and lacy handkerchiefs. Ellie held up a pair of long undies, the legs full of row after row of lace.

"Augh!" She tossed them aside. Next, she found a camisole, which wasn't bad, made of soft cotton without too much lace. In her time, these were bought with the express purpose of being sexy and enticing. Ellie had the feeling that in Peavine, Nevada, they were everyday wear.

She heard Lucky banging pots and pans in the kitchen as she buttoned a navy skirt over the white blouse she had pulled from the closet. The skirt hit just above her ankles, and she wondered if anyone would notice that she must be taller than Elizabeth. She shrugged, then dropped to her hands and knees with her head in the closet looking for shoes.

"Oh, no," she groaned as she plopped on her fanny. There were two pairs of lace-up-heeled boots neatly placed on the bottom of the cupboard where the clothes hung. No flats, no slip-ons, no tennies. Ellie's mouth twisted in consternation as she looked over to the edge of the bed where she had kicked her hiking boots.

With a sigh of resignation, she tugged on a pair of the lace-up boots, grunting as her toes slammed into the end. Apparently, there was more than height where she and this Elizabeth person varied. Of course, she doubted anyone would notice the size of her feet. A trip to the clothes store was definitely in order.

By now, the rich smell of coffee wafted through the house to Ellie's nose. She stumbled once finding her way to the kitchen when her skirts wrapped around her legs. Perhaps if she wore a slip beneath them, they'd not trip her up.

When she walked through the door, Lucky's mouth dropped and the skillet he had been holding fell back onto the stove.

"What?" Ellie was still aggravated with his wake up call so early this morning, and didn't need him staring at her. She found a cup and poured herself some coffee. "Ah," she sighed as the first mouthful of caffeine slid down her throat. Now, if she only had a cigarette.

"You look real nice all gussied up, Miss Elizabeth," Lucky finally sputtered, then blushed and ducked his head, avoiding her glare.

"My name is Ellie."

"Well, you look and sound just like her, when you ain't swearing," Lucky sassed her right back.

Ellie raised a brow, wondering where the reticent Lucky had acquired his nerve so early in the morning. Perhaps he had an independent streak after all.

"But you gotta do something 'bout your hair; and get rid of that thing strapped to your wrist. We don't got them either."

At his comment, Ellie glanced at her wristwatch. She yelped, "You woke me up at six in the damn morning."

As though in response to her uncharitable attitude, a resounding blast rattled the window panes. Coffee sloshed in Ellie's cup as her whole body shook. Before she could question, another boom echoed through the valley.

"What the hell?" Ellie thumped her cup onto the table only to watch it shimmer and shake almost to the edge. She reached to catch it and everything stopped as suddenly as it started. She stood, arm outstretched, waiting.

"You ain't never heared dynamite blasts?" Lucky questioned and Ellie guessed her face gave her away.

"Are they trying to blow up this house?" Her heart still thumped too fast.

"Nope. That blast come from the Golden Fleece, if I heared right. That's clear up the slope to Peavine Summit."

"How in he...heaven's name do the people stand it? Don't the walls tumble right in on them?" Ellie thought the noise and initial trembling was worse than the earthquake she had encountered in Chili several years ago.

"Sometimes worse than others -- 'pends on how deep the shafts are and how many blasts at the same time. I suppose if'n all the mines blasted at once, it would fair ring the trees bare of branches. Most days is spent hauling ore and shoring up the walls so they can dig some more."

Ellie shook her head in wonder. It seemed she'd better figure out a way to get home fast. She had no desire to be buried under a pile of rock if some match happy miner lit too big a fuse.

"I'm going out."

"You can't do that. Zeke said so," Lucky stated in a panic, waving the spatula at her like that was going to keep her in place.

"Zeke's not my keeper," she stated, walking back down the hall, Lucky right on her heels. Knowing she'd never get far if she couldn't get rid of him, she stopped and turned. He nearly smacked into her.

"Lucky. I have to go to the bathroom and do something with my hair."

He didn't move.

She sniffed. "Is that your breakfast burning?" That sent him back to the kitchen in a hurry. Ellie used the time to escape through the front door. She'd worry about her hair later.

Since it had been dark when they got to the house last night, she had no idea which way was which, but in glancing down the road, it appeared town lay to the right. Only Elizabeth's house and one other faced the road she walked before she came to a cross street.

She closed her eyes trying to recall the layout of the ghost town. So many of the buildings had fallen down over the years, and she was sure some hadn't even been built in 1870. In fact, she couldn't remember having seen Elizabeth's house before last night, but then she hadn't gotten too far afield that day before Zeke found her by the creek.

Taking a chance, she turned and walked to the left. She figured Peavine couldn't be that large and she could always backtrack. The buildings on the right side of the street were at least fronted by a sidewalk of sorts, so she stepped up onto the platform. Somewhere in the back of her mind, she hoped this was all a big farce, and she'd step back into the ghost town where she started and would calmly wait to be rescued.

She couldn't help the sigh which escaped as she noticed the people out and about. There weren't many; mostly men all wearing old fashioned typed clothes, but they were all gawking at her.

She hoped, having eluded Lucky, that the store would be open because she suddenly felt uncomfortable out in the open. Mentally, she reviewed her list of supplies until a sudden thought struck her and she stopped in the middle of the walk.

The bank sign across the street made her realize she was broke. How could she buy clothes and cigarettes with no money? She cocked her head and stared at the sign. Calhoun's Bank & Trust. Jesse had said Elizabeth's father owned the bank.

Ellie had no idea where Mr. Calhoun was; he certainly hadn't spent the night at the house. However, she decided as long as she had to play-act as Elizabeth, she was entitled to her money; or her father's money. Whatever. She just hoped they had heard of 'charge it' here in the hills of Nevada.

"Elizabeth?" Ellie didn't connect the name with herself until someone touched her elbow. Reflexes honed from living in New York made her jerk back and quickly turn around.

"I'm sorry. I didn't mean to startle you, but you seemed in a daze. What are you doing here, anyway? I thought you left town." The suave gentleman standing in front of her came right out of a very old movie. Dark gray suit, white shirt with a starched collar and stick pin in his tie. He even had a handlebar mustache and a bowler-style hat which he swept off slicked back hair as he nodded to her.

Ellie panicked briefly, wishing now that she had stayed put until Zeke had time to brief her. Who was this guy? How was he connected to Elizabeth? "Why would you think I left town?" She questioned out loud, hoping to glean some insight without giving the game away. Her question raised his eyebrows, and his explanation only slightly squelched her uneasiness.

"That crazy old coot, Lucky, sat on your porch when I came to pick you up for dinner at the hotel. He said you had left on the stage because an aunt had died in Belmont. I didn't realize you had any other relatives."

Ellie didn't like the insinuation in the man's voice and she definitely didn't like his proprietary grip on her arm. She pried his fingers loose and took a step back. The conversation she'd had with Jesse last night echoed inside her head. This had to be Clayton Scott, the lascivious mine owner whom Jesse detested.

While the man now respected the small space she put between them, there was still something about him that Ellie didn't trust. Too many years in the big city, she supposed. His slick looks and mustache made him out of place in Peavine, but he conveyed the perfect villain for a melodrama. Somehow that description fit with everything else Ellie had been experiencing.

She decided to be cautious until she could find out more. She offered him a sugary smile and sorrowful words. "I realized too late that there was nothing I could do for poor Auntie, so at the first opportunity, I got off the stage. Fortunately, a farmer was heading for town to get supplies." Deciding to play on his sympathies, she sighed before adding, "There's just so much death...you know." She looked at him from beneath her lashes.

The man immediately took her hand and patted it. "My poor Elizabeth. It must have been extremely difficult thinking about attending another funeral when your father so recently--"

Ellie's gasp cut him off, and she knew her expression couldn't have been any more genuine if she were actually Elizabeth. Her eyes opened wide. Elizabeth's father was dead? Could his death be related to the trouble shadowing Jesse? Panic squeezed the breath out of her. What had she gotten into -- murder and mayhem?

She pulled her hand out of his clammy one and said without thinking. "I think I should get back home. I need to see Jesse." As she turned to go, he grabbed her arm.

"I don't want you around him."

Ellie quickly thought over what Zeke had told her. "We are supposed to be engaged, after all."

"You know that's just a sham. Before I left New York, you had promised yourself to me." He stepped closer and Ellie could smell his cologne -- a cloying musk. "In fact, you had already given me much more than a promise."

Oh, boy -- murder, mayhem, and sex! Definitely things Ellie hadn't counted on. She didn't know the complete story and doubted that Zeke did either. Even so, she took a gamble. "If you want things to work out, you have to give me some space, and time."

"Time?" The man sounded incredulous. "You've been back over eight months. That's more than enough time to convince Jesse--"

"Morning, Miss Elizabeth." Their conversation was interrupted by an old miner walking by.

Clayton glared at the intruder; Ellie smiled and nodded.

"I'm coming over tonight," he whispered.

"No." When he gave her a suspicious look, she hastily added, "Zeke and Lucky are sticking close for some reason. We need to act...innocent. Let things settle for a bit."

She could tell he didn't think much of her idea, but knew she couldn't let him near her. "Besides, I need to convince Jesse--" She let the sentence hang, hoping he'd finish the cryptic line he had started, but he just scowled.

"Fine, but if this takes much longer, I have a plan of my own that'll get the job done much quicker." He didn't wait for a reply, but turned and strolled across the street to the bank without a backward glance.

Ellie gapped after him, stunned at what he had revealed. She rewound the conversation and played it over in her mind. Actually, he had said very little, but insinuated a lot. They definitely had a plot hatched, and while Ellie didn't think Elizabeth had anything to do with her own father's death, she didn't put it past Clayton Scott.

She shook off the morbid shadow and decided she would have to discuss what she had learned with Zeke and Lucky after she got her supplies. Regardless of not wanting to be here, she had been drawn into their lives, and she couldn't walk out of this make-believe town and leave them in the lurch. Damn it, she was just too soft hearted.

Fortunately, though still early, the door to Murphy's Mercantile and Feed Store opened beneath her hand. A bell tinkled overhead as she entered. She stood just inside the door, amazed at the sight which greeted her. Only once before, in a tiny hamlet in the mountains of Switzerland, had she ever come across a store that contained anything and everything needed for survival, and then some.

Bolts of cloth and all manner of clothes lay on tables; pots and pans, shovels and hoes hung from hooks overhead. Dried legumes filled bushel baskets on the floor. One side of the room stored barrels labeled pickles, whiskey, molasses, and vinegar. Shelves lined the walls from floor to ceiling and contained everything from coffee, spices and wine to jars and tins of food.

Since there weren't any other customers in the store at the moment, Ellie quickly moved to the clothes. A cursory glance at the inside waistband revealed no sizes, so she held up pants to find something that might fit. She had grabbed a few pairs of tan jeans and two flannel shirts before she realized that not only were there no customers in the store, there was no clerk either.

She tilted her head. There -- she heard humming. Someone was here; just in the back someplace. Strangely reassured, she scurried from area to area, grabbing things she thought she would need. She couldn't find any cigarettes, but found pouches of tobacco and papers.

"This is getting to be a real experience," she muttered under her breath.

"Elizabeth. My goodness sakes, you're out and about quite early this morning." The chipper voice soon attached itself to a body as a young, brown-haired woman came through a curtained doorway. "We normally don't see you until afternoon."

Ellie rolled her eyes. It appeared that she and Elizabeth actually did have something in common. Unfortunately, it wasn't knowledge of who all these people were. Ellie began to wonder how she'd fake her way through another conversation when Zeke came bursting through the doorway.

"Morning, Miss Sarah." He grabbed the hat from his head as he hurried over to where Ellie stood. "Morning, Miss Elizabeth," he repeated the greeting just as politely, then under his breath lectured her. "I thought I told you to stay put."

Ellie gave him a spiteful smile and replied sweetly, "It is a wonderful morning, Mr. Zeke. Why, I've already had a very delightful conversation with Mr. Clayton Scott." She took pleasure in seeing the shocked expression on his face before she turned back to the counter where Sarah stood.

"Mr. Zeke?" Sarah giggled. "I don't recall ever using that name on him before, although now that I think on it, I don't rightly recall ever knowing his last name."

Ellie lost the thread of Sarah's conversation as her gaze scanned the shelves. "Oh, my Go...goodness." She corrected herself just as Zeke coughed. "Potato chips; and pork and beans." She grabbed cans of Van Camp's Beans in Tomato Sauce off the shelf. Although she had never heard of Saratoga Chips, she recognized the potato chips by the picture on the front of the cloth bag. There was life in the 1870's after all.

She dumped her treasures on the counter before a startled Sarah. "Elizabeth," Sarah paused, apparently not sure how to address the pile of merchandise now laying before her. "I realize losing your father must be such a burden, and perhaps you sometimes forget?"

Ellie watched Sarah's gaze float from item to item. Zeke poked her in the ribs. She glanced down, and this time saw her items through Sarah's eyes. Geez. Potato chips were probably bad enough, but flannel shirts, jeans and tobacco? She offered a weak smile, her gaze beseeching Zeke even though she hated, really hated, to admit she needed help.

Zeke rolled his eyes to the heavens, but did pull her out of the fire. "I'm sure glad you 'membered all those things

Jesse and us needed, Miss Elizabeth. My ole mind is getting feeble."

Ellie shot a glance at Sarah to see if she bought the story. If not, she was too polite to say so, and began writing down the purchases on a small pad. When she reached for the Pork & Beans by Ellie's hand, she paused instead to finger her wristwatch. Ellie gritted her teeth for the quizzing she was sure would follow.

"Is that one of those new eastern fashion ideas? I must admit it's a fair piece easier than always looking at my...chest." Sarah fingered the watch pinned to her bodice and gave Ellie a grin. Ellie laughed.

"I keep telling Papa to let me go back east shopping to bring the styles to Peavine, but he insists Mr. Strauss's jeans are radical enough."

Sarah continued chatting away as she wrapped Ellie's purchases. "I really am glad to see you, Elizabeth. I heard last night that you left town on the stage, and I couldn't help but wonder if you would have been back in time for the wedding."

"Wedding?" Ellie squeaked. The only wedding she had heard mentioned was Elizabeth's and Jesse's, and she sure wasn't planning that. She gave Zeke a look.

Zeke politely smiled. "I plumb forgot about you and Henry getting hitched. What day's that wedding gonna be, Miss Sarah? You know Lucky is awaiting to celebrate." Sarah blushed nicely, Ellie thought, and Zeke could be a real charmer when he wanted.

"Just a week from this Friday." To Ellie, she added, "You know how shy Henry is. He was half afraid to ask, but was so pleased when Jesse said he would stand up for him, since you were going to be my maid of honor."

Ellie didn't know how to respond, so just smiled as Sarah handed her the bundles. "I'll just send this ticket over to the bank on your account." Sarah slid the paper into a drawer and Ellie wasn't about to argue.

Once they were outside the store, Zeke stopped Ellie. "Sarah's wedding to Henry was the biggest shindig Peavine had in a while. I'm thinking the accident was after the wedding, so we got some time to figure out what really happened a'fore it happens all over again."

"Who's Henry?" Ellie really did need to get everyone in this melodrama identified.

"Henry Jefferson. He works as a teller at your daddy's bank."

"Yeah, you really do need to tell me about daddy's bank," Ellie added, but Zeke already had his lips puckered up in thought.

He snapped his fingers and burst out, "Now I recall. The only other big doings in Peavine is the Independence Day celebration and picnic, and that's when Lucky and me got ourselves in trouble. And that means we got less than a month."

Ellie was feeling benevolent, having her arms wrapped around real clothes, real junk food, and the makings for real cigarettes. Besides, Zeke just said she had less than a month to rough it in Peavine before she could go back home. She gave Zeke the first genuine smile she'd felt since landing in this strange place and imitated his drawl. "Well then, Zeke, I think we'd best get back home and figure us out a plan."

Chapter 4

Lucky wasn't easily pacified for the ruse Ellie had pulled to escape him. She finally had to eat some of his cold eggs and biscuits. Considering all the information she had gathered on the streets, she didn't feel it was a bad sacrifice. He did make her a fresh pot of coffee, which the three of them drank while they talked.

"I don't understand Jesse's attitude. Why wouldn't he recognize that I'm not his real fiancée? I wore different clothes; I definitely acted different." Ellie hiked one foot over the other knee as she talked, unlacing the tight boot and tugging it off. It plunked onto the floor. "Actually, now that I think about it, he didn't act much like a fiancé at all." The other boot thudded. "He didn't even kiss me good night."

Silence met her pronouncement, and Ellie looked up from massaging her sore foot. Both Zeke and Lucky sat stone cold still, mouths gapping and faces red as tomatoes.

"What?" Ellie dropped her skirt from around her knees and stood to get herself more coffee.

Zeke began to wheeze and Lucky coughed. "Your. . .your feet." Lucky sputtered.

Ellie looked down. Her feet peeked from beneath the hem of the blue skirt. She wiggled her toes in relief, then frowned. "Sorry, I should have fixed them. They look that bad, huh?" She had meant to redo her toenail polish the other night at the hotel, but had never gotten around to it.

"I ain't never seen painted toes on nobody 'cept the girls from Miss Molly's down at the Gold Strike Saloon." Lucky whistled as he scooted forward in his chair, bending down to get a closer look.

Ellie scurried to her chair and self-consciously curled her toes under her skirt.

"Lucky, how many times I gotta tell you it ain't polite to talk about them girls in front of a lady." Zeke pointed out the common courtesy to his brother and Ellie wondered if she would ever begin to understand the workings of history.

To take attention from herself, if that were even possible, she questioned. "We were talking about Jesse?"

Zeke looked at her, his expression blank.

"You know," Ellie prompted, "his attitude towards Elizabeth -- towards me."

"Well, you gotta understand that Jesse and Elizabeth growed up together. Seems Jesse always wanted to marry her, and I guess back then, she felt the same. So Jesse, he thinks Elizabeth's just about perfect, don't you know. Even when she says she won't marry him 'til he's rich, he still treats her like a princess." Zeke snorted with disgust for the entire mess, and Ellie guessed he never had a lady love.

"But then, how come Jesse wouldn't notice I'm not the same person?"

Zeke questioned, "You mean 'sides the fact you've been back east for the past years?" At Ellie's nod, he continued, "Sometimes, you see what you s'pect to see, or what you're used to seeing. We called you Elizabeth, and so he just figures you're who we says."

Ellie thought about that as she excused herself for a minute. After digging through Elizabeth's things, she returned to the kitchen where she sat back down with her findings. Just as she did, a dynamite blast sounded in the distance. The floor shook slightly. Ellie shivered, knowing she would never get used to that sound. Especially since it seemed to predict doom for Jesse.

"Why don't you two have to help Jesse at the mine?"

"He says me and Lucky should be retired, if you ever heared of such nonsense. Even if my old bones creak some, I can still earn my keep." Zeke sounded thoroughly offended that a man of his age should contemplate not working. "Anyhow, he pays us to run errands for him, getting things from town and such. Jesse's got some workers -- the smallest group of miners in the area -- but they're loyal to him, leastwise." Zeke finished.

"Can you be sure?" Ellie had been a newspaper reporter before she landed the job with the travel magazine, so questions naturally popped into her head.

"Yeah. Clayton Scott manages Fravel Mines, like the Golden Fleece, and he always tries to hire Jesse's workers away, but they won't go. 'Sides, Jesse gives 'em a piece of stock in the mine along with their wage. When he hits the motherlode, all of 'em are going to be rich." Lucky answered, screwing up his face as he watched her work. "Whatcha doing? I thought you couldn't sew."

"This isn't sewing; it's mending."

"Ain't that the same thing?"

"No, besides, I didn't see any of these at the store, so I'm making my own." She had confiscated several pairs of Elizabeth's frilly, long-legged underwear, cut the ruffles off, and was putting in a hem. She held a pair up for inspection. They'd still be longer than her bikini briefs, but they'd work.

"But ain't they supposed to have the ruffles on 'em?" Lucky asked, even though embarrassment tinged his cheeks pink.

Ellie gave him the look, as she was beginning to think of her usual expression when it came to Lucky. "Do you know anything about life in my time?"

"We couldn't get us to town, you know. We just had to depend on seeing what the people who came to Peavine had about them."

"And did you ever see any women with long, ruffled legs?"

"Well, no, I guess not."

Ellie shrugged. "There you go." She bit the thread and folded the last pair onto the pile at the table. She scooped up the scraps and, not finding any place to throw them, dropped them back to the floor for now.

She collected her cigarette papers and tobacco and tried, for the hundredth time it seemed, to roll herself a smoke. She had one end twisted shut when the whole thing tilted and the tobacco slid out the open end. Her shoulders slumped; Lucky smirked, and Zeke sighed.

"You should quit. If'n you can't make 'em, you shouldn't be smoking 'em."

"Shut up." She said without animosity, pushing him the makings as she had earlier. He sighed again, but expertly dumped tobacco into the curved paper he held just right between his fingers, pulled the draw string pouch shut with his teeth, then rolled it up into a smooth cylinder. She held her hand out, snapping her fingers and stopping him just short of licking the paper shut.

He grinned as he handed over his creation. "It'll cost you." He reached for another paper, quickly making himself a cigarette and striking a match for both of them.

"It has already cost me far more than you can ever realize," Ellie replied, looking around the room. As homey as the kitchen was with its pot-bellied stove and gingham curtains, it still sat in the middle of a mining town in 1870.

Deep in her subconscious, Ellie knew she was stuck here. She vacillated between belief and denial, but for the moment had resigned herself to the month Zeke believed they had to figure out the problem. A shiver sliced down her spine, and she wondered what would happen if they didn't get Jesse's trouble straightened out.

"You promised to tell me about Jesse and what you think happened." She crossed her arms on the table and gave Zeke a level look. "We haven't exactly seen eye to eye, but as long as I'm stuck here, I might as well help. I can't do that until I know everything. Then, we can get it over with so I can go home."

Lucky and Zeke exchanged a look and Ellie's stomach lurched. No, they had said she could go home in a month. One month, her brain echoed; one month, she prayed. She couldn't even contemplate otherwise.

"Spill it."

* * *

Zeke and Lucky spent the remainder of the day at the kitchen table, drinking coffee and giving her details about Jesse's and Elizabeth's lives. It was probably fortunate that

Elizabeth had been away to finishing school and had only returned to Peavine eight months ago. Any mistakes Ellie made could always be attributed to her eastern book learning, as Lucky put it.

Most of the time, they spoke of Jesse, who they treated with near reverence. It seemed the man had gone through some pretty rough times, but despite it all, was nearly perfect -- or so they said. According to them, Elizabeth's father, Wendell, and Jesse's father, Warren, had been mining partners until '65 when Wendell decided to sell out and start a bank to finance other mining ventures. Zeke seemed to think that Wendell had kept some interest in the Nightingale Mine even after he started the bank.

Clayton Scott took over management of the bank when Elizabeth's father died two months ago, and apparently had alot of money in the bank because of his interests in Fravel mines. The question Zeke and Lucky couldn't answer, though, was whether Scott had any actual stock in the Nightingale mine.

"How long has Scott lived here?" Ellie asked.

Zeke shrugged. "'Bout a year, maybe less."

Did he hold an interest or mortgage in Jesse's Nightingale Mine because of Elizabeth's father's former partnership? Did he have a vested interest in the bank, or just the management of it? What motive did Scott have to want Jesse dead? There were far too many questions left to be answered.

Though they didn't speak of Jesse's mom, they said his father died in a mine accident in '62 when Jesse was twenty. Then, Wendell Calhoun had died mysteriously just two months ago.

Ellie had said the deaths were probably coincidental, but she began to think otherwise as Zeke finally explained her reason for being there.

"'Bout the trouble Lucky and me got into on Independence Day," Zeke sullenly began as dusk fell outside. "Jesse had decided to work late, promising Miss Elizabeth he would be into town afore the fireworks."

"How do you know that?" Ellie asked, lighting the lamp on the table to chase away the shadows. It was like hearing a ghost story.

"'Cuz we was the ones what come into town and told Miss Elizabeth," Lucky stated. Mournfully, he added, "Jesse was close, he said, real close to finding the biggest vein in all of Nevada. All the assay reports said so. Most nights, even after he sent the other miners home, he'd stay below, chipping away, looking for the mother lode."

"Well, if you were in town and Jesse was in the mine, how did you two end up de...how come you were still around when I--?" Ellie still couldn't say the word dead out loud. Somehow that would make it too final.

"When we got to town, Miss Elizabeth and Mr. Scott was on her front porch, real cozy like." Lucky sounded as though he were the one betrayed, instead of Jesse. "We gave her the news, and Mr. Scott said we should go on down to the saloon and have us a drink. Said he'd make sure Miss Elizabeth got to the fireworks if'n Jesse didn't show up in time."

"Well, you could hardly be blamed for--"

"We was his friends. We should've been there." Agitated, Lucky jumped up, slamming back his chair.

"Zeke, what happened?" Ellie had a feeling she wasn't going to like the end of this story.

"Right in the middle of the celebration, we heared this explosion coming from the ridge. It was a hellava lot louder than any fireworks. The whole town went running 'cross the creek to the noise, but it was too late." Tears welled up in his eyes and Ellie placed a hand over his in comfort. "Smoke and dirt was bellowing out of the Nightingale. Since Jesse wasn't standing nearby, we knew he had to still be inside, so Lucky and me raced in."

"Oh, God." Ellie clapped a hand to her mouth in agony.

"There was aftershocks, and we got knocked out by falling rock. Next thing we know, some voice is telling us we gotta hang around Peavine 'til we figure out a way to fix things."

Macabre images flashed through Ellie's mind. Seances she and girlfriends had at slumber parties when they were young suddenly seemed so pathetic. She examined Zeke and Lucky closely. They were definitely solid and very much alive -- now -- regardless of how she had found them when she first arrived at Peavine ghost town. If they had been ghosts and had come back to the land of the living in 1870, what did that make her?

She shook her head to clear the confusion. "I don't get it. Doesn't Jesse know he died? Don't all the people in town know it?"

Zeke gave her a hopeful look. "That's just it. When we found you and you looked so much like Miss Elizabeth, we figured we had a chance to make things right. We took you into the mine and--"

"You took me into a mine? A dark mine?" Ellie practically shrieked, instantly going cold all over at the thought of being inside a dark, dank underground hole where there was no light and no way out.

"Well, yeah, that's how we got you here."

She shot him a murderous look.

"Anyhow, we come back to Peavine at a time a couple weeks afore the accident. That's why everybody's going about their business."

"Well, just tell Jesse the truth and he can deal with Scott and then there won't be an accident. And I can go home."

Zeke gave his head a sad shake. "If'n it took over a hundred years for us to get back here, I don't figure it'll be that easy to set things right. 'Sides, we got no evidence, just suspects."

"And they would be?" Ellie hated playing twenty questions.

"Clayton Scott and Miss Elizabeth."

"That figures," Ellie stated and proceeded to tell the boys about her conversation with Clayton Scott. "I'm still not sure what he expects me to convince Jesse to do, but I'm sure we'll find out soon enough."

"Scott already manages the bank and if he's messing with Elizabeth, he can marry her and own the whole thing. Why do you think those two would want Jesse dead?" Lucky asked.

"That's what we need Ellie to find out," Zeke replied. "I just know it's got something to do with Jesse finding the motherlode."

"It doesn't make sense right now, that's for sure." Ellie shook her head, hoping to sift the pieces into some semblance of order.

"Well, they're about the best suspects we got right now," Lucky added. "'Sides, they was the only two people not up at the mine site on Independence Day."

* * *

Zeke and Lucky honestly felt Elizabeth had tried to kill Jesse -- actually, had killed him. Remembering his handsome face, Ellie found it hard to imagine, but she supposed greed could supersede passion. That hypothesis was all they had to go on for the moment.

Something wasn't quite right with the whole scenario, though. It didn't make sense to kill Jesse if he had nothing to do with the bank, which held all the money. Ellie felt sure the bank also held the key to this mystery. Unlike her nineteenth century twin, Elizabeth, Ellie did have a head for business, and planned to take a careful look at the dealings of one Clayton Scott.

She pumped water and heated it for a bath. As she lit two more candles to keep the darkness at bay, she decided the underhanded Mr. Scott could wait until morning.

She crunched another potato chip and marveled at the things that were available in 1870. In her naiveté, she had assumed modern conveniences had been invented in modern times -- specifically in the twentieth and twenty-first century during her life span.

It was silly to be thrilled by such little things as potato chips and scented soap, she thought, sniffing the small bar appreciatively, but a person didn't miss something until she had to do without. She eyed the small stash of pre-made cigarettes Zeke had left her. If she smoked more than that, he had said, she would just have to learn to roll her own. Or quit, he had reiterated.

Yes, life was just full of little treasures to stockpile and savor. She banged her knee on the side of the tub as she adjusted her body so hot water covered most of it. She decided to reserve judgment on copper bathtubs until later.

She reached for the glass of wine from the table. Zeke had brought her a bottle after she threatened to go to the saloon herself. She took a sip and settled her head against the back of the tub, grinning as she wiggled her painted toes against the far rim. Perhaps she would start a woman's movement right here in Peavine. She chuckled, knowing the few women she had seen in town that morning were basically two types. Matronly wives of the rich, and the kind who were already very liberated.

She closed her eyes and thought of Jesse Cole instead. Twinkling eyes came to mind, tiny lines fanning out from the corners when he smiled. Regardless of the rough life he led, she recalled he had smiled quite a bit that day. So much about him made sense now, whereas it hadn't when she thought he was a weekend visitor to the mountains.

His strength and ruggedness were natural characteristics of the kind of work he did. Zeke had said there was a lot of timber cutting needed for braces and shafts, in addition to the hard work with a pick and shovel. Ellie had no doubt Jesse did quite a bit of his own work.

In order to learn more about him, she would have to get him away from the mine for awhile. Ellie soaped her body and washed her hair, wondering if she had what it took to divert a man's attention from his work. She had never purposely set out to seduce a man.

She recalled how a stray lock of jet black hair had fallen over Jesse's forehead, giving him the look of a fallen angel. She definitely wouldn't have any trouble being seduced. She just hoped it would work as well the other way around.

Chapter 5

Ellie surprised herself the next morning by lighting a fire in the stove without burning the house down. She figured the idea must be to keep a fire burning, because the coals in the bottom of the stove quickly ignited the other tinder she shoved through a hole.

Lucky hadn't come over this morning to bug her, and while she considered that a good thing, she would have liked someone around to cook. A search of the cupboards produced a tin of coffee. As she put a pot on to brew, she convinced herself she could be a pioneer. After all, how hard could it be?

While she waited for her morning coffee, she ventured out the back door and immediately revised her opinion. An old-fashion outhouse stood further back in the yard, the quarter moon cut into the door causing Ellie to recognize it. They actually looked like that, she thought, smiling at all the times she had seen them portrayed in movies and such. A huge pile of sawed logs lay in a heap by a flat-topped tree trunk with an ax sticking from it. When Ellie looked closer to the house, she found a small stack of wood, but realized she would have to find someone to cut more before long.

The morning sun was barely up, but Ellie could already feel the heat rising from the earth. If not for the breeze which seemed to continually blow down the mountain and through the trees, she knew it would be intolerable, especially without central air conditioning.

A distant boom echoed and the ground shook. Ellie jumped. Several more blasts quickly followed. She prayed quickly that the dynamite blasts were no more than work in progress, and not a premonition of doom. Her gaze wandered in the direction of the mines which ran along the eastern slope of the Sierra Nevada mountain ridge.

It awed her to think she was within walking distance of some of the richest gold, silver and copper mines in the history of the United States. Just past the back of the house to the trees, and a little beyond that to the creek. And if she walked along the creek a little ways, she would come to Jesse's cabin.

His image immediately rose to Ellie's mind; eyes of indigo blue and full of laughter, broad shoulders and a tall, trim body. She couldn't imagine any woman wanting to hurt him, but then she hadn't lived in the 1870's for more than a few days and didn't know what motivated people here. Greed, jealousy and hatred were definitely factors which existed in her world. While she hoped things hadn't always been that way, somehow she doubted it had changed over the years.

She had a crime victim and she had a final result, unless they could somehow change the course of history. While Zeke and Lucky might have lived during the times, they didn't seem to understand the why of things. It looked like Ellie would have to find the motivation that had gotten Jesse Cole killed -- or would get him killed on the fourth of July.

Ellie heard the coffee sputtering from inside and hurried through the door to the kitchen. Her coffee was boiling over and splattering onto the fire. Without thinking, she grabbed the handle, forgetting the entire fixture was made of metal and conducted heat.

"Damn." she swore, dropping the pot back onto the stove and shaking her hand in the air. She quickly jerked at the pump handle, sighing as cold water rushed over her blistering hand. Patting it gingerly with a towel, she swore again, feeling royally sorry for herself and her plight.

It took two cups of coffee, after cooling, and her last rolled cigarette before Ellie felt ready to tackle the problems Zeke and Lucky had discussed with her last night. But as with everything else in her life, Ellie dug into a project with a vengeance once she knew the parameters.

She decided to start with Jesse -- the one who needed protecting -- and work her way back from there. In this case, Zeke had explained who belonged to who and who was dead and alive, but that left alot of holes. The biggest lack of information concerned Clayton Scott. He hadn't lived in Peavine as long as the rest of them, and his background appeared dubious.

From her brief encounter with the man yesterday, a very obvious connection could be made between him and Elizabeth. That connection wasn't one Ellie wanted to pursue, so she decided to tread lightly. She definitely needed Clayton around until they could uncover the whole plot, but she didn't trust the man and didn't know if she could pretend otherwise. She knew Clayton Scott wanted more from Elizabeth than Ellie would be willing to give.

Ellie pulled on a pair of jeans without thinking before she realized that probably wasn't the way to approach Jesse. While he might have excused her dress the other day, she figured she better act as close to Elizabeth as she could. To that effect, she dug through the closet in search of something suitable.

Elizabeth must think highly of her appearance, for all the clothes Ellie found were full of frills and lace, and entirely too dressy for life in the town of Peavine. Of course, if Elizabeth had recently returned from some east coast boarding school, that might explain the fancier attire.

Ellie tried to view Elizabeth's wardrobe as she did her own. Three categories divided her clothes -- work, play and party. Using that criteria, Elizabeth had no play clothes and very few work things. Ellie finally decided to wear the blue skirt again, this time with a cream colored blouse. It appeared a trip back to Murphy's was in order.

Another dig clear to the back of the wardrobe led to the discovery of a worn pair of slip-on shoes. The leather was scuffed and soft, and when Ellie put them on she sighed with pleasure. These would be much more comfortable than the heeled boots she had worn yesterday.

An hour later Ellie ventured outside. She swung a picnic basket from one hand and pulled the door closed behind her. The warmth of the day made her wish for a pair of cutoffs, but she guessed a skirt was cooler than jeans would have been. Cooler, but not as comfortable, she thought caustically, as she grabbed a handful of said skirt and hiked it up as she stepped down from the porch.

Instead of turning towards town, Ellie headed for the trees, and as she remembered, soon came to the creek. The grassy bank spread along both sides, and the crystal water tumbled along. It might be fun to come down here and swim sometime, she reflected.

Once she got to the area of the creek where the stones acted as a bridge, she hesitated. The spaces between them looked a lot further apart than they had the other night. She worried her bottom lip as she decided whether to use the stones or just wade across. She couldn't see to the middle and wondered if it might have some deep pockets.

She definitely didn't want to ruin her new found shoes, so she slipped them off and laid them on top of the basket. She took one step towards the water and decided something had to be done with her skirt, too, because there was entirely too much of it. She grabbed it in one hand, then realized that made her unbalanced to walk on the stones. Finally, she bent over, grabbed the back hem and brought it up between her legs and tucked it into the front waistband. The procedure brought the whole thing up around her knees like a pair of bloomers.

* * *

Jesse watched Elizabeth's actions with interest from the trees on the other side of the creek. He smiled when she took off her shoes, but gaped in astonishment when she hiked up her dress and bared her legs. His heart beat faster as she tentatively took a step nearer the water, and he knew it wasn't fear that she would fall in. After all, it was only about a foot deep in most places.

Deciding his men could do without him for awhile, he crossed his arms over his chest and leaned against a tree, watching her progress. He had started into town three times last night to see her. Each time, he'd talked himself out of it, thinking perhaps she would already be abed, or that he shouldn't push her for an answer to his proposal, even though that had been exactly what he wanted to do.

Then today, he'd had to ask twice when something was said, had told Lucky to go to town for supplies but hadn't given him a list, and when he showed back up later, had told him to go to town for supplies again. Normally, he worked right down in the mine with his crew, but his supervisor, Carlos, had just told him to take a break.

Jesse jerked upright and stepped forward as Elizabeth teetered on a rock in the middle of the creek, but before he could move, she'd regained her balance and proceeded on. He didn't understand the profound effect she had on him, and had thought to stay away from her to see if he could get things back to normal.

Now, here she came instead, with a picnic basket clutched in one hand and an indecent, but enticing, amount of leg showing. Her head was bent to watch the rocks, and her blonde hair bounced around her shoulders. When she reached the last rock, she slipped again, and this time Jesse quickly moved forward to scoop her up in his arms.

Even in her astonishment, she automatically grabbed him around the neck, much to his delight. She started to wiggle loose, but when she looked up, her brown eyes flashed with recognition.

"Have I caught a mermaid?" He asked with a grin, then added, "No, I think not. If I recall, mermaids don't have limbs as perfect as these." His gaze moved up her legs.

A short gasp parted her lips and Jesse tried to recall the taste of them. It had been quite some time since Elizabeth had allowed him that pleasure, but that thought didn't stop him now.

Ever so gently, his lips grazed hers. To his delight, she didn't pull away. In fact, he swore he felt her lean into him. He pressed his advantage, his tongue seeking entrance to her sweet depths.

After her initial shock at Jesse's sudden appearance, Ellie quickly relaxed in his embrace and enjoyed his kiss.

Too much. If she closed her eyes, she could easily forget her circumstances and only recall Jesse's handsome face. Until he murmured against her lips.

"Elizabeth, what an enchanting surprise."

Ellie knew she was suppose to be someone else, but hearing Elizabeth's name on Jesse's lips when he kissed her effectively doused her passion.

"Put me down," she managed to say without emotion. Even when he released her, though, she held on long enough to get her footing and not slip down the bank. As quickly as she could, she put some distance between them.

Jesse shrugged and gave her a half-hearted smile of apology. "Sorry, but seeing you exposed so enticingly just caused me to act loco."

His comment, and the direction of his gaze, caused Ellie to blush. She quickly jerked her skirts down so they fell to the ground, and slid her still damp feet into her shoes. Her behavior probably wasn't proper for the times, even if they were supposed to be engaged. Regardless, she had enjoyed Jesse's kiss, probably more than she should have. She'd have to remember to ask Zeke the proper courtship procedure with regard to kissing.

Jesse stuck his hands in the pockets of his jeans and just stood there with a big grin, staring at her. She scowled, looking down at her attire to see if everything was buttoned.

"What?"

He shrugged, making his entire upper body undulate. Ellie swallowed hard. The movement, so casual to him, caused ripples of desire across her stomach. She wanted to see him naked, the thought came unbidden to her mind. She blinked and shook her head to clear it. Getting involved with this man wasn't part of the deal. Less than a month and she'd be out of here.

Endless moments seemed to pass as they stood on the banks of the bubbly creek staring at each other. Ellie couldn't read his thoughts, but from his stance, the sensual curve of his lips, and the passion flaring in his blue eyes, she could make a fair assessment.

A sudden fit of jealousy came from nowhere and smacked her hard in the chest. If she and Zeke and Lucky managed to change history and save Jesse this time, she didn't want Elizabeth to come back and get to keep him. If Elizabeth was involved as they assumed, Ellie wanted to make sure she got caught and sent away. Jesse deserved better than a back-stabbing bitch.

"Why such a frown?" Jesse broke the silence.

Knowing she couldn't tell him, Ellie searched for an explanation. "I, ah, wondered if my potato chips got soggy when you splashed while grabbing me." Ellie mentally groaned.

"Potato chips? You brought me lunch?" Jesse's grin was back in place, and Ellie's heart melted just a little more. He took the basket from her and grabbed her hand, pulling her up the bank. "Come on."

Ellie laughed at his exuberance as she scrambled to keep up with his longer stride, lifting her skirts out of the way. He led her along the creek to a grassy knoll where a huge tree canopied the water with its leafy branches. A cool breeze swept along the earth, rippling the grass.

Ellie brushed her hair out of her face as she watched Jesse take the blanket from top the basket and spread it on the ground. Suddenly shy about being alone with him, especially after their kiss, she couldn't quite decide how to proceed. Perhaps some generic questions might work to move herself to safer ground.

"Don't you have to work?" She accepted his outstretched hand and stepped forward, dropping cross-legged to the blanket but making sure her skirts covered her legs. His callous-roughened hand engulfed her much smaller one, the warmth of it radiating clear up her arm. Think generic, she cautioned herself.

"I never work so hard as to ignore a beautiful woman when she comes to see me." He winked at her. "Especially when she brings food." He delved into the basket and Ellie suddenly wished she knew how to make fried chicken and potato salad and cherry pie.

Apparently Jesse didn't mind her lunch of ham sandwiches, lemonade and potato chips, because he wolfed it down like a starving man. She contented herself to munch on chips, spending her time absorbing him. He had sprawled on his side on the blanket, propped up on one elbow. He took a swallow of lemonade and then held up a single potato chip.

"Isn't it a marvel what modern man can invent?" He held the chip to her lips and Ellie automatically took it, her lips grazing his salty fingers. Body parts lower than her stomach began aching. Think generic wasn't working.

"Like what?" She found it hard to concentrate on the conversation.

"Making potato chips; iceboxes to keep food from spoiling."

"Hot dogs and ketchup," Ellie added, thinking back to picnics in her youth.

"Hot dogs?" Jesse looked at her in shock. "I know they do things different in the east, but don't ever tell me you ate a dog."

Ellie began to giggle, and soon rolled to her back in hysterics. Jesse's expression was priceless. But how could she explain something which apparently hadn't been invented yet?

She opened her eyes to find Jesse leaning over her. "Oh."

"I haven't heard you laugh in too long a time, El. I know since your father died, it hasn't been easy. Still, it's time to get on with your life." Before Ellie could think, he lowered his head and kissed her -- a kiss so light and gentle she might have imagined it. Except for her rapid heartbeat and the tantalizing smell of him which filled her head.

As quickly as he had come to her, he retreated to his side of the blanket. "Tell me about your time in the East. When you first came home, I had the feeling you wanted to go right back there for good, but lately, you seem to have settled in."

What could she tell him about the East, especially not knowing where Elizabeth had gone to school or what she

62

had studied. She decided to stick as close to the truth as she could, and hope that Jesse hadn't been east of the Mississippi.

"New York is, well, New York." She began with a shrug. "Very cosmopolitan, you know. It's the center of fashion and trade."

"Is that all they taught you in that finishing school of yours? Fashion?"

Indignant, Ellie rose to her knees, hands on hips. "I know three languages, can program a computer, and--" She broke off at his look of astonishment.

"What's a computer?"

Oh, boy, now she'd done it. "It's, ah, new type of musical instrument." Struck by genius, she thought of the computerized keyboards all the pop stars used.

Jesse cocked his head to the side. "Musical instrument? And where do they use this?"

"At the opera." Hoping to get him off track, she continued, "I love the opera. We used to go every opening night for the new performances. The costumes were spectacular, and the music divine."

Apparently Jesse wasn't fond of music, because he rolled to his stomach in disinterest. "What else?"

"I also studied poetry, so I spent alot of time at the coffee houses and at poetry readings."

That caught his attention. "You actually like poetry now?"

"Yes, why?"

"I don't believe you. Who's your favorite?"

"Robert Frost," Ellie answered without hesitation.

"Ah-ha! I knew it! You don't like poetry, you just said that to rile me. I've never heard of Frost."

Ellie arched her brows. "What does a woodsman know about poetry?"

Jesse was acting like a child, but when he blushed at her comment, she felt she had injured his male pride.

"Mother had a fondness for the romance poets, so I grew up surrounded by books, especially the early poets.

There's something magical about the lyrical rhythm of the epics they wrote." He gazed beyond her.

"I tried to read poetry to you. I even tried my hand at writing you a sonnet, but you laughed at me and called me a sissy."

Ellie was appalled anyone could be so callous. Even though she wasn't at fault, she felt compelled to apologize. "I'm sorry, but I don't remember doing that."

"You were only ten at the time and I fourteen." Jesse's gaze slid away from her and Ellie thought perhaps the hurt was still there.

It seemed important to her to make it up to him. She gave him a gentle smile as she spoke. "Robert Frost is a fairly new poet from the New England area, so it's not surprising you haven't had the chance to read him yet.

"Part of one of his poems aptly describes my life here at Peavine, I think." She closed her eyes as she quoted, "'Two roads diverge in a wood and I, I took the one less traveled by, and that has made all the difference.'"

Jesse stared, enchanted, as Elizabeth quoted poetry to him. Her face was serene, her voice a soft caress of the words. He shook his head in wonder. "You have really changed quite a bit, Elizabeth," he stated when she finished her short recitation. She frowned at his comment, and he wondered if she had misconstrued his compliment.

"I must go." She stood and began to gather their picnic things, stuffing them back into the basket. "I'm sure you have work to do."

"Well, yes, as a matter of fact, I probably should get back to the mine." Jesse scrambled to his feet as she tried to jerk the blanket out from under him. "Elizabeth, what's wrong?"

She looked at him then, but the tenderness he had seen earlier was gone, along with any hint of the laughter they had shared. "Nothing is wrong. Good-bye." She started down the path, only to turn half way around again. "And I told you I preferred being called Ellie, not Elizabeth."

"El--" He called her back, but she had already disappeared through the trees.

Ellie paced around the table in the kitchen, stopping to snub out her cigarette. "Damn, damn, damn!" She stomped a foot in agitation.

Lucky walked in the back door in the middle of her tirade. "Boy, Miss Elizabeth, how many times do I gotta tell you--"

"Just don't start on me, Lucky." Ellie turned on him. "And don't call me Elizabeth!"

She hated the woman, even though she had never met her. Ellie had only been in Peavine a short time, and already she felt something for Jesse Cole. And what did that man do but call her by another woman's name. It was irrelevant to Ellie that Jesse didn't know any better; that he thought she was Elizabeth. Somehow she felt he should know the difference.

By the time Zeke arrived, Lucky had fixed Ellie dinner and the two of them were playing poker at the kitchen table. Ellie guessed by the expression on Zeke's face that he didn't approve of the haze of smoke, nor the near empty whiskey bottle on the table. She shrugged.

"Wanna join us, Zeke?" She asked, squinting up from her cards. Zeke ignored her and glared at Lucky, who gave his brother a lopsided grin.

"I thought you were gonna come up with a plan to get Jesse outa this mess." Zeke issued the flat statement and Ellie hypothesized that he didn't want to play poker. Looking at her cards, then at the owl-eyed Lucky, she threw in her hand.

He had consumed far more whiskey than she had, which was why more money lay in front of her. She had wanted to get drunk, damn Jesse Cole's hide, but in the end decided to use it to loosen Lucky's tongue and find out everything he knew about the man.

That hadn't worked. Either Lucky didn't know anything, or whiskey wasn't the way to get him to talk.

"Just exactly how involved is Jesse with Elizabeth?" She decided to get answers out of Zeke.

"What's that got to do with finding the murderer?"

She blew upward at the hair hanging in her face. Trouble with Zeke was he did know things, and was smart enough to keep them to himself.

"I already have a plan for getting at that information." She waved away his concern with a flick of her wrist. Ellie had decided on a course of action while Lucky was at the saloon. However, some morbid imp in her head wanted to know about Jesse Cole's love life. "I need to know if Elizabeth's been making out with Jesse. Don't you think it might be strange if I, as Elizabeth, suddenly decide not to anymore?" Although that'd be a cold day in hell.

Zeke turned the brightest red Ellie had ever seen a person turn. "Making out?" The words squeaked out of his mouth.

Ellie grinned. "Yeah, you know, sparking. Don't tell me they don't do that in the 1870's. Explain to me about kissing."

"Oh, boy." Lucky slapped a hand to his forehead just before sliding off his chair onto the floor in a drunken stupor.

Chapter 6

Ellie didn't see Zeke or Lucky for several days after that. She imagined Zeke didn't want to explain things to her, and Lucky was sure to have a hangover -- one which Zeke would rip him about. It didn't matter, because she had things to do and would just as soon not have to explain herself to them.

First, she conducted a thorough search of the house. The Calhoun residence was small by modern standards, but she supposed it was equivalent to Country Club for Peavine, Nevada. There were only two bedrooms, the kitchen, a formal dining area and the front living room, or parlor as Lucky called it. Then, off one bedroom, she opened a door leading to what could only be Mr. Calhoun's study.

She couldn't find any indication that things at the bank weren't on the up-and-up. It would help if she knew exactly what to look for, but since she didn't witness the first go-round of the accident, she'd just have to wing it. She looked behind the pictures, pulled books from the bookcase and tossed back the rug on the floor, but couldn't find a safe. Of course, why would a banker need a safe at home when he could keep all his stuff at the bank.

Sitting cross-legged on the floor, she debated her next move, and knew a trip to the bank would be necessary. There had to be a paper trail to help her understand what was going on. However, today was Saturday, so she'd have to wait a couple of days.

Being in Peavine equated with being on vacation in Ellie's book, for the inactivity made her more tired than working. Used to a very active life, she tried to keep busy Saturday straightening up the house, even though it wasn't hers and wasn't really messy. She washed the dishes, rinsed out a few personal things and hung them on the line out back, took a nap and finally decided to walk downtown to the store.

Judging by the duskiness of the sky, it was later than she thought, and she hoped the store would still be open. She was out of eggs and potatoes -- about the only things she knew how to cook without a microwave. She also needed to find out, without asking if possible, how to get more ice for the icebox. That sounded dumb, but unless she could find Zeke or Lucky, she couldn't just come right out and ask when she supposedly lived here all her life. She didn't even know how healthy keeping food on ice really was, but figured if people weren't dropping like flies because of such a "marvelous invention", then she could survive, too.

Whooping and hollering echoed along the boardwalk as she turned the corner to town. When she stepped past the post office, she could see hordes of men crowding the doorways of the saloons and spilling out of the boarding house. Amazed, she wondered where they had hidden all week. The other day when she'd ventured out, she hadn't seen very many people at all.

"Well, howdy there, honey." Rough hands grabbed her around the waist and sour breath assaulted her senses. "Are you a new little piece of sugar from Miss Molly's sent here just for me?" Coarse male laughter accompanied the question.

Ellie reacted the instant the man touched her, but his strength and size overpowered her as he lifted her right off the sidewalk. "Let me go, damn it!" She swore between gritted teeth, swinging her arms and feet at her attacker.

None of her self-defense classes had included lessons on fending off an assault while wearing an ankle length skirt that kept wrapping around her legs. Ellie couldn't find any skin to bite, and digging her nails into the man's forearm didn't faze him. She threw back her head, hoping to conk him on the chin, but instead left her neck exposed to his slobbery kisses. Bile rose in her throat.

"Looks like ya got a handful, Tom. Need some help?" Several male voices added to the clamor as panic knotted in Ellie's stomach.

"Naw, I like a little fight in my women." The man called Tom roared with laughter as Ellie fought all the harder.

"It's too bad this particular lady isn't your woman. Now put her down." A calm but steely voice made itself heard over the crowd.

Tom turned to the source of the command; Ellie's body flopping like a rag doll as she flew in a semi-circle, still clutched in the giant's paws. Her relief at seeing Jesse quickly died when she noticed all he had to back up his dictate were wide shoulders and a brave stance. No gun or knife; no sheriff. Not that it mattered, apparently, for Tom immediately dropped her, and when Ellie teetered to the side, his previously rough hands gently set her upright.

"I'm sorry, Mr. Cole. Is she your woman? You know I'd never mess with her if'n I knew she was yours." The huge man, sounding so contrite, almost garnered sympathy from Ellie, until she recalled how brutal he'd been before Jesse appeared.

She whipped around to give him a piece of her mind, but Jesse caught her forearm and gently but strongly pulled her back against his side. Even though his gaze never left the gigantic miner, Ellie had no trouble hearing his softly whispered, "Don't even think about it," before he spoke out loud to the group of men. "Women should always be treated as ladies, regardless of whether they work at Miss Molly's or are the banker's daughter."

Ellie frowned at the derogatory tone he used when labeling her "the banker's daughter." She didn't know Miss Molly, but from earlier remarks, could only assume she either owned the saloon or a brothel; maybe both. Jesse's words didn't really answer Tom's questions, and Ellie wondered if he didn't think of her as his lady, or if she just didn't qualify as a lady at all.

The men quickly dispersed after Jesse's admonishment, and without a word he turned her around and herded her towards home.

"I have errands to run." She stated as way of explanation for her appearance, though she didn't know why she felt the need to excuse herself.

"It's Saturday night."

"What's that got to do with anything?"

Jesse stomped onto the porch at Elizabeth's house before answering. "For God's sake, Elizabeth, I'm usually an easy going man, but the past few days you've tried my patience in more ways than one. Not to mention I left a perfectly good beefsteak to rescue you."

For once, Ellie was glad Jesse called her Elizabeth. The name somehow excused her from feeling guilty at causing him such trouble. At the same time, the fact that he was eating steak while she had eaten her last two eggs -- scrambled -- made her mad. "That still doesn't explain all the men on the streets. And what's so special about Saturday night?"

Jesse ran a hand over his face in exasperation. "Have you forgotten everything since you came back home? The majority of men working the mines aren't married, so they live right up at the mine sites in tents during most of the year. If Tom wasn't one of my own miners, it probably wouldn't have been so easy to get him to let you go. Those men only come down to town on payday, which is Saturday, and then it's not always just to get a home cooked meal and a bath."

Ellie actually blushed at the implications, but that raised another question. "If Saturday night is so special, why didn't you come over to take me out?"

"Why would I do that?" Jesse looked at her with a startled expression. "While I will admit you've been on my mind alot lately, I don't see the need to do things different than before."

"Before what?"

An arresting grin on his face, he crossed his arms over his chest and leaned against the porch rail. He raised one eyebrow and gave her a totally male, I'm-everything-you-ever-wanted, look. "Before you threw yourself at me the other day."

Ellie hadn't quit sputtering in anger before he leaned forward and quickly kissed her on the forehead, then turned and stepped off the porch.

"I most certainly did not throw myself at you."

Rich laughter met her denial.

Refusing to give him the last word, Ellie responded in the heat of anger. "Well, if you're too busy to take me out on a date, then I'll just find someone who will."

That stopped him. He turned, standing in the shadow of the house, holding his hands up in mock surrender. "OK, I'll take you to church tomorrow. Will that do for a date?"

Secretly pleased with herself, if only for a small victory, Ellie smiled. "Yes, I think that will do nicely." She gave him a little flip of her head and turned to go into the house.

Only in visiting with the minister after church the next day did Ellie find out that Jesse always took Elizabeth to church. The fact of the matter was both their fathers had been responsible for seeing the church built in the first place, and in recognition, the families had the very front pew together.

* * *

Ellie knew she had a quest to fulfill within the month, but it had become difficult to keep that separate from her growing infatuation for Jesse. Even when he made her mad, she wanted to spend time with him, to get to know him and what he liked to do and...well, more. At the same time, she knew she had to cultivate Clayton Scott's trust to uncover the exact plan he had to take over the Nightingale Mine. After the little trick Jesse pulled Sunday, Ellie decided Clayton could very well serve an additional purpose in making Jesse jealous. She just hoped she could keep him under control.

71

While she would prefer Clayton not be at the bank when she arrived, she had to assume he would be. With that in mind, Monday morning Ellie chose a frilly dress with lots of ribbons. Lucky stopped by and stood there gapping at her like she was a Martian. When he opened his mouth, and Ellie just knew he was going to make some crack about her attire, she frowned so quickly he turned tail and ran without even having a cup of coffee.

Henry's eyes widened when she opened the door to the bank. He stammered when addressing her, and Ellie had the uncomfortable feeling she had once again done or said something inappropriate for this time period.

"Miss...Miss Elizabeth. I haven't seen you here since Mr. Calhoun...died." The last word came out a strangled whisper, but at least she now understood his nervousness.

Ellie couldn't help but be moved. She reached past the bars of the teller cage and patted Henry's hand. Even though Mr. Calhoun wasn't her father, she felt empathy for Elizabeth and the people of Peavine. A shiver ran down her spine. Heaven forbid, but she was beginning to assimilate herself into 1870.

"It's all right, Henry. I'm sorry it's taken me so long to come in again."

"Well, you never did come in much." Henry amended his earlier statement, then apparently embarrassed by his outspoken words, he began stammering again. "I mean...other than to get money..." He finally gave up, staring down at the paper in front of him.

Ellie laughed, trying to defuse the situation. "I've decided to take a more active interest in banking, Henry. Could you please point me to Mr. Scott's office?"

If Henry thought it strange that she didn't know where the office was, he didn't say as he reached around his partition and pulled open the half gate so Ellie could enter the back of the bank.

"I'm sure Mr. Scott won't mind if I borrow his office for just a little while, do you think?" Ellie pasted on a smile as she opened the massive wood door to an office directly behind the teller's cage.

Well, hell!

"Good morning, Elizabeth. You're out and about early this morning. Do I dare hope you came all this way just to see me?" As suave as ever, Clayton rose when she entered and moved around his desk to take her hand in both of his.

Ellie sincerely hoped her facial expression didn't give away her surprise at his being there, nor her hesitation as he kissed her gloved hand. She wanted him to be gone so she could check the bank records, but now if she just turned around and left, he would get suspicious.

She forced a smile and very politely accepted his offer to take an early morning ride in his carriage.

Ellie thought about Clayton Scott's role in this reenactment of history. Because of the type of man he was, she had known it wouldn't be hard to garner his interest, even before she understood Elizabeth's relationship with him. Now, however, it would take real acting to keep him interested and at the same time at a distance.

As the carriage bumped over the uneven road towards the outskirts of town, she pretended to study the passing landscape. Peavine was situated in a little valley with the Sierra-Nevada Mountains on its west side. The lower range where the town sat was covered with trees and Ellie knew alot of that timber was used in the mines.

She wasn't well versed in tree types, but did recognize pine, fir and juniper as they drove closer to the wooded area. She realized that the trees also helped keep the temperature from extremes, since the breeze over the mountains remained cooled as it wafted through the trees.

She would have continued to tune Clayton out as he rambled on about his mining interests and the bank, but then he began talking about the sweet music they could be making together, and she had to interrupt.

"Really, Clayton, you shouldn't be talking like that." She scooted to the outside edge of her seat, trying to put some space between them. Ellie sure didn't know where Elizabeth had found this one, but he was slick. For every inch she moved, he moved two. When she reached down to scoot her dress over, he grabbed her hand and brought it to his thigh, driving the single horse rig with only his left hand.

"My talk didn't used to bother you." His jaw tightened as he shot her a glance and his hand squeezed hers. "You're different, Elizabeth, and I'm not at all sure I like the change."

Of course she was different, but she wondered how Clayton could have ascertained so much in so little time. When Jesse had told her that, he had smiled and said he liked the change.

She glanced around for something generic to talk about. Apparently Clayton was heading for the mines on the east slop, north of where the Nightingale stood. Thank goodness. Ellie didn't want Jesse to see her with Clayton, even though her earlier wish had been to use him to make Jesse jealous.

She only hoped she could pacify Clayton, increase Jesse's interest in her, find out the scheme behind the accident, and not go insane all in the same month! Her head started pounding just thinking about it, and she didn't realize she had groaned out loud until Clayton pulled the carriage to a stop.

One arm snaked around the back of her shoulders, pulling her close against him. "Are you all right, my dear? You look flushed."

Using the opening he gave her, she touched the back of her hand to her forehead, fluttered her eyelashes, and moaned, "I do feel somewhat faint. Perhaps it would be best if--" She hadn't even finished the sentence when he bent his head, stopping her words with his mouth.

His kiss wasn't at all what she expected from Clayton, whom she felt had an evil core. She thought he would be hard, but while his lips were firm and hot, he kissed her with the expertise of someone who practiced, and apparently put a whole lot of time into that practice.

Somewhere in the back of her mind, Lucky lectured that she shouldn't be kissing Clayton, and especially not enjoying that kiss. Ellie mentally gave him the look, and relaxed in Clayton's embrace. It might be fun having two guys chasing after her in Peavine, Nevada, because she definitely didn't have any aversion to kissing. At this rate, it wouldn't be hard to continue her masquerade. She'd just have to keep her dance card straight.

Those thoughts, and kisses, were interrupted when Clayton began to move. While his mouth nibbled its way down her neck, his hand conveniently wandered over her hip, down her leg, and was in the process of hiking up her skirt. Now that, Ellie figured, was not part of the little game they played.

Grabbing his wrist with one hand, she brought her other palm up flat against his chest. "Oh, my." She really didn't have to act, for she found herself short of breath from his kisses. "I do believe you should take me back to town."

"Elizabeth, quit being a tease. You can only tease a man so much." He murmured the words, his voice still soft and caressing, but Ellie could feel the tension in his arms as they tightened around her.

This time, she more forcefully pushed him back. Damn, every time someone called her Elizabeth, it just ruined the game. However, in this case, it helped clear her mind and made her realize how foolish she had just acted. Where did she draw the line between welcoming his advances in order to ferret out the information they needed, and being true to Jesse?

That thought stayed with her on the ride back to town. Though he acted the gentleman, she sensed the increased tension in Clayton and hoped she wouldn't have to spend much time with him. If push came to shove, she knew she didn't have the strength if he wanted to overpower her. And who would come to her rescue -- Zeke and Lucky?

She poured herself a glass of lemonade when she got home and sat at the kitchen table contemplating the day. She almost choked as she reflected on her emotions. She just hadn't expected to enjoy kissing Clayton. But while his kisses were breathtaking, somehow the little tingles and fevery aches she had felt with Jesse had not been there with Clayton.

So, it was a worthwhile experiment, she told herself. Having kissed both men, Jesse definitely aroused more erotic sensations, which only seemed right to Ellie, since she had more intense feelings for him. Besides, they already knew Clayton was the evil one, and would do whatever it took to get rid of Jesse. That thought made her feel guilty for having kissed him, but more determined to resist him the next time.

None of this should matter, she fumed, because neither man was hers. Not that she wanted them, she sternly reminded herself. She had a life in a different century, and would be out of here soon enough. She crushed out her cigarette and cursed Zeke and Lucky, who had gotten her into this mess in the first place.

* * *

The next day, she covertly watched the bank from the corner. When she saw Clayton leave, she scurried across the street and through the bank doors, determined to check out the books for possible discrepancies in the records.

"Mr. Scott's not here, Miss," Henry stated politely as she hurried through the gate and behind the counter.

"Oh, that's OK, Henry, I'll just wait for him in his office." Ellie didn't give him time to reply but quietly closed the huge oak door and headed right for the back side of Clayton's desk. It had to figure that if something were fishy, he wouldn't keep the records with the rest of the bank's books. Any bank examiner worth his salt would find a problem within the hour.

It took Ellie less time than that. The bottom drawer to the desk was locked, but the key was in a tray in the middle desk drawer. Foolish man, she thought, as she pulled out a ledger and a cursory glimpse at the pages showed it to be some kind of payment book. Both Jesse's and Elizabeth's fathers' names were at the top of each page.

Hoping to find some dates or description of what the amounts of money were for, she quickly flipped to the front, but in the process, an envelope fluttered out from between the pages.

The front of the envelope had Jesse's name on it, and she quickly took out the papers, scanning the spidery writing. Though some words were impossible for her to decipher, it looked to be some kind of codicil where someone's ownership in the Nightingale mine reverted back upon death. Did that say Wendall or Warren? Whose death?

She shook her head, trying to unravel the words, when she heard Clayton's voice through the door. She grabbed the book, shoving it back into the drawer and slamming it shut just as Clayton came in. His surprise at seeing her seated in his chair behind his desk couldn't be any greater than her surprise at seeing him standing there.

She swallowed, trying to moisten her suddenly dry throat. Under cover of the desk, she stuffed the paper and envelope into her handbag, speaking to cover the sound of rustling paper.

"Hello...Clayton. I've been waiting for you."

His brows rose in an expression of disbelief. It wouldn't do at all for him to find out what she had really been up to. "Two days in a row, my dear? After yesterday, I wouldn't have thought to see you again quite so soon. Or did you remember that my advances were to your liking after all?"

Had he deliberately spoken loudly so people in the outer office could hear, since the door remained slightly ajar? Ellie decided she didn't have to take that kind of behavior, but before she could stand, he had rounded the desk and moved behind her, pushing her back down in the chair with rough hands on her shoulders.

He bent forward, his breath hot against her cheek as he slid his hands up and down her bare arms. "Seeing you here like this, I have this erotic picture in my mind of you laying naked on my desk," he kissed her ear as he spoke, "begging me, not for a loan, but for--" The last word was lost as his tongue darted out and licked her ear, but Ellie couldn't mistake his meaning.

She jerked backward, sending the chair into Clayton's stomach and slamming him into the wall. Yesterday she could handle, but this, she hadn't planned on. Regardless of whether Elizabeth had already given herself to Clayton, Ellie knew with a certainty it wouldn't happen in this reenactment.

Clayton's fingers dug into Ellie's shoulders. "You little bitch," he swore under his breath, then surprisingly, he laughed. "Ever since your father died, you've turned into a cold fish, and while I might have accepted it for awhile, I won't anymore. We're two of a kind, Elizabeth, so if you want to play rough--"

His words were cut off when a verbal scuffle and stomping boots grew louder just outside the door. Before Ellie could remove Clayton's hands from her shoulders, Jesse stormed into the office, his beautiful mouth an angry slash and fire in his blue eyes.

He stopped just inside the door, his gaze turning dark and stormy as he took in the scene. Ellie groaned as she realized what it must look like from his viewpoint. Again, she struggled to free herself, but Clayton's grip was totally possessive and Ellie immediately realized his intent.

"Well, well, my dear, look who's here. We really didn't want an interruption, but as long as you don't bother knocking, what do you want, Cole?" Clayton's words were snide and insinuating, and Ellie's heart twisted when she saw the look of anguish that crossed Jesse's face as he watched Clayton's hands caress her.

How could she ever make him understand this wasn't what he thought? And why on God's green earth had she ever found Clayton attractive? Even if the two men hadn't been in the same room, she wouldn't have chosen Clayton over Jesse. Elizabeth might like the bad guy attitude, but the evil emitting from him burned straight through the padded chair and into Ellie's back. Her cheeks flushed with embarrassment that Jesse would think she had thrown herself at Clayton. Especially after he had accused her of doing the same to him. What must he think of her?

"Let the lady go, Scott. Then you and I will talk." Jesse waved a fist at them, a crushed paper in his hand.

There was that word lady, again, Ellie thought; and as before, she wasn't too sure that Jesse meant it in a nice way.

"I don't think so. Elizabeth, here, has a direct interest in the bank, don't you, dear?" He squeezed her arm to get a response, and though Ellie nodded only slightly, her gaze beseeched Jesse not to listen to the evil words.

"I want to know what the hell you mean sending me this mortgage notice and saying I'm behind on payments. I don't owe you any money!" Ellie had never seen Jesse mad before. The anger in him was an almost palatable thing, and it was aimed straight at Clayton. He wouldn't even look at her when he spoke.

"It's really quite simple. Your father was buying out Elizabeth's father's interest in the Nightingale mine."

Ellie could feel Clayton give an indifferent shrug, but she never took her eyes off Jesse. She kept hoping he would look her way so she could express -- what? With Clayton's hands all over her, how was she to convey anything to Jesse so that he would not hate her?

Jesse frowned. "I thought that agreement became null and void upon their deaths."

"Ah, well, if that was their intent, they should have put it in writing, because I have the ledger showing there is still money owed. Therefore, Elizabeth's father still held an interest in your mine. Until the note is paid, I have that share, because I bought out the loan before Wendall died." The gloating in Clayton's voice caused Ellie's stomach to drop to her toes.

Ellie watched as red crept up Jesse's neck and into his cheeks. For reasons she hadn't determined yet, these two men didn't like each other, and Jesse especially didn't like the fact that Clayton held something over his head.

"I'll buy out the note, then. How much is left?" Jesse's voice was determined, but Ellie wondered where he'd get the money.

Clayton just laughed. "Why would I let you do that? You keep telling everyone who'll listen that you're close to the motherlode. If you can't make the loan payment, I can take over the mine. Even if you make the payment, I still hold the rest of the note, so if you do strike pay dirt, I'll collect a tidy sum for my investment."

"You bastard," Jesse cursed. "If you think I'll let you have one speck of dirt from the Nightingale, you're crazy. I'll shut the mine down first."

"Tsk, tsk. Then I'd get it all, wouldn't I, because you wouldn't be able to make your payments. It would seem that little loan has become a real nice investment for me. Unless, of course, you can come up with a paper that says the loan was canceled, as you seem to think."

Clayton's hands had relaxed on Ellie's shoulders, and now he stroked her with an absent-minded touch. Ellie had the eerie feeling his thoughts weren't on her at all, but on the money he would have and the riches within reach if Jesse forfeited on the loan.

She looked at Jesse as he stared Clayton down. She could see his hands clinched at his sides and realized what control it took for him not to hit Clayton. A vein throbbed in his neck and he swallowed convulsively, as though taking a bitter pill. How she longed to soothe the wrinkles from his brow and bring a smile to his face once more.

Yet even knowing she would rather leave with Jesse and try to kiss away his anger, she decided for the sake of the game, she'd better stick with Clayton. She definitely didn't want to kiss him into submission, but his role in this mystery was more important than Jesse's -- at least right now. They already knew what would happen to Jesse if she didn't help. How could she go with one man and not make another angry? Before she could announce her decision, Jesse balled the paper up, threw it across the room, and stormed out of the office.

Ellie sat in the chair where she'd been since Jesse first burst into Clayton's office, too stunned to move, even though Clayton had since let go of her.

"What is that noise?" Clayton asked, eyeing her suspiciously.

Ellie glanced down at her lap and found her hands nervously snapping and unsnapping her purse. She forced herself to sit still and not tuck the handbag under the edge of her skirt as her brain screamed to do. As calmly as she could, she stood and moved to the door.

"Well, that was certainly exciting. If you don't mind, I think I'll go home now." She reached for the door knob, but Clayton's fingers circled her arm.

"I thought you had come to see me. It seems we have unfinished business."

She shrugged off his hand, anger seething through her at his callous manner. "I think I've seen quite enough of you for one day, thank you very much." At the look of incredulity on his face, she added, "Regardless of what you may think, I do not like to be manhandled." With that parting remark, she sailed through the door and had almost made her escape when he again caught her elbow, at least gently this time.

"Henry, I'm taking Miss Calhoun to supper and then seeing her home," he told the teller as he opened the door for her. That was the last thing she wanted, but somehow it seemed prudent to accept his offer. Ellie inclined her head slightly and proceeded him out of the bank.

However, when he moved to her side, his hand brushed her purse, and again she felt the weight of the stolen documents inside. There could be only one thing to do. She had to dump the purse, but where?

"I must stop at Murphy's for a few things. It's really not necessary for you to take me to supper. I'm sure you're very busy and I'm perfectly capable of getting home myself." She tried unsuccessfully to remove her elbow from his grip.

"Nonsense. It is my duty as a gentleman."

"Excuse me if I disagree with your personal assessment." Ellie was still angry with his treatment of her, and angry at herself for enjoying that first kiss.

Her comment stopped him on the boardwalk, and he pulled her aside from the other people walking along, his fingers painfully pinching her arm. "It seems to me you are the one being disagreeable, Elizabeth. It wasn't that long ago your attitude was much more pleasing. As I already told you, I won't tolerate it anymore."

Nothing else was said as they crossed the street and he opened the door to the store. As quickly as she could, she collected a few cans of food and hurried to the counter. She just hoped Sarah would play along with her.

"Hello, Sarah. Would you ring these up for me, please?" Since there were several other people in the store, Sarah didn't take the time to visit with Ellie, for which she was glad. However, when she had totaled the purchases, Ellie knew the hardest part was to come, and she only hoped Sarah was preoccupied enough with her customers not to notice Ellie's lie.

"I want to thank you for letting me borrow your purse, Sarah, and I'm sorry it took so long to return it." She pushed the beaded bag toward the young woman.

"But--" Sarah started to protest.

"I know. It's been so long, you probably forgot it was yours." Ellie stared intently at Sarah until the girl seemed to mentally absorb her thoughts.

Slowly, she took the purse, glancing from Ellie to Clayton and back. "Oh, uh, you're right. I had completely forgotten." Then, almost as an afterthought, she added, "Will you come to coffee tomorrow, Elizabeth? Mrs. Carter says our dresses are done and she needs one final fitting."

"Yes, of course, I'll come." Clayton tugged on her elbow and she knew she had to leave. Damn, it was a pain in the rear to have so many people pulling her in so many different directions.

As they walked away from the store, Ellie decided she might as well ask questions. "Why would Father keep Jesse's mine, or allow you to buy out his interest?" She couldn't stop herself from adding, "You didn't treat him very nicely today."

Clayton snorted in disgust. "Why does it matter? He's a hick -- he has no culture. You saw his reaction."

Ellie knew that wasn't true. Jesse quoted poetry, and from what she had gathered, that wasn't the extent of his learning. "You taunted him terribly; what did you expect? And why won't you discuss a buy out? It's not like you don't have other interests."

"What make the difference to you anyway?" His tone held anger, and Ellie knew she couldn't let him think she really cared about Jesse.

Still, she had to get the information. "So, you won't let Jesse buy back his loan?"

Clayton gave a harsh laugh. "You are such a soft touch. You really have no head for business, do you? If you were a banker, you'd be forgiving every man's loan who brought you a sob story, and your bank would go under. Besides, maybe I won't have to do anything with Cole's loan. Mining accidents happen all the time. Now, don't worry about it. Just let me take care of things and we'll have it all."

His attitude frightened Ellie. There was definitely a plot underfoot which spelled trouble and Elizabeth must have been right in the middle of it. Something about Clayton's casual disregard for Jesse's life bothered her, and she felt an urgent need to see him and ascertain that he was all right.

Chapter 7

Jesse had stormed back to the mine, yelling at everybody, even though he knew damn good and well none of his workers were at fault for what had happened at the bank. Zeke had tried to pacify him, telling him things would work out if he had some patience, but even Zeke hadn't had an answer when Jesse informed him Elizabeth had been in Scott's office.

In fact, Zeke had gotten so riled, Jesse had had to calm him down. Zeke had then yelled at Lucky and the two of them raced off, Zeke muttering about someone named Eleanor and what he'd like to do to her.

Now, as dusk settled across the town and a cooling breeze blew down from the mountains, Jesse had to wonder why he was sitting on Elizabeth's porch waiting for her to come home. He ground his teeth when he recalled how Scott's hands had been all over her. From where Jesse had stood, she hadn't seemed a very willing partner, but she hadn't seemed inclined to move away, either.

Nor had she followed him when he stormed out of the bank. He doubted he would have talked to her anyway, he had been so mad at Scott's high-handed attitude. But the fact of the matter was, they were sort of a couple, and he had sort of asked her to marry him a long time ago. Ironically, it had never bothered him a bit that she seemed in no hurry to marry, until recently.

Over the past week she had consumed his thoughts, not to mention bothering other body parts as well. There had been no hesitancy in the way she kissed him, but just as quick she seemed to get mad at him. Hot and cold; fast and slow. No wonder his mind was in a continual state of confusion. Would he ever figure that woman out?

Just thinking about Elizabeth caused an ache in the lower reaches of his anatomy, so he consciously shifted his thoughts to Scott. A slow, burning anger heated his insides over the snide way Scott had rubbed in the fact that he held the note to Jesse's mine. Not the bank, but Clayton Scott personally.

That hadn't set right with Jesse. He searched his mind for a conversation he'd had with Wendall -- how long ago? Months before his death, Elizabeth's father, who had been as close to Jesse as his own father, had ventured up to the Nightingale. Wendall had talked mostly about old times when he and Jesse's father had first started prospecting.

In recalling his visit, Jesse felt sure he'd mentioned an agreement with his father as to the disposition of the mine upon either parent's death. Unfortunately, if such an agreement existed, Wendall had probably kept it at the bank. Just one more reason for Jesse's anger against Clayton Scott.

The last bit of sunlight faded behind the mountain, night shadows now concealing his scowl as he sat on the porch rail with his back against the wall. In the distance he could hear voices and knew Elizabeth was heading this way, probably with the fancy pants banker in tow. Regardless of her earlier behavior, Jesse felt an incredible need to see and talk with her. Instead of making himself known, however, he slid further back into the shadows as the couple approached the porch, not the least guilty about eavesdropping on their conversation.

"Thank you for dinner and for seeing me home, though it wasn't necessary." Elizabeth stopped walking at the gate and turned, as though she didn't want Scott any further.

"I'll come inside," the man responded. It was a demand, not a request, and Jesse's hair bristled at the underlying threat. He turned in the darkness and planted both feet on the porch, ready to step forward.

"No, I think not." Her voice held a stubbornness he hadn't heard before.

"Elizabeth, I told you I wouldn't play dandy to a tease." Clayton grabbed her arm and Jesse made his move, not waiting to see how Elizabeth replied.

With long strides he bounded off the porch and wedged himself between Elizabeth and Scott. "She said to get lost." He didn't have to straighten up to be taller than the banker, but he did anyway, planting his hands on his hips, although he longed to plant them in the other man's face.

Jesse was happy to note Elizabeth's relieved look at his presence. Perhaps she wasn't as fond of Scott as he had previously thought. She twisted out of the man's grip and moved to the porch. Clayton stared angrily after her, his piercing gaze slicing past Jesse before he turned on his heel and stormed away into the darkness.

"Will you come in?" Elizabeth's soft words reached him, but she didn't wait for a response, leaving the door wide as she hurried inside to light a lamp. Jesse stepped up on the porch but didn't enter the house. He watched as she moved about, the glow of the lamp softening the curves of her silhouette as she moved across the room to another lamp.

Once again an ache formed, this time lodging against his heart. Why did he keep wishing he could give her everything money could buy? She had grown up in the lap of luxury with a father who gave her everything and then some. At times, Jesse had even considered her spoiled. Her recent behavior reminded him of the old Elizabeth; the one he had always wanted to love and cherish.

"Are you coming in?" She had moved to the door to question him again.

"No, it's late."

She cocked her head and though the light was at her back and he couldn't read her expression, Jesse heard the confusion in her voice.

"Why did you stop if you didn't want to see me?"

"I...was angry today...but not at you. Even so, I shouldn't have said the things I did while you were there. It's just that," Jesse sighed, not understanding his need to explain his behavior, but wanting her to understand anyway. He ran his hands through his hair in frustration.

"I know," she said, reaching out to pull him into the house. She quietly closed the door behind him. "Let's make some coffee."

She left him to follow as she wound through the house to the kitchen, carrying one of the lamps with her. He straddled a chair and watched her putter around the kitchen, stoking the fire and putting the coffee pot on.

"Look, Jesse--"

"Elizabeth--" They began at the same time. She laughed, and the sound was such a delight that he simply sat there staring at her. When she didn't seem inclined to continue, he nodded his head slightly for her to proceed.

"Sometimes things aren't exactly the way they appear," she begin, fidgeting with the sash at her waist and not looking at him.

Jesse's heart sank. "You've decided Clayton Scott is a better investment of your time." He tried to keep the emotion out of his voice, knowing it was her choice to make.

"God, no!" Her head snapped up and she gave him a wide-eyed stare. "Why would you think that?"

Now Jesse really was confused. "Maybe it had something to do with the way his hands were all over you at the bank today." Remembering just made him mad, so he turned aside.

In seconds, Elizabeth had rounded the table and squatted by him. When he wouldn't look at her, she turned his head, hands on his cheeks. "You can't possibly think I'd prefer him over you."

"Then why--"

She put a finger to his lips. "If I tell you, you have to promise not to go after Clayton."

Jesse snorted. "I won't promise any such thing."

Elizabeth started to get up and he grabbed her arm to stop her from leaving his side. She flinched, then quickly tried to pretend she hadn't. Jesse looked where his hand held her. Just above his fingers, a light bruise showed.

"That son of a bitch. I'll kill him." Jesse threatened in a flat tone, even though his heart beat painfully, his hand shaking as he slid the sleeve of her dress up further. Definite bruises circled her slim arm -- the exact kind of marks a man's hand would make if he grabbed her too tightly.

"Someone has to figure this mess out." Elizabeth continued.

"Stay away from him." He growled at her, trying to hide the rage he could barely control. The thought that Scott would dare hurt her consumed him with loathing.

"Would you really care so much?" She asked softly, leaning close enough for him to smell her sweetness.

"How can you even ask that?" Jesse groaned, dropping his head so his forehead rested on hers. "Lately, you've been starting fires in me no amount of cold water can douse. It damned near killed me to see you in his arms."

She gave a little sigh. "I told you, it's not what it seems, but you have to have patience."

"That's what Zeke said."

"Well, sometimes Zeke does know what he's talking about."

"Then explain it to me so I'll know, too." A throbbing headache had started behind Jesse's eyes, and he wondered if any explanation could cause it to stop. He turned in the chair so he could rest his head in his hands.

Elizabeth seemed to hesitate.

"Come on, El, you know I hate secrets."

"It's just that we don't have any hard evidence yet."

"We?"

"Zeke and Lucky and me."

"Zeke and Lucky?" Jesse laughed. "Those two don't have enough sense to come in out of the rain at times. What else could they possibly be up to?"

Elizabeth grimaced at his tone. "They know some things you wouldn't believe."

Jesse quirked a brow, wondering just exactly what those two old miners had told her. "Such as?"

"There may be a plot afoot to take over some of the mines in the area and Clayton may be behind it."

Jesse started to object, but she silenced him with a look.

"I was at the bank today trying to look at the records," she continued. "There must be something to indicate what he's up to."

"There's an easy way to find out. It's called my fists." Jesse didn't consider himself a man with a temper, but truth to tell, he was mad as a hornet right now.

"No, damn...darn it. You can't just waltz in there and pound it out of him. If we tip our hand before it's time, he'll destroy the records and then you'll have nothing."

"What records are you talking about?"

"That's just it. I don't know for certain. I just have to find a discrepancy -- something that's out of place."

"And how come you know about these records?"

Elizabeth looked away and Jesse began to wonder. After all, she seemed pretty chummy with Scott. Could she be playing both of them against each other?

"You know I never had anything to do with the bank. After father died, I didn't care what happened and let Clayton run it. Lately, some things he's said and done have made me wonder if that was a good move. That's why I went to the bank. I'll do what I must to find out if he's up to something illegal."

"And that includes letting him fondle you?" The instant the words were out of his mouth, Jesse wished he could call them back. But jealousy gnawed at his gut, making him say and do things he never thought he would.

Instead of getting mad, Elizabeth smiled. "Are you jealous?"

Jesse leaned closer to where she knelt between his legs. "Yes." He was a plain spoken man and above all things, honest.

There was a twinkle in her brown eyes, and a mischievous twitch at the corner of her mouth. "Well, he did kiss me the other day."

Jesse swore an oath, and her face broke into a wide grin.

"I tried to remember what your kiss had been like, but just couldn't recall." She shook her head, the movement causing her hair to wave, the silky tendrils just barely caressing his cheek as she leaned toward him.

Jesse couldn't stand being that close to her and not touching her. He gently pulled her closer, his mouth covering hers. Instant heat flared deep within and spread like wildfire through his veins. Her arms circled his neck and she ran her fingers through his hair, but when she arched her back and pressed her breasts against his chest, Jesse lost it.

Growling deep in his throat, he scooped her up and plopped her down on his lap, hugging her tight. Their kiss lengthened as Elizabeth tentatively touched his lips with her hot tongue. Jesse let her take the initiative, and soon they were gasping for breath. Struggling for control, he breathed in her scent -- fresh air and wildflowers -- and tried to content himself with burying his face in her silky hair. She snuggled close, peppering his neck with hot little kisses until he thought he'd die. Any thoughts of her choosing the banker over him flew out the window.

"I'd better get out of here or I might not be able to leave at all." The emotional seesaw he'd been on all day tilted him dizzily and he knew it wouldn't take much for him to fall right off.

"Would that be so bad?" Her innocent question sent his blood thundering.

"I'd like nothing better than to stay, but it wouldn't do your reputation any good."

With one last kiss to his chin and a sigh, she moved away from him. "That's probably true. I know it's difficult, but I do have to keep Clayton happy, too." She made a face.

Some of Jesse's anger returned. "If he lays a hand on you--"

She put a finger to his lips. "He won't, believe me." She gave him a gentle kiss on the lips and scooted off his lap. Jesse felt bereft. He didn't want her anywhere near Scott, so he tried to find a way to keep her to himself.

"What would you say if I take you to Steamboat Springs for a few days? My foreman can handle the mining operation."

"We can't. Sarah's wedding is in two days."

Jesse refused to take no for an answer. He wanted her out of Peavine until he could figure out what was going on. While he realized Elizabeth had an inside track to the bank records, there were some things he could investigate on his own.

"We'll go right after the wedding then."

Elizabeth smiled as she answered. "I guess one way to keep you out of trouble is to keep you out of the same town as Clayton Scott."

That wouldn't solve the problem, thought Jesse, but he didn't want her to worry so he kept his mouth shut.

* * *

Sarah's wedding day dawned cloudless, but turned hot. From the little room off the sanctuary, Ellie surveyed the crowded church and wondered how these people lived without air conditioning. Most of the ladies waved fans, their pastel colors fluttering among the pews like so many butterflies.

Well, it would soon be over, and she could escape to her house for a cigarette, strip down and cool off. Ellie thought of the way she had been living of late. Lucky only stopped early in the morning, and she hadn't seen much of Zeke. So, after her habitual cup of coffee in her bathrobe and instructions from Lucky not to cause trouble, she would spend the day alone, and practically naked. It was just too hot for clothes, so she had settled on a chambray shirt with the sleeves rolled up. Since it hung to her knees, she'd worn it for a house dress.

Yesterday at midday, she decided a cool bath might help, so had filled the tub with cold well water from the kitchen pump. She had lulled around for over an hour,

91

pretending she was back in New York at her condo swimming pool.

She had even begun sleeping naked, and the sensuous feel of the sheets against her skin had invoked dreams of Jesse Cole. Now, she stirred restlessly, peeking around the door jam to catch sight of him. He hadn't come back to see her in the past two days and she could only hope he wouldn't confront Clayton.

She had told Lucky what had happened on her porch. He shook his head, a low whistle escaping, reiterating Ellie's fears about a confrontation. Though they wouldn't say, Ellie had the feeling Zeke was keeping a close eye on Jesse.

"Isn't it time, yet? I'm so nervous." Sarah's shaky voice brought Ellie back to the present, and she turned away from the door, knowing there was nothing at the moment she could do about Jesse and Clayton.

"Yes, I just saw Henry step through the door at the other end." Ellie smiled as she straightened Sarah's veil. "You make a beautiful bride, and I wish you all the happiness in the world." She hadn't known Sarah long, but Ellie considered her a friend.

"Oh, Elizabeth. One day soon, it'll be you and Jesse getting married." She dabbed at her eyes beneath the gauzy veil. "I'll probably cry like a ninny then, too."

Ellie hugged Sarah close, knowing she couldn't keep the desperation off her face at those words, and she didn't want Sarah seeing it. There would be no wedding for Elizabeth and Jesse; not if Zeke and Lucky had anything to do with it. As for Ellie and Jesse; Ellie couldn't even contemplate that.

"You ready, pumpkin?" Nate Murphy stuck his head through the doorway. Sarah's father had been more nervous that she, and Ellie had finally sent him outside to visit with the guests as they arrived.

With a final squeeze of Sarah's hand, Ellie picked up her bouquet of wildflowers and stepped lightly into the foyer, pausing briefly at the very back of the church until the organist began the wedding march. She knew she looked her best in the dusty rose satin dress Mrs. Carter had made. When the seamstress had delivered the dress yesterday, Ellie had spent plenty of time staring at it hanging from the door of the armoire. She felt like Cinderella going to the ball, for none of her gowns for the opera had even been this elegant.

As she started down the aisle, her gaze collided with Jesse's and time stood still. Her heart beat erratically, heat infusing her body that had nothing to do with the temperature outside. Jesse's gaze smoldered, causing an ache to start in the very core of her, just as though his hands were caressing her skin.

She forced her feet to continue their march towards the alter. Why couldn't it be Jesse and me getting married? The question came unbidden to her mind. She refused to listen when her logical self firmly stated that she didn't belong to this world.

Instead, she recalled the passionate kiss they had shared; their conversation in the kitchen a few nights earlier. She had been speaking as herself, not Elizabeth, when she had practically begged him to spend the night with her. She -- Eleanor Weaver -- wanted Jesse with something akin to obsession. It had nothing to do with her original purpose for being in Peavine and everything to do with being a woman.

What she felt for Jesse had made it extremely difficult not to tell him how she knew so much about Clayton and what he had planned. She doubted Jesse would understand how she had come to be in this century. Ellie had to try even harder not to implicate Elizabeth because that would have meant tying herself to the crime in Jesse's eyes.

Ellie came to stand slightly off to the side at the front of the church. As Nate Murphy gave his daughter in marriage to Henry Jefferson, she concentrated on the young couple. She would just have to live for the moment because there didn't seem to be much she could do about fate.

Henry, for all his reserve as a bank employee, looked full of youthful exuberance, his gaze lingering on his bride with total disregard for anyone else in the church. Sarah, also, had a look of pure love and utter devotion, and Ellie envied them this moment.

She glanced at Jesse, who stood on the other side of Henry. He wasn't watching the wedding ceremony at all, for his gaze was intent on her. What she saw in the stormy blue of his eyes was deep and dark; a magic passion mixed in the heart of the mines and running as swift and hot as molten gold.

In that moment, Ellie realized she wanted to spend a lifetime with Jesse Cole, not just a few weeks or a month. Her mind echoed Sarah's words as Ellie silently pledge to love Jesse forever.

* * *

Ellie should have known there would be a dance following the wedding. Zeke had said it was the biggest event Peavine had seen for awhile. Fortunately, by the time they ventured from the church to the community center attached to the rear, a wonderful breeze had swept the air clean, and clouds blocked the worst rays of heat from the sun as it made its westerly descent.

Once the wedding dinner had been served and the dishes and tables cleared away, everyone in town was ready to kick up their heels and dance. Several musicians sat on a make-shift stage tuning their instruments, and the townspeople mingled and visited as though they hadn't seen each other in ages.

Ellie had to smile at this slice of small town life. When she went to the local market in New York, she rarely ran into anyone she knew. Yet here in Peavine, Nevada, she had friends and acquaintance from all walks of life.

"Beggin' your pardon, Miss Elizabeth." The giant who had accosted Ellie the other night stepped in front of her, blocking the light from nearby lanterns. She had to step back and tilt her head to even see his face. She knew, in the midst of all this company, the man wouldn't try anything, but she still felt leery after the way he had manhandled her.

"Yes?" She was sure the surprise showed on her face. Tom had spruced up pretty damned good, a clean shirt stretching tight across his massive chest, his string tie dangling midway down his front.

"I was hopin'," the man's face turned beet red, but he doggedly continued, "well, that is, I'd be honored if'n you'd consider havin' a dance with me," he finished in a rush.

Although Ellie wasn't at all sure just how they might accomplish that, given the man's size, she didn't have the heart to say no. Instead, she flashed him a smile and nodded in the affirmative, and his chest puffed up in gratitude.

The night sped by in a whirlwind of laughter and dance, and Ellie barely had time to catch her breath between sets. She had done her fair share of dancing, but found it hard to keep up with these miners! Officially, because she had been maid of honor and Jesse the best man, they were paired together for the bridal march, but it wasn't the type of dance that promoted intimacy. After that it seemed she was fair game. Even Lucky dragged her around the dance floor to a lively jig, where Ellie stepped fast if for no other reason than to keep her toes from getting smashed beneath Lucky's stomping boots.

She knew she shouldn't sulk because Jesse danced with other women. Most of them were already married, and a few were very young daughters of the residents of Peavine. None of the bar girls were present, of course, as would be fitting any society function of this time, she supposed. Still, she found herself glowering every time Jesse twirled past with a laughing woman on his arm.

Much later in the evening, she finally convinced Jesse to fetch her a glass of punch and meet her outside. Arm in arm, they strolled through the dark, around the back of the community building and towards the tree line.

Ellie commented on the stillness. "It's so quiet -- not even the stamp mill is running tonight."

Jesse laughed. "It's not often everything shuts down in Peavine."

"Yes, I know, but even on normal days there's no traffic noise, no sirens." Ellie bit her tongue the instant the words came out and hoped the darkness would cover the blush she knew heated her face.

"Sirens? Traffic?" Jesse's steps slowed.

Realizing her slip, Ellie shrugged. "You know, the hustle and bustle of the city. Oh, it doesn't matter. I really rather like Peavine better."

Jesse tugged her to a stop. "Do you think it a good idea to be away from the crowd?" He asked her, though he didn't turn around and head back towards the lighted hall.

"I'm a big girl, now, or haven't you noticed?" Ellie knew she was being deliberately provocative, but since her revelation during Sarah's wedding she had this all-consuming fear that something would happen before she had time to tell Jesse how she felt.

Her comment must have set off warning bells in Jesse's mind, because he turned to face her. "There's nothing wrong with my eyesight, El, but I also know your father wouldn't want you doing something you would later regret."

Ellie put a finger to his mouth. "It's my life," she whispered just as she replaced her finger with her lips. Beneath a blanket of stars with the creek as their symphony, she tried to express how she felt. She needed him to know, no matter what happened at the end of the month, that she, Eleanor Weaver, wanted him with a passion that had somehow spanned the centuries.

She wrapped her arms around his waist to pull him close, and yet it wasn't enough. As he slanted his mouth across hers, she slid her hands into the hip pockets of his pants, massaging his buttocks.

With a groan, Jesse pulled her down on top of him on the soft grass. His hands roamed up and down her satin clad back, pressing her closer still. The fragile control he had been keeping on his emotions where she was concerned slipped another notch.

Since returning from school, Elizabeth had changed. She wasn't the Elizabeth he'd known, and he found himself drawn to her on a different plane. Where before he was comfortable with their relationship, her nearness now made him uncomfortable and aroused. Her kisses fired his imagination with fantasies of making wild passionate love to her.

At one time, she had been a hesitant participant in his advances. Now, she took every opportunity to touch him, and he often felt her gaze at the most disconcerting times, so intense it heated his blood and made his body throb. Like in the church earlier today, he had found himself squirming uncomfortably under her seductive gaze.

"God, woman." Sucking in a breath as their lips parted, he searched her face. Her gaze seared him with passion. As he pulled her down to continue their kiss, Jesse wondered just when, in the last two weeks, had he come to love this woman more than life itself?

Elizabeth put her hands on the ground by his head, lifting herself away from him, her hair spilling loose from its pins to fall seductively around her face and shoulders.

"Did I tell you how very beautiful you are this evening?" Emotion clogged his throat, making his voice deeper than normal.

Elizabeth laughed delightedly, then she gave a funny little shrug and her dress slid off a shoulder, giving Jesse an enticing view of creamy skin and the swell of her breasts. It proved too much to expect him not to touch. He traced a finger along the edge of the material, even though he half expected her to stop him.

She didn't, but instead gave a throaty sigh and rolled to the side onto his discarded coat, leaving herself open and vulnerable to his caresses. Jesse kissed a path from her ear down her throat to the curve of her shoulder.

His only thought was of how soft she felt; how pale her skin looked against the dark tan of his hand as he caressed her arm before pulling her close. The heat of her beckoned him and he lost himself in her kiss. She smelled of the wildest flowers in the hills, and the erotic scent stopped his brain from functioning.

Ellie nearly moaned aloud as Jesse caressed and kissed her shoulder. Even though she had ached for his touch, the actuality of it sent her into spasms of delight. Her rational self knew Zeke wouldn't approve of the depth of her involvement with Jesse. That made no difference. She craved his touch; she wanted a memory for when she wouldn't be able to touch him ever again; for when he became dust from the past.

She knew they couldn't be together forever, but she also knew she'd never forget him. Where had he been when she was looking for love in her own time? "Make love to me, Jesse," she begged, breaking the kiss but leaning into him even closer, so that her breasts brushed against his linen shirt.

His answer was a groan as he rolled her to her back. She could feel his hardness against her hip -- the pulsing length of him pushing against her. A surge of power such as she had never experienced before swept through her.

"Please," her ragged plea vibrated the still air around them. "I need you."

He rewarded her plea with a growl as he lifted himself to his knees beside her. Passion-dark eyes bore into hers, before his gaze slid across her as his hands had done. She could feel heat burn in her cheeks as his potent stare lingered on her heaving breasts, for she couldn't catch her breath. She wanted him with a fever that scorched her.

"Why?" Fists clinched on his thighs, Jesse sat so still that it took Ellie a moment to realize he had spoken.

"I didn't know two people had to have a reason when they felt like we do." Ellie was confused, for in any of her dealings with men, not one of them would have turned down the invitation she was issuing only to Jesse.

"No, I mean why now, Elizabeth, after all this time when you've put me off and delayed giving me an answer to my proposal?"

There was that damn name again, Ellie fumed. She wiggled to a sitting position, adjusting her dress back up on her shoulders. She couldn't summon the energy to be angry with Jesse because he didn't know she wasn't Elizabeth.

When they made love, and she knew they eventually would, it would be her, not Elizabeth, he loved. She would make certain of that. But her silent vow didn't make him saying Elizabeth's name out loud any easier.

"What is it? What did I say?" Jesse scrutinized her and Ellie knew her face had given her away. Fortunately, before she could find an answer, a horn blared in the distance.

Both she and Jesse started at the noise, and Jesse jumped to his feet, turning in a circle to locate the source of the racket. Within seconds, more horns honked, followed by the beat of a drum. Ellie saw Jesse's shoulders relax and a smile started at the corner of his mouth.

"They've begun the shivaree!" The smile gave way to a full toothed grin.

Damn, but he was one handsome man, Ellie moaned as he straightened his clothes. A glint of light created shadows which played off the planes of his face. A lock of hair fell across his forehead as he fumbled with his tie, and suddenly the entire scene was right out of some high school prom movie. Ellie began to laugh, holding out a hand for him to pull her to her feet.

Instead of letting go when she regained her balance, Jesse pulled her closer. With a touch softer than the breeze, he brushed the hair back from her face, tucking a lock behind her ear. He placed a gentle kiss on her forehead, and it stirred Ellie more than the deeper caresses they had shared earlier.

With a rueful shake of his head, he stepped away from her. "I don't understand my lack of control around you anymore."

Ellie gave him a self-satisfied smile. One of these days she would make sure he lost whatever control he had left. But for tonight, she excused him with a shrug.

"Maybe it's the moon," she said.

"There is no moon tonight."

"Perhaps I really come from a galaxy far, far away -- from the future, even, and I've cast a spell over you."

He laughed as he tugged her back toward the lights of town. "Now that, I'd believe."

Chapter 8

Ellie, Zeke and Lucky were having a strategy meeting in the kitchen a few mornings after Sarah's wedding. Frankly, Ellie was glad for the company because even though Jesse had told her they would take a trip to Steamboat Springs, problems at the mine had kept him occupied.

On top of that, it had been raining since late the night of the wedding, the streets were a sea of mud, and neither freight nor anything else was coming in or out of the town. That left very little cause for excitement.

Zeke had been kind enough to bring her some tobacco, but Ellie found herself toying more with the strings on the pouch than ever actually making herself a cigarette. Instead, here she sat in a kitchen in the middle of 1870, more concerned for Jesse Cole than she had ever been for anyone in her entire life.

"Look, I've been to the bank and can't find any indication that something fishy is going on. The only paper I confiscated is in a handbag at Sarah's, and she won't be back from her honeymoon for two weeks. Even so, I don't know for sure that paper will do us any good." Ellie tried to recall exactly what the paper said, but the handwriting had been hard to read.

"Henry must have thought I was crazy when I asked if an audit had been done at my father's, well Elizabeth's father, death." Ellie had become so ingrained in the life at Peavine, at times she actually thought it was her house, her town, and her problems. She became especially possessive when it came to Jesse.

"Aren't there any controls over the banks out here -- any bank examiners?" Frustrated, Ellie did roll a cigarette,

100

unconsciously going through the motions and actually getting one made.

"Hurump," was all Zeke said when she waved it under his nose.

"I just can't figure Scott's angle, even though I happen to have a very good business sense and a great grasp on money."

Lucky cast her a quizzical look. "You can't cook. How can you know about money?"

With a sigh, Ellie got up to pour more lemonade. "If you were married, Lucky, you wouldn't have to ask. Every woman knows about money." She began to pace, thinking better on her feet.

"Isn't there a mint in Carson City?" At Zeke's nod, she continued. "Wouldn't you think they'd have records? I mean, they print money and coins and stuff. Maybe they also keep bank records? How far is it from Steamboat Springs to Carson?"

Lucky shrugged but Zeke answered. "'Bout twenty miles, but how you going to get to Steamboat? That's a good twenty more miles from here."

"Automobile?" She deliberately drew the word out, motioning with her hands like she was driving a car.

"You can't be saying stuff like that." Lucky became so agitated Ellie almost felt sorry she teased him, but he flustered so easy.

Zeke calmed his brother with a look. "You know she don't mean that."

"Train?" Ellie felt that a more logical choice.

"Only got it built from Steamboat to Carson." This from Lucky with a smirk of satisfaction that he could get back at her.

"Well, Jesse said he's take me to Steamboat Springs, so I guess I'll just let him figure it out. We know Clayton is involved in what happens to Jesse. We just have to find some evidence, otherwise what good is that knowledge?"

"What good is any evidence if he blows Jesse up, anyway?" Zeke turned her question around and Ellie felt like they were in a Catch 22. "Instead of running off to

Steamboat with Jesse, maybe you'd best be letting Scott court you so he spills his guts and we know what to look for this time so as history don't repeat itself."

"I've been doing that," Ellie replied defensively, "but your Mr. Scott isn't exactly a gentleman. I think he'd just as soon toss me in bed as court me."

Zeke blushed a bright red. "Well, hell, we didn't mean you had to . . .will you be able to handle him if he invites you to?"

"I can't believe we're having this conversation." Immediately, an image of dark hair and twinkling blue eyes came to mind, and Ellie knew what her answer would have been to an invitation from Jesse. Clayton, though, she had already found cold, unfeeling, and brutal.

"Don't worry, Zeke, I won't jump into the wrong bed, but could we step up the timetable on this melodrama so I can get home?" The more she thought about Jesse, the more she realized it was too late to save her heart. The best thing she could do was get out before she hurt Jesse.

Zeke shook his head. "You know I can't do that. That's the one thing that can't change even a second."

* * *

The skies had cleared and Jesse had the timbering completed at the Nightingale by early the next morning. When he came by the house, Ellie was more than happy to take off for Steamboat Springs. She figured she'd ask him about traveling on to Carson City once they were on the road.

"Where's the buggy?" She asked when she opened the door for him, seeing only a couple of horses tied to the post at the fence.

"We can get there faster riding. Besides, the road will be nothing but ruts and a wagon would probably get stuck more often than not."

Ellie couldn't say no, even though it had been years since she rode. How could she, when he stood there all tall and handsome in tight jeans and a slouchy hat, his eyes

102

twinkling and a rough stubble of beard on his chin making him look all the more rugged. Damn, but he made her hungry.

"Well, load my bag and then come in while I change." She left the door open and headed for the bedroom. Luckily, she had the jeans she'd worn when she entered this century. Thinking about that day as she slid out of her skirt and blouse, she was surprised how easily she'd fallen in with the styles of the day and dressed in skirts or dresses all the time. She really hadn't even missed her shorts and tees.

Sliding into the Levi's brought a smile to her face. She had forgotten how comfortable they were, and how much freedom they afforded. She stomped into her new boots, grabbed a hat Lucky had left behind and, tucking a flannel shirt in at the waist, she hurried back into the front room.

"Sorry, I can't ride a horse in a dress. Did you grab my bag?" Silence met her question and she looked up from buttoning her jeans. Across the room, Jesse stood with his mouth open, her bag dangling from one hand.

"What?"

"You can't--" Jesse cleared the squeak from his throat, "--can't ride to Steamboat like that."

"Why not? It's no different from what you're wearing."

"Yeah, but I'm a man."

Ellie knew exactly what he was getting at, and decided to cause him a little discomfort because of it. With a provocative sway of her hips, she sauntered to him, demurely blinking her lashes as she looked him up and down. She raked a fingernail softly along the stubble of his beard and gave him her most seductive smile. "I can see that," she cooed, "but what does it have to do with me wearing jeans?"

Jesse swallowed hard and wondered how in the hell he had gotten into this conversation. She had a way of turning the merest comment into a sensuous, sexual bantering that he was hard pressed to keep up with. He hadn't gotten any sleep at all the night of Sarah's wedding, and his body refused to calm down until well into the next day. The more he was around her, the more she confused him. Even when

103

he wasn't around her, the merest thought of her sent his body reeling.

Now, he decided not to fight what she offered, and let things happen according to the way nature meant them to be. He was tired of refusing her just for the sake of misplaced gallantry. Besides, he thought wickedly, what would the provocative Miss Elizabeth do if he took her up on her offer? Was it all a tease, or did she mean it? On this trip to Steamboat, he meant to find out.

Sweeping an arm around her waist, he pulled her close and kissed her. Her incredibly sweet body responded immediately and she melted against him, circling his neck, her hand knocking his hat to the floor. Her carpetbag thudded along with it as Jesse wanted both hands free to feel the curves of her lush body.

His initial shock at seeing her in Levi's had given way to hunger. The tight pants outlined every curve; the indentation of her waist, and the long, slim length of her legs. But even as his lips devoured her and his hands sought out her curves, anger took over.

Jerking his head up, he held her at arm's length. "What the hell are you thinking, wearing that get-up? Do you want every miner and locoweed in the territory sniffing around you like Tom did that night? How am I suppose to look after you when you go around dressing like that?" He hadn't meant to sound so gruff, but the thought of anyone else seeing her sweet derriere made him crazy.

Elizabeth looked at him with wide eyes. "I can't wear a dress to ride a horse. Since you didn't have the brains to bring a buggy, you'll just have to get over it."

Jesse backed up a step, eyes widening and brows lifting. Where just a moment ago, Elizabeth had been pliant and willing in his arms, now she shouted right back at him. She bent over to retrieve his hat, then planted her fists on her hips and stared him right in the eye, and he couldn't help but laugh.

"I don't think it's my brain you have to worry about on this trip, missy." He picked up her bag and grabbed his hat, and when he turned to see how she reacted to his message, he found her staring at his backside. This would prove to be a very interesting trip, indeed.

* * *

Jesse had said it was only nine miles to Reno from Peavine and another twelve to Steamboat Springs. For some cockeyed reason, Ellie thought they would be there in an hour -- two max. Two hours down the road and a sore behind hadn't even gotten them to the outskirts of Reno. Ellie tried to keep her mind off her pains by observing the landscape.

The area around Peavine was covered with shrubs and little grass, even though the side of the mountain boasted several types of trees. The further down the hills they had come, however, the flatter and more sparse the vegetation. Reno sat just to the east of the Sierra's, but far enough away to be out of the lush forest area of the Carson Range.

Ellie wondered if they even called it that in the 1870's. Afraid of putting her foot in her mouth, she kept a careful eye out for signs as they approached a toll bridge.

Jesse paid their fifty cents per horse toll to cross the bridge over the Truckee River. What Ellie assumed was the start of Reno at Fuller's Crossing was only a hotel built by a man named Lake, appropriately named "Lake's Hotel." She started to question Jesse on how much further they had to go when several more buildings came into view. She was decidedly happy to see them.

"When they started talking about horsepower, they sure didn't mean you," she muttered to the mare as she slid to the ground. Although Daisy was docile, Ellie hadn't ridden in years, and her body let her know it. Her legs turned to jelly, and she grabbed the saddle horn to keep from dropping in the dirt.

Jesse came around to her side, eyeing her curiously. "Did you give up riding like everything else when you went to school?" His tone implied what a stupid idea he thought that was, so Ellie knew better than to say she had.

"Of course not," she responded, "I ride all the time." Motorcycles, subways, jet-skis, she mentally added so it wasn't a lie. She groaned slightly as she bent forward to get the kink out of her back.

"Pull your shirt out," Jesse whispered fiercely.

Ellie grinned as she complied, recalling that while the trip into town had taken longer than she expected, it definitely hadn't been boring. Jesse's gaze had kept straying to her fanny, and she knew he couldn't get over the fact she wore jeans, much less rode astride. He would open his mouth to say something, then snap it shut in a stubborn line.

The problem was, his gaze had unnerved Ellie as much as her jeans did him. Her stomach had tightened and she'd grown warm all over. She wondered how Jesse managed to keep such iron control over his emotions when she had been very close to grabbing him and kissing him senseless.

With a sigh, she jerked the shirttails out of her pants so they hung down over her butt. For now, she'd placate him and keep unwanted attention off herself. Though she was sure it didn't hide her identity, she swept her hair up under her hat instead of letting it rest on her neck in a ponytail.

"Wow, Reno's sure changed since the last time I saw it." Ellie couldn't help exclaiming, glancing down the single dirt street with wood-faced store fronts. Not exactly the glitz and glamour of neon signs in the twentieth-first century.

"What do you expect for a town that's only been around for two years? With the amount of gold and silver coming out of the hills right now, it'll continue to grow. I'm just surprised they haven't started paving the streets." Jesse's remark brought laughter to Ellie's lips, but even though he grinned at her in return, she knew he couldn't possible understand the humor she saw in his comments.

"I only need to check on the supplies Zeke ordered last week," he said, hopping the steps two at a time. "Then we'll grab a drink to wash down the dust and be on the road. I want to get to Steamboat by sundown."

"Sundown?" Ellie glanced around, knowing it couldn't be much past noon.

"We've got another three or four hours at least. I'd just as soon get to the hotel before dark." Jesse gave her denimclad legs another look, and Ellie realized he didn't think it would be safe for her to be seen after dark. Given the rough and tumble look of the miners walking past, she would have to agree with him.

For the first time, she noticed Jesse wore a gun. It just hadn't occurred to her that crime was rampant or that she wouldn't be able to defend herself with the karate she had learned. The incident with Tom at Peavine hadn't escalated because Jesse had been there to help her out. While she didn't mind his being there, she didn't want him taking unnecessary risks for her.

* * *

After hours in the saddle, Ellie wondered if she'd ever be able to walk straight again. She had just considered questioning Jesse about whether he actually knew how to get to Steamboat, when she could see steam rising high in the air in front of a low range of hills. Several sprays shot up at various intervals and different heights, and although they looked like they formed a straight line, Jesse said they were scattered all over the plateau.

"Listen," he said as they drew nearer.

In the quiet of the landscape, Ellie could hear a puffing sound, easily matched to the tall columns of steam. She laughed in delight.

"That's why the town is named Steamboat Springs -- after the sound of a steamboat on the river."

"Cool," Ellie exclaimed, reverting to slang.

"No, actually, they're very hot, and although the water is used in the bathing houses it has to be cooled somewhat first." Jesse turned in the saddle, the leather squeaking softly beneath his weight. "Didn't your father ever bring you down here when he came on business?"

Ellie shrugged. "If he did, I don't remember." She really did try not to lie to Jesse, but lies of omission would probably send her to hell anyway.

Jesse checked them into the hotel and ordered Ellie to relax at the bath facilities and he would see her for supper. The hotel was the most commodious in town, according to the clerk, and Ellie had to agree when she saw her room. Lightly sprigged curtains blew in the breeze from an open window, and the feather bed was thick and fluffy. She opened her small carpetbag and shook out a dress to wear for dinner.

"Would you like to follow me, Miss?" A pretty girl wearing a maid's uniform curtsied at the door.

"Do I need anything?" Ellie felt like she was back in college and visiting the group shower facility in the dorm.

"No, Miss." The maid led the way down the hall and stairs to an outside door. "There are fifteen sets of medicinal baths here, but this one is especially reserved for hotel guests." She led Ellie next door to a group of private bathing chambers. Each was complete with a huge tub, fluffy towels on a stool, and what could only be a decanter of liquor. Steam hung heavy in the air and Ellie sighed. Heaven.

The maid continued to chatter as she turned to help Ellie undress, but eyeing her jeans, her mouth opened and no words emerged.

Ellie just laughed. "What is your name?"

"Rainee," the girl answered with a blush.

"Well, Rainee, you were saying?"

The maid blinked twice, glanced between Ellie and the bath water, and finally returned to her speech. "The vapor baths are beneficial to persons afflicted with the rheumatic complaints, and in some cases cutaneous diseases."

"Wow, I'm impressed." Ellie couldn't keep the laughter from her voice, and her own grin brought a smile to the maid's face.

"I'm not even sure what those big words mean, Miss, but we all had to learn them to keep our jobs." The girl, who couldn't have been more than sixteen, was fortunate she had a good speaking voice and pleasant face. Ellie realized there weren't many jobs for young women in this era, and this one was at least off the streets.

"I'm not sure I know what they mean either, but I can almost guarantee they mean this water will make me feel go-ood." Jacuzzi, here I come, Ellie thought as she shucked the last of her clothes and lowered herself into the tub. "Ah, does that make my rump feel better after being on a horse all day."

Rainee giggled again. "Will there be anything else, Miss?"

Ellie thought of her cigarettes, left forgotten on the kitchen table back at Peavine. Well, she was no doubt better off without them. With a sigh, she waved Rainee away and settled back to enjoy her beneficial, rheumatic-and-disease-divesting vapor bath.

* * *

Dinner proved a rather unromantic affair at the public dining hall which was part of the hotel. Crowded with miners and any number of people camping on the outskirts of the small town just to use the mineralized hot springs, the room was far too noisy to carry on any type of conversation. Ellie had wanted to broach Jesse about going on to Carson City, but now was not the time. He had intended this as a pleasure trip, and Ellie decided not to change his mind just yet.

Regardless of the atmosphere, Ellie couldn't resist staring at Jesse throughout their dinner of steak and potatoes. He had indulged in a trip to the barber and his smooth shaven cheeks shined bronze in the candlelight. His dress shirt looked slightly wrinkled, but Ellie thought that made him all the more endearing. In fact, there wasn't much about Jesse Cole that she didn't find fascinating.

That thought should have scared her to death, for she considered herself an independent woman of the twenty-first century; one who shouldn't think of a man in terms of eternity and essential for each breath she took. But as she caught his eye over peach cobbler and coffee, she came to the conclusion that was exactly how she felt, and surprise of surprises, it felt good.

Ellie overheard someone at a nearby table mention the upcoming Independence Day celebration being planned in Steamboat Springs and her heart fell. What good did it do caring for Jesse like she did; for opening her heart to feelings she had always kept buried? She had less than two weeks to try and save his life and then what? She could only assume she would go back to her own century when she had accomplished what Zeke and Lucky had brought her here to do. She couldn't even contemplate what Jesse would do after she left. What if he married Elizabeth? The thought made Ellie groan.

"Are you all right?" Jesse reached across the table and took her hand.

Ellie hadn't realized she'd moaned out loud. Her gaze collided with his. Those beautiful blue eyes, fringed with sooty lashes and little crow's feet, looked at her with concern, and something more. It was that other emotion Ellie wanted to pursue. If her time here was limited, why should she waste any more of it wondering 'what if'?

"It's too crowded here. Will you walk me back to my room?"

* * *

Ellie lit only a single candle when she entered her hotel room. She hadn't gotten used to the dark, but she knew that Jesse would take away any fears she had. Butterflies fluttered against the walls of her stomach. She wished she hadn't eaten so much at dinner.

"Well," Jesse cleared his throat. She turned towards him. He stood at the threshold, his manners showing, for she understood he thought her reputation would suffer if he was found alone with her.

She wanted to scream that she didn't care what people thought; that she wasn't Elizabeth and that she loved him. Oh, God, even as the words echoed in her mind, she knew they were true. Boy if that wouldn't make her editor laugh; to know that the urbane, European-touring Ellie Weaver had fallen in love with a very western, very earthy miner.

"Come in for just a minute or two," she pulled him into the room, closing the door behind them. While Jesse Cole might be a miner, he was also a very well educated, extremely sexy man. Suddenly it didn't matter in the least that he was one hundred twenty-eight years old, given her date of birth. She wanted him, and knew she would have to make the first move.

Never one to be timid, she still hesitated in front of him. Would he accept what she offered, or would he spurn her for being a whore by his standards? Did she dare take a chance? She took his hat out of his hands and tossed it on the chair by the door. Her gaze collided with his and she knew there would be no turning back. His brilliant blue gaze burned bright with passion.

"Ellie," he whispered her name, and she melted against him. Strong arms circled, crushing her breasts against his chest. Even as his head lowered to kiss her, Ellie's hands were trembling at the buttons of his shirt.

Her movements stilled when his lips touched hers. He had kissed her before, but she had always felt he held a part of himself back. Now as she opened to him, an urgency took over that had never been part of Jesse. A groan escaped and Ellie grabbed hold of his shoulders under the impact of a passion so jolting, so electrifying, goose bumps raised over her body.

He had finally lost control. All the times before when she had teased him, taunted him, she had wanted more than he seemed inclined to give. Suddenly that attitude was gone, replaced by pure man who appeared ready to give her all, and then some.

"Ellie, Ellie." Her name was a litany on his lips as he kissed a heated path to her ear. Nibbling on her earlobe, his breath hissed as she finally was able to get her hands inside his shirt to bare skin. Lord, how she reveled in the feel of firm muscles, quivering beneath her touch.

"Who are you?" His feverish question gave her pause, but he continued before she had a chance to fabricate a lie. "Why, after knowing you half my life, do I feel I don't know you at all?"

Ellie peppered his bare chest with hot kisses, hoping to make him forget there might be anything strange about her. She wanted this night. With only a dozen or so days before the accident, she longed to spend all of them in Jesse's arms. Zeke, Lucky and she had carefully gone over every detail they knew. With Elizabeth out of the picture, this time there should be no accident.

There was no doubt in her mind that sometime on the fourth of July, she would be thrown back into her own time, and Zeke and Lucky and Jesse would all remain alive and well this time, in Peavine. As long as she had to abandon him, she wanted to leave him with memories of hot, sizzling nights.

Jesse groaned at her forays, and Ellie refused to stop, intent on making him forget everyone and anything except her. She slid her hands between his belt and his back, massaging his spine. She kissed the tip of his chin, the corners of his mouth, before his hands held her head and stopped her meandering. Firm, hot lips slanted across hers, his tongue darting out to tease her own.

Jesse couldn't recall much about undressing either of them except the exquisite desire that burned through him with each piece of clothing she removed. His thoughts were jumbled, and he couldn't begin to figure why Elizabeth -- Ellie -- affected him so strongly in recent days. Ellie -- the name seemed to fit her better, for it was softer, more feminine than the formal Elizabeth. But Jesse knew the adoption of a nickname wasn't what was making him crazy at the moment.

In the past, whenever he tried to kiss or caress Elizabeth, her response had been lukewarm at best. He hadn't pressed her, since they weren't married, and Elizabeth had assured him she would give him what he wanted after they did marry. After he found the motherlode, he amended.

The thought crossed his mind that she had most definitely changed her ways, but when her hands slid down his ribs to the buckle of his trousers, he honestly couldn't find fault with the new, sensuous woman who smiled up at him. He gloried in her sight, felt ten feet tall -- her knight in shining armor -- and he knew in that moment that he would love her from here 'til eternity.

The bed creaked beneath their weight as Ellie pulled Jesse down on top of her. It felt so right, his chest pressing her down deeper into the mattress. Her hands wandered across his back, the muscles bunching beneath her fingers. She couldn't get enough of the feel of him, his hard, taut skin so different from her soft curves. Sensation exploded deep within her when he found her nipple, nipping lightly before sucking it into his hot mouth.

"Jesse, take the ache away, please." Her head rolled from side to side, the cravings building to fevered pitch in the very core of her being. She arched her back, her breasts jutting upward, aching for his touch. He slid to her side, still suckling, one hand exploring her bare skin and dipping lower to caress secret passageways. Ellie just about came off the bed.

"Did I hurt you?" Jesse's hand stilled, his gaze searching her face.

"Do you have any idea what you're doing to me?" Her voice, low and husky, sounded unfamiliar to her.

Jesse's smile was slow and seductive. "I think I have a fair idea." His hand began to move again, this time brushing the inside of her thighs, sliding across her skin from hip bone to hip bone, not touching where she needed him the most, yet intensifying her pleasure.

Ellie reached for him, but he tucked his hips in close to hers and though she could feel his manhood against her, she couldn't get her hands on him. "That's not fair," she pouted and he kissed the corner of her mouth. "I want to touch you."

With a growl, he moved on top her, pushing her legs open with his knee. "One touch will send me over the edge, sweetheart, but your words can easily do it anyway." She arched her hips and with one smooth thrust, he buried himself deep within her. Ellie cried out in pleasure.

Jesse stopped his movements, his shaft pulsing deep within her hot, moist womanhood. He hadn't meant to take her so suddenly, but her words, her movements, the very stars in the sky caused him to need her desperately. Any further thought was blocked as Ellie began to move beneath him.

The pressure built incredibly fast, the passion singing through his veins with every stroke deep within her beautiful body. Her legs hugged his hips tightly, her arms wound around his shoulders to keep his chest brushing against her breasts. He couldn't breathe, but didn't need to. He couldn't think but didn't want to. He wanted and needed only her movement with him, to hear her gasps of pleasure against his neck, and know that wondrous delight of her body.

Without warning, Ellie pitched headlong into a tide pool of sensation, flooding her with heat and rapture. Her legs trembled against Jesse's sides; her arms quivered. Seconds later he tightened against her, thrusting deep, meshing his hips solidly with hers. Ellie didn't breathe until he collapsed against her, then rolled to the side.

The repercussions and guilt began immediately as Ellie felt cool air against her fevered skin where only moments ago Jesse had kept her warm. She called herself every name in the book, knowing she had no claim to Jesse; no right to make a demand such as this on him.

Everything she had learned about him led her to believe he would demand commitment. She didn't have the right to give him that commitment, whether she loved him or not. And she sure as hell couldn't make a commitment for Elizabeth, knowing the woman had stabbed him in the back and become a traitor.

Jesse nuzzled her neck and Ellie ached for him all over again. "I love you," he whispered. "I think I started loving you when we first met and you were only twelve. But you were always just there. I didn't realize just how much you meant to me until you fell off that horse in front of my cabin and I thought you were hurt."

Ellie wanted to stop his confession. It hurt too much. He had made love to her -- Ellie Weaver -- and she had given herself to him unconditionally because she loved him. But even when he mentioned her own unceremonious fall into his life, she didn't know for sure who Jesse loved. And time was speeding by way too fast for her to figure it out.

Chapter 9

Repercussions and guilt didn't make Ellie stop wanting Jesse and she proved it to him time and again during the night. She longed to keep him away from danger; to slow the time when Elizabeth would return. She could use the trip to Carson City as an excuse to stay out of Peavine, if only for an extra day or two. She might tell Jesse it was to find the reasons behind Clayton Scott's behavior, but deep in her heart she knew differently. She desperately wanted one more day -- maybe two-- with Jesse Cole.

Even so, Ellie woke alone the next morning. Apparently, the pleasures they had shared in each other's arms could amount to nothing more than just that. She told herself it didn't matter, but the funny thing was, she couldn't convince her heart to quit breaking nor the tears to quit flowing.

Later, Ellie laid on the bed fully dressed with a wet towel over her eyes, hoping the cool water would lessen the redness before Jesse came. He had sent a message with Rainee that he'd be by later to get her for brunch. Actually, Ellie needed the time to decide how best to approach him. 'The morning after' had never been a concern for her, mainly because there hadn't been any men in her life whom she allowed that close or for that long.

She felt it would have been easier if he hadn't left her room. Then, she could have showed him how she felt, because if she were truthful, she wanted nothing more than to haul Jesse's hide back into bed. She might tell herself it was one way to keep him safe, but she just plain loved making love to him! She sighed, turning the rag to a cooler side.

Keeping Jesse naked and in bed with her for the next two weeks was impractical to an extreme. Besides, would that be something Jesse wanted? Had he left in the night because he regretted what had happened? She didn't regret a moment of their pleasure, and only hoped he felt the same. That would at least make the next two weeks interesting, regardless of what Clayton Scott intended.

A knock at the door ended Ellie's deliberations. Butterflies jiggled around in her stomach, and she held her breath as she crossed the room to open the door.

"Good morning, El." Jesse gave her a heart stopping smile and held out his hand.

Ellie's heart turned over at his smile, and come what may, she knew at least for now things would be alright. She reached out and took the single, black-eyed Susan he clutched. Turning towards the mirror, she tucked the flower into the tie of her braid where it lay over her shoulder. That way she could see it all day.

"There weren't many flowers." Jesse sounded nervous, and in the mirror's reflection, Ellie could see him turning his hat round and round in his hands.

"You didn't take some lady's last flower out of her garden, did you?"

"Of course not." He went from nervous to affronted. After a pause, he grinned and added, "Well, actually the only other one had lost half its petals."

"Jesse, it was her last one--"

"I offered the lady on the porch money, but she wouldn't take it once I told her what I wanted to do with the flower."

Ellie tilted her head to study him, noting the tense set of his shoulders. "And that would be?"

"I wanted it for the loveliest woman in all Nevada. I figured since she already had my heart, she needed a flower to keep it company."

"Oh, Jesse." Ellie's lips trembled and she just knew she was going to cry. Jesse circled her with his strong arms, and for this brief moment in time, Ellie felt loved and wanted and perfectly at peace. She only wished it could last, and that was the reason she cried.

Jesse awkwardly patted her back, fumbling with his hat and not quite knowing what to do. "Sh, sweetheart, I didn't mean to make you cry." He hadn't expected her to be sentimental; she had rarely been in all the time he had known her. However, he had to admit he had woken up this morning with a different frame of mind, so he supposed she could, too.

Jesse had slept like the dead after he left Ellie last night, but woke up discontent. The reason had stared him in the face from the pillow next to his head. It was empty. He longed to wake up beside Ellie, holding her tight in the winter to keep warm and snuggling next to her cool, satin skin in the summer. He'd probably make a fool of himself for wanting her all the time, but she aroused the demons in him.

Yet now, as he held her, he kept those feelings bottled up inside. He searched his mind for some phrase from all the books his mother had given him, but the classic poets' words somehow seemed shallow and pretentious when compared to the beauty standing before him.

Her face glowed; her brown eyes sparkled with gold through tears left unshed. In those eyes, he saw the love for which he had been waiting a lifetime. He didn't have to struggle to see past her spoiled exterior. She no longer resembled the pouting young woman who had returned from her high-brow eastern school full of herself.

No, whatever airs she had brought back to Peavine were gone now, replaced with an open-hearted goodness and smiling face. He started to tell her again that he loved her, but a shadow flickered across her gaze.

It was gone so swiftly he could have imagined it. Then she touched his lips with a gentle finger; her hand caressed his cheek and no words were needed for him to understand that she loved him, even if she couldn't say the words. For the moment, he contented himself with her touch, the look of adoration in her eyes, and the fierce need which once again tightened his muscles and started his heart pounding.

* * *

Jesse knew he shouldn't be gone from Peavine more than a day or two, but he wouldn't deny Ellie anything.

118

Even so, he seriously doubted any Carson City bank or even the Nevada State Court House would be able to give them the answers to the questions she felt needed asked.

He sighed as he bought their train tickets. He was smitten for sure. Why else would he have agreed to go traipsing all over Nevada in search of evidence that he owned the Nightingale mine. He knew it belonged to him, or it would when he paid off the loan. Ellie, on the other hand, seemed to need proof that Scott wasn't trying to swindle him and take over.

"Train should be on time," he said to Ellie as he walked across the platform to where she paced.

"Lucky said the train didn't run here," she glanced up and down the tracks, eyes bright with curiosity. She suddenly gabbed his shirt front, her voice panicky. "Jesse, what if we can't find the answers? What if there's an accident?"

A sense of déjà vu swept through Jesse, leaving him icy cold even in the early morning sunshine. Why did he have the feeling they were acting out parts in a play where the ending was already written and the outcome determined?

His stomach clinched as the train whistle echoed in the distance, almost as a warning.

Ellie turned away from him, nervously twisting the thin straps of her handbag. Now that she'd blurted out her worries, she avoided his gaze, staring instead down the tracks as though willing the train to appear.

He studied her from beneath the brim of his hat, watching the sway of her hips as she paced along the platform. Ellie stopped then started, then stopped again. In-between her pacing, she'd dig through her handbag, looking for something, appearing frustrated at not being able to find it.

Ellie, not Elizabeth. It wasn't just her name that was different. Just about everything from the way she walked and talked to the incredible way her eager gaze racked him while he undressed her last night. That, especially, fell beyond his understanding. Nowhere in Jesse's somewhat limited experience with women could he explain Ellie's sudden and erotic desire for him. Even though he definitely wouldn't complain about that, it was almost as though she was an entirely different woman than the one he'd always known.

But that was ridiculous. People didn't become other people overnight. The changes in Elizabeth; even her desire to use a nickname, had come about from her associations back east. That was all.

Jesse stepped back, pulling Ellie with him as the train ground to a stop, great puffs of steam escaping from beneath its wheels. Whatever worries had plagued her disappeared as she eagerly climbed aboard the passenger car.

"Oh, my God, this is incredible," she exclaimed as she walked down the narrow aisle, touching each bench back, running her hands over the polished wood and chrome of the headers.

She plopped down on a bench by a window, eyes wide. She patted the bench beside her and he sat, scooping off his hat and crossing one ankle over the other knee. "You'll never make me believe you haven't ridden a train, so why are you so excited?" Jesse cocked a brow at her in question.

"But I--" she broke off as she so often did and Jesse shook his head. Then she turned toward him, sliding her arm behind his shoulders. She smiled impishly and fiddled with his hair. Goose bumps rose along his skin at her touch. She glanced around to see if anyone watched, but no other passengers had entered this particular car as of yet. Before he could guess her intention, she leaned forward and kissed his ear.

"I meant," she whispered, "I've never ridden this particular train, and I've never done it with you." Her tongue tickled his ear and Jesse jerked his hat from his knee to his lap.

Damn! What she said caused images of their lovemaking to career through his brain. However, her breathy whisper in his ear gave a whole new meaning to the jerky movements of the train as it drew down the tracks.

"How long will it take to get to Carson?" Her fingers were in his hair again, and although she didn't whisper now, she remained close enough that her breast still brushed his arm.

"Too damn long." Jesse squirmed on the hard wooden bench, everything about her causing him extreme discomfort in the lower regions of his anatomy.

"Will we stay over, or do our business and head back home?"

"Sweetheart, the business I'm thinking about is going to take too long to get done in one night." He knew she understood when her eyes opened in surprise and her sweet mouth formed a small oh, but she didn't looked shocked in the least. Instead, she dazzled him with a smile and settled snugly against his side.

"I'm glad," was all she had to say as she rested her head on his shoulder.

Jesse was certainly glad that the only other passengers walking past to find seats were men, and each eyed him and winked in appreciation of the beauty he had resting against him. Jesse could certainly be glad he didn't have to contend with any matronly outrage.

With a sigh, he contented himself to sit quietly for awhile, breathing in her scent and feeling the weight of her against him. In his constant search for that big strike; the one that would make him and all the men who worked for him rich beyond their wildest dreams, he had neglected many things in his life.

Looking back, he wished he had more schooling, instead of always working alongside his father. He couldn't speak in the eloquent words of Clayton Scott, even though his mother had made sure he learned the basics of reading, writing, and manners. Ellie didn't seem to mind so much now, but would it make a difference later in their married life?

And speaking of -- he wiggled his shoulder to get her attention. "Hey, don't go to sleep. We need to talk about getting married."

Ellie jerked upright and scooted away from him. She began shaking her head even before she spoke. "No! No, we don't, not now. We need to find out about your mine." She spoke in a panic and began fidgeting with her purse strings again.

Jesse read the only thing he could into her statement. "You mean you're still not going to marry me until I find the gold? After last night, I think it's a little late to back out." His mother had taught him responsibility and he wanted to tell her there was no alternative. At the same time, he wanted her only if she came to him of her own free will, because she loved him. Last night, he had thought she did.

She stared out the window for some time; her shoulders drooped. A large sigh escaped. When she turned to face him again, her eyes sparkled with tears. She placed a gentle hand to his cheek. "Oh, Jesse, I do want to marry you. You can't imagine how much. But now's not the time to talk about it." The train lurched to the side at that moment, and a crooked smile touched her lips. "Besides, a rattling train isn't exactly the most romantic place to propose."

"I've already proposed -- dozens of times. I just haven't gotten you to say yes." What was it about her that kept him coming back for more, even when she left for years to study back east; even when she hung around unsavory characters like Scott?

She leaned forward and gave him a peck on the cheek. "Don't pout, Jesse. You must have patience. Now, tell me about this train we're on. After all, it wasn't built when last I was here."

He shook his head, deciding she was right and there would be better opportunities to press his advantage. But he made himself a promise that she would be his wife, with or without the damn gold.

"They say when this is finished, it will be the most crooked railroad in the world because its whole course is one big curve. I'm not sure where the construction is at this point, but trains began running to Carson just last October. It's expected the whole route will cost about three million."

"Good lord, that's a lot of money for -- how much road?"

"The entire railroad will connect Reno, Truckee, Meadows and Steamboat, then Washoe and Eagle Valleys down to Carson City; a total of fifty-two miles. A very necessary investment."

Ellie gave him a look of wonder. "Three million dollars' worth?"

"Considering the worth of the Comstock ores transported to the quartz mills, not to mention the necessary timber and cut lumber needed by the mines to continue production, and I'd say it was worth it. Besides, this train travels at twenty miles per hour, which is twice as fast as the stage."

Ellie giggled at him and Jesse wondered why she thought he was so funny.

"Wow, a whole twenty miles an hour."

He frowned. "You don't think I'm serious about marriage, and now you laugh when I say this steam engine is the fastest thing around." Jesse shut his mouth and crossed his arms over his chest, determined not to say another word until they got to Carson City.

Ellie giggled harder.

* * *

Ellie rubbed the small of her back as she stepped onto the wood platform of the Carson City train station, stretching sore muscles. She knew she hadn't been fair to Jesse on the train, in both teasing him unmercifully about what they had done the night before, and about the speed of transportation. Sometimes she wished she could tell him about the future; not just speeding cars and traveling to the moon in rockets faster than he could conceive, but all the wonders of the modern world.

Jesse threw their bags into the back of a buckboard and motioned for her to climb aboard with the old man handling the reins. She might miss pizza and cold beer, but at the moment a soft cushy car seat was much preferable to another ride on a wooden bench.

"Is it too far to walk?" She questioned, refraining from rubbing her sore fanny.

Jesse shrugged, digging a coin out of his vest pocket for the driver and instructing him to drop their bags at the Warm Springs Hotel.

"I suppose you want to get right to work, looking for clues to this intrigue?" He questioned as he took her arm and turned towards town.

Frankly, the instant his hand touched her bare elbow, Ellie's thoughts immediately raced ahead to the night, barreling right past all the questions in her mind about the bank records and Clayton Scott and Jesse's mine. Never had she let a man interfere with her life to this extent; and would wonders never cease, she didn't even mind.

"Well, if we're walking past the bank, wouldn't it make sense to scope it out?" She made herself concentrate on matters at hand, instead of the delicious warmth of his hand on her arm.

"Scope it out?" Jesse echoed her words as he held the door to the bank open for her.

Ellie patted his cheek in an affectionate manner and breezed past him without explaining herself. As she hoped, he didn't ask what she meant.

Cyrus Connors, according to the name plate, sat behind a huge desk to the right of the teller's cage, and Ellie decided to start with him.

"Good afternoon, Mr. Connors, my name is Elizabeth Calhoun, from Peavine, and I would like to ask you some questions about my father's bank."

The rotund man immediately stood and Ellie was gratified by the male chivalry of this century -- until he spoke. Instead of addressing her, he barely acknowledged her introduction with a slight nod of the head, instead turning his attention to Jesse.

"Sir?" He questioned.

"Jesse Cole, owner of the Nightingale Mine at Peavine Summit." The two men shook hands, leaving Ellie beginning to steam like the springs at Steamboat.

Mr. Connors came around his desk and pulled up another chair in front. "Please, have a seat, Miss Calhoun." Again, he extended her a courtesy, but spoke only to Jesse.

"What can I do for you, Mr. Cole?"

"Actually, it is Miss Calhoun who has the questions about the Calhoun Bank & Trust of Peavine, which as she said was--"

"--owned by my father." Ellie interrupted.

Connors gave her an annoyed glance. "Perhaps your questions could best be answered by your father, then." The condescending sound of his nasal voice quickly grated on Ellie's nerves. She clasped her hands tightly together.

"Perhaps if my father were still alive, I wouldn't find it necessary to ask you questions, sir, since apparently you don't have a clue as to what's happening." She could feel Jesse's hand on her arm. She hoped it was in support of her because she didn't like to think he'd act like a male chauvinist.

"Really, Miss, I am sorry, but what would I have to do with your father's bank?" His eyes suddenly widened and he stuttered, "I hope you're not implying I had something to do with his death?"

"Honestly, why do men always think of themselves?" Ellie muttered under her breath as she sat back in her chair exasperated. Jesse chuckled beside her. He placed a gentle hand on her shoulder and Ellie took a fortifying breath.

"Your sign says Carson City National Bank, does it not?" At the man's nod, she continued. "My father owned a bank. When he died, wouldn't someone from this national bank have been contacted to do an audit?"

"Why?" The man questioned, sounding just like Lucky.

Ellie threw her hands up in exasperation. "You mean that any records of my father's transactions would only be at that bank? No one else has copies?" The man nodded. She stood to leave and Jesse rose with her.

Cyrus Connors scooted around his desk, reaching for Jesse's hand in a greedy grasp. Ellie supposed he thought maybe Jesse would bring his gold to this bank.

"I do apologize for any misinformation you may have gotten from this...female," the man sputtered ingratiating, "but you must know that all banks are solely owned and operated, so I couldn't possibly have anything to do with her father's bank, or his death," he added hastily.

His back was turned to her, and he spoke in a low voice, but it was still plenty loud for Ellie to hear. "If I were you, I'd marry the little gal and get her with child so she can't be out and about and meddling in men's business." He nodded his head in emphasis.

Ellie swung her handbag around to clobber the idiot, and would have succeeded if Jesse hadn't glanced over the man's shoulder and intercepted her projectile. He tucked her purse under her arm and latched on to her hand, tugging her away from the banker and out the door before she could control her anger enough to get a word out.

"That imbecile." The word escaped and even though Ellie could see Zeke cringing in her mind's eye, she was mad.

"Whoa, baby, calm down," Jesse used his claim on her to pull her close, transferring his hold to circling her waist.

Ellie jerked to a stop on the boardwalk and swung around to face him. "You're not taking his side, are you?"

"Do I look like a fool?" Apparently Jesse knew how to be politically correct.

Ellie pursed her lips to look at him, knowing no way in hell Jesse Cole would ever be anyone's fool. Well, except maybe Elizabeth's, if they didn't get him out of this mess.

She blew out an irritated breath. "Why did he talk as though I didn't exist and didn't know anything?"

Jesse gave her a look Ellie had come to know meant he was thinking too much about what she said. That could lead to trouble if she didn't learn to curb her tongue. "One of these days," he said, shaking his head, "I'm going to take a trip back east; to Boston and New York and all those places

126

you've been. The way you talk sometimes, it's as though you lived on a different planet."

Same planet, different century, Ellie thought wryly, before generating an excuse, as always, for her actions. "That's still no excuse for boorish behavior."

Jesse shrugged, cupping her elbow and setting them in motion again. "I can't keep apologizing for all the stupidity of other men, Ellie. You'll just have to believe I try my best not to be like them."

Ellie gave him a smile. "I know you're not, and believe me, I appreciate it more than you can know."

Their walk had gotten them to the courthouse, but a few questions and a quick examination of the assayer's records showed no liens against the Nightingale Mine at Peavine Summit. The Registrar of Deeds did say sometimes private deals with anonymous backers were made to raise money for the mining ventures on the Comstock, but they certainly didn't keep those records. That information made Clayton's claim appear all the more valid.

"Do we have time to go to the Mint yet today?" Ellie asked, squinting into the bright sunlight to the sandstone building across the street.

"You are certainly full of energy, aren't you?"

Jesse sounded as though he would rather be sitting in a bar drinking a cold beer, and Ellie certainly couldn't fault him for that. But given the uncooperative nature of the men she was encountering, she knew she'd find no answers at all without Jesse at her side. That thought grated on her liberated nature.

"Look, I'm doing this for you, you know. I realize that you shouldn't be away from the mine for long, so the sooner we get this done, the sooner we can get back to Peavine."

Jesse looked surprised that she would think of him. Men, she thought. If she only had more time, she'd teach him a thing or two about liberated women, supportive males, and the world of equality.

As it was, she contented herself to exploring the Carson City Mint with him. They were told that the nearby prison had quarried the sandstone to build the building, and it had only been operational since February. The first coin struck was a Seated Liberty dollar, bearing the CC mint mark. Jesse traded some of his change for one and gave it to Ellie as a keepsake.

They had taken the entire tour and listened to a weasel-looking man talk in a monotone for over half an hour before Ellie had to conclude that as much as she hoped otherwise, the mint would not provide them with any information. She had the feeling she was confusing it with a federal reserve bank. Even so, when they were introduced to Abe Curry, the superintendent, Ellie felt compelled to ask him about bank records in Peavine.

"Ma'am, we mint coins, like double eagles, half eagles, and that seated Liberty dollar you're fiddling with. We don't keep records on what banks do. That's their business." With a sharp nod of his head, he excused himself, professing to be needed in the coiner's department.

"Damn," Ellie swore, softly, hands on hips outside the Mint's doors.

"When did you start swearing, El?" Jesse asked, his voice full of humor. "I think I'd better start keeping Lucky and Zeke up at the mine more."

Ellie shrugged, not wanting to debate her language, background, or the lack of information they had gathered in their fruitless search for evidence against Clayton.

"What now?" Jesse took off his hat as he spoke, wiping the sweat from his brow with his sleeve. Late afternoon sun glinted off his hair, and Ellie reached up to touch the wayward curl that always hung across his forehead.

She knew what she wanted. A cold glass of wine, a cool bath, and Jesse Cole, not necessarily in that order.

He smiled at her and Ellie's heart melted. Bittersweet country songs floated through her mind, one phrase coming unbidden to her lips. "'I'll do anything you want me to, just to see you smile.'"

That widened the grin on Jesse's lips. "Anything?"

Chapter 10

Anything proved to be a no-holds-barred, free-for-all, night of loving. Ellie had never been treated so royally -- from the scented bath Jesse ordered to the champagne dinner of mouthwatering roast beef, potatoes, and a whole basket of fresh fruit.

It was his gentle, yet turbulent love making, though, that Ellie would treasure for the rest of her life. She smiled at the oxymoron, knowing it was the only way she could describe what had happened last night. He had taken her to the height of passion with breath-taking intensity, and in the aftermath he had kissed and caressed her into a gentle slumber, only to awaken her and repeat all those wondrous feelings.

Her mind full of the rapture of the night before, Ellie never heard the door open, and squealed in fright when Jesse called to her.

"Come on, sleepyhead. Either get out of bed right now, or I dump you into last night's cold bath water."

"Go away," she mumbled into her pillow.

"Are you always so agreeable in the morning?" She could hear the laughter in his voice. Reaching blindly beside her, she grabbed the pillow and heaved it in his direction.

The instant his callused hand grabbed her ankle, she knew she was in trouble. Casually, almost seductively, he pulled her to the end of the bed. When she tried to kick him with her free foot, he grabbed and twisted her legs together, forcing her to roll over. She watched him as his gaze swept up her naked form. Passion flared.

"Why don't you come back to bed instead?" Ellie stretched wantonly.

Jesse groaned and Ellie thought she'd won, even though he was fully dressed. A surprised squeal escaped when he grabbed her and lifted her clear off the bed. He walked through the door to the bathing area, holding her over the tub.

Ellie wrapped her arms around his neck, begging him not to drop her. The devil's own grin lit his face as he pried her hands loose and plopped her into the tub. Prepared for the cold water from last night, Ellie had to sigh as the warmth of it both surprised and delighted her. Just another instance when Jesse Cole proved his thoughtfulness and earned her love.

"There's only one train to Steamboat Springs today and I need to be on it, so hurry up, or you won't get breakfast."

"I go nowhere without coffee," Ellie shouted as he closed the door behind him.

Within minutes, a knock on the door and a cautious, female voice announced she had "missy's" coffee if she would be allowed to enter.

"A hot bath, fresh coffee and the love of a good man," Ellie mused. "Life can't get any better than this."

* * *

Late the next day, Ellie wondered if she had jinxed herself by speaking those words. They had reached Steamboat Springs and retrieved their horses, but several miles from Peavine her horse had thrown a shoe. With the supplies they'd picked up in Reno, they certainly couldn't ride double. When Jesse had insisted she ride his horse and he'd walk, she had said if he had to walk, so would she.

"Ouch!" She groaned when another stone on the rough trail twisted her foot sideways.

"If you weren't so stubborn, you wouldn't have blisters from those ridiculous boots." Jesse glared at her.

"It's not my fault the horse threw a shoe," she retorted.

Jesse sighed. "Elizabeth, I never said it was. Why are you so intent on causing an argument?"

Ellie had come to realize Jesse only called her Elizabeth when he was mad at her. That suited her fine, because it somehow absolved her from blame. At the moment, though, that fact was neither here nor there. The closer they got to Peavine, the more nervous Ellie became.

Would Elizabeth still be gone? Could she keep Clayton at a distance? Those were minor questions up against the biggest one weighing on her mind since they had made love in Steamboat.

Could she follow through with their scheme and willingly leave Jesse when the time came?

Ellie studied him as they walked along the trail which grew steeper as they ascended towards the mining town. Her gaze slid over jean-clad legs and tight buttocks, past a slim waist to his shoulders, straight even in the heat of midday. He had one hand wrapped around the reins of both horses and the other hovered close to his holstered gun.

Ellie hurried to catch up. Her gaze jumped from his gun to his face and she saw his eyes flicker, continually surveying the terrain.

"Are we in danger?" Her anger was forgotten as she sidled closer.

"Wherever there are men and fortunes in gold, there's danger."

Ellie giggled.

Jesse glared at her. "What's so funny?"

"You sound so serious. Can't you just consider this an adventure? I do."

He snorted. "I'll bet. Sometimes, lately, I think every day is an adventure for you."

"You don't know how true that is," Ellie muttered to herself, but refused to be drawn into another argument. She skipped forward and turned in front of him, momentarily walking backwards. He didn't stop until she'd circled his neck with her arms.

"Then we might as well add a little spice to the adventure," she whispered just before she kissed him. She hung on, even when he tried to pull away, and finally his lips softened under hers and he kissed her back.

131

"El, we're out in the open, in broad daylight," he protested.

"So?" She kissed him again.

"So, I can't remember," he murmured, wrapping his arms around her to draw her close.

Jesse's experiences with Ellie over the last few days had been unique, to say the least, and while he could have sworn he heard bells a time or two, this was the first time he'd ever heard fireworks. It wasn't until she jerked her sweet mouth away from his with a yelp that he realized the popping sounds he heard were gunshots.

The horses shied away as rock chips flew. Jesse released the reins, pulling his revolver with one hand and keeping his other arm around Ellie as he pulled her behind some rocks on the hillside. A rocky incline with few trees made it more difficult to scramble up the slope away from the direct line the shooters seemed to have of the path.

"What the hell is going on?" Ellie scrunched down, back against the rock that hid them from view.

Without taking his eyes off the opposite hillside, Jesse replied, "You sure have taken to swearing alot. Surely they didn't teach you that at your fancy ladies' school."

His comment was met with a sigh. "Look, Jesse, if someone's going to kill us out here in the sticks, there's something you need to know about me."

Jesse shot her a look. "Thanks so much for your faith in my ability to protect you, Elizabeth." He let sarcasm seep into his words. "Would you mind keeping your confession to yourself until I get us out of this mess?"

Compounding the assault by unknown shooters, thunder erupted close enough to cause the hair on the back of Jesse's neck to prickle. Great. All they needed was a gully washer to finish them off.

"I hope you weren't going to confess that you can't swim," he commented dryly, even though he knew that wasn't an option and that they'd have to reach higher ground. If it did rain hard enough to cause a wash down through the hills that surrounded them, they'd never survive the onslaught of water.

132

"Jesse, I--" Her comments were cut off by another round of gun fire, this time coming from further down the path, followed by receding hoof beats.

Jesse held his fire. It wouldn't do any good to shoot into the brush and trees without having a target in his sights. He'd end up killing his own horse by mistake.

"Jess--"

Jesse finally turned, keeping his head low and back against the rock for protection.

"All right, Elizabeth, spill it if you just positively can't wait until we get back to Peavine. Which, by the way, will now take quite a bit longer, given that holding on to you caused me to lose my grip on the horses. Chances are, they're already back at the stable." Thunder rumbled closer behind him, and Jesse knew no one would come looking for them before morning if a storm broke loose.

Now that she had his attention, Elizabeth didn't seem inclined to talk. Jesse reloaded his revolver before sliding it back into his holster, then he turned towards her. Her eyes were closed, her face white. Her arms were clutched across her chest. Jesse didn't like her frightened expression.

"I didn't mean it; about the horses being your fault." Jesse relented. They had been teasing each other just moments before the shots rang out, and although frustrated, Jesse really hadn't meant for her to take him literally.

"I think I've been shot," the thready whisper barely reached his ears.

"What?" Jesse jerked away from the rock, frantically searching her body for a pool of blood. Not immediately seeing any, he straddled her legs and gently probed her skull with his hands. "Where?" The word left his mouth at the same moment he saw her arm.

It took less time for Jesse to clean the graze on her upper arm and wrap it with his handkerchief than it did for his heart to return to a normal beat. Even when she gave him a weak smile and assured him it didn't hurt too terribly bad, his heart refused to quit pounding against his chest.

"Come on, we gotta get up the hill to the old Ramsey mine." Jesse tried as gently as possible to get Ellie to her feet.

She swatted at his hand. "I'm not going into any dark mine."

Even though the gunfire had stopped for several minutes now, Jesse knew the danger wasn't over for a storm seemed imminent. A crack of lightning punctuated his thoughts. "I doubt you could swim hard enough or hold on long enough to survive a gully washer."

He scooped Ellie up and shuffled up the slope, zigzagging his route in case anyone still observed them. Whoever had been shooting at them must have high-tailed it out of there, thinking they had accomplished their job when Jesse quit firing back.

Ellie looked past him to the threatening sky and sighed, pushing against his chest. "Put me down. It's my arm that's hurt, not my legs, and we'll never make it the way you're puffing for breath."

Jesse smiled in spite of himself, happy that she grumbled at him rather than fainting at the sight of blood, especially her own. And though he refused to admit she might be right, it proved much easier to take her hand and lead her up the steep slope to the deserted mine.

Fat drops of rain hit them as Jesse jerked the boards off the face of the mine. Excavated, then deserted early in the Comstock run, the rotten boards gave easily beneath his gloved hands. He figured they'd make good firewood.

One rumble of thunder and the heavens opened on them. "Grab that board and get inside, quick." Jesse grabbed what he could and dashed further into the mouth of the cave. He only hoped no wild critters had decided to make their home in the shallow entrance. As a word of warning though, he spoke over his shoulder as he stacked the wood for a fire. "Don't venture too far back. I don't know where the shaft drops."

When silence met his statement, he glanced up to find Ellie still outside the mouth of the mine.

"Get in out of the rain, for Crissake." When she didn't move, Jesse skirted the fire and reached to pull her inside. She jerked back so fast it surprised him and he lost his balance, almost ending up in the fire.

"What the hell is the matter?" He yelled, but when she lifted frightened eyes to him, he felt like a heel. Perhaps it was the after effects of the attack, or her getting shot, though Jesse knew the later wasn't serious.

He approached her softly. "El, come inside, out of the rain." He could see her shiver, and her blouse now clung to her curves like a second skin.

"It's dark."

Jesse glanced around. "Yes, the storm's going to make it dark faster tonight." He reached for her hand but she tucked both behind her back.

"It's dark in the mine. I can't go in there." Her voice quivered.

Her comment stumped Jesse. "Ellie, mines have always been dark. We used to play hide and go seek in the Nightingale while our pa's worked."

The rain had brought a chill to the air and Ellie was getting wetter by the minute. Reason didn't work, Jesse thought, perhaps anger would.

"Get your butt inside before I blister it like I threatened to do years ago when you wouldn't listen to me."

That caught her attention. She crossed her arms over her chest and took two very small steps into the cave. "That must have been a very long time ago, Jesse Cole, because I certainly don't remember it."

Since his comment had the desired effect, Jesse let it go and turned to put more wood on the fire so she could dry. "Move over here close to the fire."

"I'm f-f-fine," she stuttered and Jesse could hear her teeth chatter.

"For the love of St. Eligius," he muttered, jerking off his shirt. "Here -- put this on and give me your wet one."

She continued to stare fixedly at the fire, pulling her soaked shirt off, and her chemise, and pulling on his dry chambray. She never looked at him, and while his breath quickened at the sight of her breasts, nipples peaked with cold, she seemed not to notice her nakedness.

He cleared his throat. "Since when did you become afraid of the dark?" His voice was gentle but it didn't erase the haunted look from her eyes.

"A lifetime ago," she whispered, squatting down with her back to the wall, stretching her hands to the heat.

Jesse looked at their meager supply of wood, knowing it wouldn't last til morning. He could keep her safe when the light from the fire died, if she'd let him. How odd that he never knew about her fear before. Last night...it suddenly occurred to him that there had been a lamp burning last night in her room.

"Look, I need to find some more wood." He took one of the larger boards that burned on one end to use as a torch. "Take that bandanna off your arm and rinse it off in the rain and clean that cut. It's not bad, but there's no sense letting it get dirty." He hoped giving her something to do would quiet her fear.

Jesse ventured as far back as he dared but couldn't find anything remotely resembling firewood. When he returned to the fire, he stood mesmerized at the sight of Ellie, sitting cross-legged, the creamy texture of her back reflecting the firelight. She was looking out at the barrage of lightning, but turned to him when he dropped his torch into the fire. Sparks flew, but his heart was already ignited by the sight of her.

"The rain's pelting the ground so hard it's creating craters in the earth and washing out grooves that are like miniature streams." She sighed. "Sometimes, I used to stand outside during a storm. There's something about the excitement and the thrill of danger."

She turned her smile on him and though Jesse couldn't for the life of him understand her thinking, he would gladly live in a cave with her forever if it made her smile like that. When he had no response for her, she shrugged as if it didn't matter.

"I couldn't tie it back on one handed." She gestured to the make shift bandage. He'd forgotten she'd have to take his long-sleeved shirt off to get at her wound.

Nature surely conspired against him, Jesse thought, as he squatted down beside her to retie his bandanna around her arm. Seeing her half naked and vulnerable, he wanted nothing more than to make love to her. Given the cold rain, lack of firewood to keep them warm, and a very hard dirt floor, he sighed and settled for holding her tight.

"There's not enough wood to keep it light all night," he murmured as he tucked her head under his chin and leaned his back against the wall.

"That's OK," she said with a sigh that tickled his neck. She kissed the pulse that beat there. "I'm not frightened with you holding me like this." She wrapped an arm around his waist and nuzzled his neck like she was burrowing in for the winter. Then all was quiet.

Jesse sat the night through, holding her close. He didn't know how he deserved her trust, much less the love she seemed so adamant to give him after all this time, but he was determined to earn both. He shifted her in his arms and his hand brushed against the knot of his bandanna. Regardless that it was only a flesh wound, someone deliberately shot at them and Jesse was going to find out who. Too many weird things had been happening lately to call them all coincidences.

* * *

Zeke was roused out of a sound sleep by the stable owner's son. He stomped into his boots and pulled his suspenders up as he hurried down the muddy street, trying to dash from cover to cover so as not to get soaked. "Dang fool boy," he muttered to himself. "This better be good."

Only one lantern lit the musky interior of the livery, but Zeke had no trouble picking out Sam in the gloom.

"Sorry to wake you, Zeke, 'specially since it's raining, but thought you'd know what to do."

"Do 'bout what?" Zeke grunted in reply as the cold rain began to seep into his bones.

Nodding to the first stall, Sam said, "Jesse Cole's horse come back, by itself, along with the mare I saddled for Miss Elizabeth when they left for Reno."

"Holy sh--" Zeke wasn't prone to swearing, but ever since he and Lucky had come back from the dead, so to speak, he'd been doing more'n his fair share. Now, he raced over to the sorrel's side, running his hands over his forelocks and withers.

"I took the saddles and pack bags off so I could wipe 'em down. The mare musta had a stone in the shoe, cuz she's limping, but ain't got the stone in there no more. Don't see no other harm, but I sure don't know why they'd come home by themselves."

Zeke couldn't think of a reason either; only Jesse or Elizabeth would be able to tell them that. It didn't look like he and Lucky'd be able to get out before first light. Damn, it was Ellie, not Elizabeth. Once he recalled that, all sorts of problems raced around his brain, refusing to let him grab hold of 'em, and plain giving him a headache.

He rubbed his forehead as he spoke. "Jesse Cole knows them hills like the back of his hand. For whatever reason he let the horses go, I sure as shootin' figure he's holed up in a mine on the hillside. Can't do nothing in this downpour, so Lucky and I'll go find him at first light. Judging from the pack bags, they was heading back from Reno, so I got a suspicion on where they put up for the night."

Sam shrugged, figuring his job was done, and reached up and turned down the lamp. "Suit yourself, Zeke. Night."

"Yeah," Zeke muttered, already trudging back to the boarding house, his mind full of questions as to where Jesse and Ellie were, and 'xactly how they got to be there.

* * *

"You're sure you took care of him?" Clayton Scott asked the man dressed in black. Water ran off the man's hat and coat, pooling on the porch and making mud out of the

138

dirt from his boots. Clayton stepped back a pace or two, not caring to have contact with the likes of him.

"I said I did, didn't I?" The answer was growled from beneath the wide brim of the black hat. Scott knew the man from reputation only, and had talked to him just once when he paid him half his fee for agreeing to get rid of Jesse Cole. Now, the man had awaken him in the dead of night to get the rest of his money.

Thunder roared and the rain continued to come down in sheets. A wind came up behind it, blowing the wetness close enough to sprinkle the highly polished wood floor. He heaved a sigh, determined to get this piece of business done.

"Wait here." He left the man standing on the porch in the rain, returning a few minutes later with a fat envelope.

"Where did you take the girl?"

"You never said anything about bringing her down with me. I ain't no baby-sitter." The man growled menacingly.

"You didn't--"

"Look. I ambushed them like you said. The girl was getting all mushy and hanging on him like a damn coat, making it hard to get a shot. When I did shoot, they both went down behind a rock."

"You fool! I wanted Cole dead, not the girl. What if you hit her?" Scott was incensed and momentarily forgot the other man's reputation.

The man, however, wouldn't let him. Grabbing the front of Scott's dressing gown, he jerked him close. Scott could see the lightning reflected off the black of his eyes -- eyes that were deep and dark and soulless. "I took care of them, I said. Either she's dead or he is. Either way, the other'll be too scared to say anything. And they sure as hell won't be able to finger me."

With that, the man released Scott's clothing, shoving him backwards into the hallway. Tucking the envelope inside his shirt, he turned and disappeared into the rain, leaving Clayton shivering.

139

Clayton closed the door, shutting out the elements and reviewing the events of the night. He'd miss Elizabeth's warm, willing body, if indeed, she had been shot. Then again, it would mean the bank and the mine could both be his. Even if Cole remained alive, he couldn't fight ownership of the mine without the codicil, which Scott had safely tucked away in his books at the bank.

Clayton tossed back a whiskey to take the chill out of his bones; a chill caused by the stormy night, not by remorse. He had none.

Chapter 11

"Jesse! Jesse Cole -- you up there?"

Ellie heard shouts and felt Jesse's leg tense under her head. She jerked upright, disoriented, when Zeke yelled again. Raising an arm to brush her hair out of her eyes, she felt the sting from the gunshot wound and yesterday flashed back across her mind.

She looked wildly around the cave and couldn't believe that she had spent the night inside its black interior. Watery sunshine took some of the dark edges off, but she still shivered. As Jesse unwound his lean frame from the uncomfortable ground, she understood how she had been able to sleep. Jesse had been there to protect her.

"Well, it looks like we're about to be rescued," Jesse said wryly as Lucky shouted after Zeke to wait for him.

Ellie groaned. It would seem her time alone with Jesse was at an end. She took one last look at Jesse's naked torso as he stretched, gave a heartfelt sigh, and waited the arrival of her two guardians.

Zeke wheezed as he entered the cave, a happy grin splitting his craggy features to see they were all right. Lucky came barreling in after him, so completely out of breath he had to bend over, hands on knees, and Ellie really thought for a minute that he would keel over. Zeke recovered first.

"I knowed you'd be here if'n you got caught in the rain 'tween here and Reno." He nodded in a self-satisfactory way. Just as quickly, his gaze darted between Ellie and Jesse and his face fell. Ellie could see a dull red creep up his neck and infuse his already ruddy cheeks, and couldn't suspect what his problem was.

"What?" she quizzed.

"You...you got--" Zeke couldn't even finish his sentence, but pointed between the two of them as if they could guess what he meant.

Ellie couldn't, but Lucky apparently had some insight into his brother's logic, because the minute his head came up, he got as red as Zeke.

"Aw, gawd darnit, what'd you go and do, Miss Elizabeth?" He actually whined, and Ellie looked at him, shaking her head.

Jesse had been preoccupied with spreading the ashes of their fire, which had long since extinguished itself, but when Zeke and Lucky kept sputtering at Ellie, he took notice.

"Just exactly what are you two babbling about? Surely the climb up that hill didn't rattle your brains that much?"

Lucky turned and said in a whisper which Ellie figured could be heard back in Peavine, "She's wearing your shirt."

She glanced down then over to Jesse. "Oh," squeaked past her dry lips. She didn't exactly know the particulars about Zeke's and Lucky's pact which had brought them back to present day Peavine. Had she disrupted the threads of history by making love to Jesse? Well, hell, she sure hadn't made a pact with anyone. Besides, what she and Jesse did was none of their business.

"My shirt was wet and Jesse gave me his," she defended him, though he hadn't felt it necessary to comment. There wasn't any sense in these two thinking something had happened when it didn't.

Jesse shook her now dry, but terribly wrinkled shirt and walked over to hand it to her. "That's right. Ellie was soaked to the skin by the time we got up here."

"Ellie?" Zeke and Lucky echoed in unison.

As always, Lucky blamed her without knowing the facts. "You told him?" He grabbed his hat off his head and banged it against his legs. "Dang it all, anyway!"

Ellie rolled her eyes and shook her head. "Aren't you the one always telling me not to swear?"

"You told him that, too?" Lucky squeaked out.

Ellie suddenly realized that he had misconstrued her comments, and thought if she didn't say something fast, he might be the one to spill the beans. "Lucky, read my lips. I told him I liked Ellie as a nickname." She looked him straight in the eyes and repeated, "Ellie is my nickname."

Zeke must have seen the need to change the subject because he quizzed Jesse. "Why would you be soaked to the skin a'fore you got here? You know good and well how fast storms come over these mountains, and I don't recall you ever getting caught in one."

"Yeah, well, he's probably not usually getting shot at, either. Besides, Jesse is a wonderful woodsman. If it weren't for him, I might have been wounded more severely than I was."

Now that took the attention off her nickname, her swearing, and Jesse's semi-naked state.

"You was shot?" Lucky shouted.

Jesse waved them towards the entrance to the cave. "I'll tell you all about it while we wait outside for Ellie to change. Then I can have my shirt back and we can all ride into town together just like nothing's wrong. You did remember to bring us some horses, didn't you?" His voice faded as he corralled the guys outside.

Ellie chuckled even as she struggled to pull her shirt on over her sore arm. Zeke and Lucky thought she couldn't keep the simplest things straight without their help. She thought to explain but never got the chance as they rode back to Peavine.

"You'd best head right to the mine, Jesse," Zeke commented, pulling his horse to a stop. "Carlos has been asking 'bout you. Me and Lucky'll see Miss Elizabeth home." Zeke had that funny tone of voice that Ellie knew spelled trouble.

"I was going to invite Jesse home for breakfast," she said, just to judge his reaction.

"You goin' to cook?" Lucky snorted, knowing full well he did the cooking for her.

Ellie shot him an evil look.

Zeke shook his head. "No, not a good idea at all."

"Zeke, what the hell is going on?" Ellie turned her glare on him.

Lucky groaned at her language.

"Miss Elizabeth." He emphasized her name and left the word hanging. It was enough to make the hair on Ellie's neck prickle. Though he hadn't said exactly what was up, she had the feeling a kabotch had been put to their plans.

Jesse leaned close, cupping her cheek with his hand to turn her head to face him. "It wouldn't do your reputation any good to be seen coming into town with me; not with the way we both look. Zeke is right about that." He stared at her with such longing, Ellie knew he didn't want to leave.

"But--"

"Let Zeke see you home. If there's any way around it, stay away from Clayton Scott. Regardless of what we didn't find out in Carson, I don't trust him any further than I did last week. Which wasn't any at all." With a quick kiss on the cheek, Jesse turned his horse away. "Get your bones up to the Nightingale with me, Lucky, so you can take my horse back to the livery."

Lucky pouted at having to leave, but obediently followed Jesse towards the tree line. Zeke rode with Ellie up to the house, then took the horses down the street to the livery while she had a hot bath. Regardless of any brewing trouble, she made him swear he wouldn't come back for a full hour.

A good soak, strong coffee and a cigarette didn't help settle her nerves at all. The more she thought about the shooting on the mountainside, the more upset she became. Her stomach churned and her fingers trembled as she held the coffee mug. She had traveled all over the world, and lived in plenty of big cities, and yet she'd never in her life been mugged, much less actually shot. She was in the travel business, for God's sake, and sure as hell didn't go anywhere other than very secure, high-dollar resorts.

She sighed, knowing that those very safe resorts didn't come close to offering the kind of excitement she had found with Jesse Cole in Peavine, Nevada. Excitement she

144

didn't want to end, even though she knew it would in a few short days. Maybe it would be better if she went ahead and left right now.

By the time Zeke returned, Ellie had jerked on her own Levi's, shirt and hiking boots and was pacing the kitchen. She jumped him the instant he crossed the threshold. "Zeke, I want to go home. Right now."

At the same time he shouted, "Miss Elizabeth is on her way back." In exasperation he ran his hands through his hair.

"Zeke, I am back."

"I mean the real Miss Elizabeth."

"Oh, God," Ellie groaned, dropping into a kitchen chair, her own problems forgotten. "How do you know?"

"I happened to be walking past the telegraph office and Jimmy Jones bumped right into me, hurrying so fast he weren't watching where he's going. Darned near knocked me right down, he did."

"Zeke, stick to the story."

"Well, I says to him to watch it, and he says how he's got a telegram for Mr. Scott. I figure it won't hurt none to have a look-see, so I says I'll take it to the bank seeing as how I'm going there, anyway. Jimmy Jones didn't mind none seeing as how I gave him a dollar." Zeke appeared quite pleased with himself, and Ellie had to admit he kept on top of things.

"And?" she prompted.

Zeke slapped a scrap of paper on the table as he spoke. "It was a telegram from Miss Elizabeth."

"No." Ellie scanned the rough handwriting. "How come Jimmy wouldn't realize I couldn't be in town and out of town at the same time?"

"I suppose if'n he figured on it a'tall, he'd figure you was just recent gone, which you was." Zeke shrugged to show his unconcern for Jimmy Jones.

"How long do we have?"

"I hurried on down to the stage depot, but Elmer don't keep much for schedules. He says the stage gets here when he sees a cloud of dust down the road a piece. So I looks at his map and figures seven, maybe eight days."

"That's cutting it mighty close."

"Yep, but just think of what could of happened if'n I didn't get that telegram. Just the same, you and Jesse was shot at, and I'm thinking there's more mischief going on than we know."

"You're right. Why would someone suddenly try to get rid of Jesse; or me?"

"There's no good reason for trying to claim jump the Nightingale 'cuz she ain't been producing much all this time."

"Yes, but I still say either Scott or Elizabeth know more than they're telling and it's directly related to Jesse's mine."

"Even so, you'd best take Jesse's advice and stay away from that man."

"Zeke, I can't do that. I'm supposed to be in cahoots with him. How can I ignore him and act like he doesn't exist? If I do, he won't tell me any more of what he has planned."

"We could figure it out on our own if'n we had to. 'Sides, you sure don't want to be doing with that snake's belly what I'm thinking you and Jesse were doing all this time."

Ellie blushed and for an instant considered telling him to mind his own business. But in reality, she and Jesse were his business. With a sigh, she shrugged her shoulders in confusion. "Zeke, there's a place he's touched in me where no one else has ever been. Even when he's gone, I can still feel him here," she touched her heart, "and here," she moved her hand to her head. "He's constantly with me; he's all I think about."

Zeke slowly shook his head. "Missy, you ain't gonna get all 'motional and mushy on us now, are you? You know we gotta change history right this time. Then you go home."

Ellie slammed back her chair as she jumped to her feet. "Don't tell me what to do." She shouted, then immediately burst into tears. She stood in front of Zeke, wringing her hands. Through tears, she searched his face as she spoke. "Zeke, I don't want to leave him."

"Oh, boy, that'll change history for sure."

* * *

Zeke had not been able to come up with any kind of answer to Ellie's anguished pleas to be allowed to stay in this century. Ellie hadn't wanted to come to this place; hadn't wanted to help with anything, but once they had brought her through the mine to Peavine, she had fallen in love.

Whether that would put a kink in history and destroy their plans, or whether things could progress as indicated, they just didn't know. And if they couldn't save Jesse this time around, Ellie didn't want to live in either century.

Ellie cried herself to sleep that night, dreams of Jesse's tender lovemaking finally giving her rest. The next morning, it was all she could manage to drag her weary body out of bed when someone knocked on the door.

Clayton's astonished look when she greeted him told her that her swollen eyes and scratchy throat didn't do much for her appearance. She didn't care. When he grabbed her arm and she winced, he didn't even look surprised. It was almost as though he had known she had been hurt. That fact did register in Ellie's fuzzy mind.

"Elizabeth, I thought we had agreed to go for a ride today." His voice, oiled and about as seductive as a snake charmer, didn't fool Ellie.

She knew, also, that she had never agreed to go for a ride with him. Recalling Jesse's warning, Ellie wondered just exactly how she could manage to stay away from the banker. He let himself into the house and closed the door when she backed up.

"Clayton, I don't exactly feel up to a ride today." She pulled her robe closer around her, tying the sash over a queasy stomach.

147

He took a step closer, looking her up and down. "Where have you been the past couple of days, Elizabeth? You look like hell."

His tone irritated her and even if she was supposed to keep him happy, she just couldn't let him get by with intimidating her. "I went to Carson on business."

He reached out to trail a finger down her cheek. Ellie shivered at the coldness of his touch. "I know you were with Cole. I told you to stay away from him; that I'd take care of him."

Ellie's ears were ringing and her head was spinning. What had he said? She tried to concentrate on the conversation, but felt as though she'd been drugged and was standing outside herself.

"What kind of business do you have with Jesse Cole, Elizabeth?" Ellie felt the danger, even though his voice remained devoid of emotion. Still, she couldn't think of any reply but the truth.

"Personal." She tried to out stare him, but her eyes weren't focusing.

He now stood directly in front of her, his chest lightly brushing her wrist as she clutched the front of her robe. He wrapped long, cold fingers around the front of her throat.

"How personal did it get, Elizabeth? Did you let him have your delectably soft body?" His fingers tightened painfully. "Did he tell you what we need to know after you sprawled in his bed?" He whispered the question just before his cool lips touched hers and he forced his tongue inside her mouth. Ellie didn't move a muscle or respond in any way.

Still holding her with just his grip on her throat, Clayton stared at her with hard, cruel eyes. "You're mine, Elizabeth, so get Cole out of your mind. He's a dead man."

Ellie closed her eyes and willed herself not to get sick. It's all part of the plan to gain information, her mind zapped out a repetitive message, but her stomach refused to listen. With a groan, she twisted away and raced to her bedroom, barely dragging the chamber pot out from under the bed before her stomach rebelled entirely.

148

She didn't realize Clayton had followed her until she sagged weakly to the floor, her back to the bed. She numbly flopped her head back against the mattress.

"Well, that's thoroughly disgusting," he said from the doorway, looking as though he thought she would contaminate him. "I suppose we'll have to postpone our little outing, but at least if you're sick, I don't have to worry about you rendezvousing with Cole."

"Go to hell," Ellie retorted, though she wished she could sound more vehement.

"That's more like it. A little spirit, but not too defiant. Come see me when you're back on your feet." Clayton laughed coarsely before adding, "Of course, you won't stay on your feet long, but I don't want you puking in my bed."

Ellie closed her eyes, shaking like a leaf. Clayton was getting entirely too bold. She only hoped she could fend him off as long as it remained necessary. Regardless of Elizabeth's history with the man, Ellie found him totally repulsive. She tried to count the number of days until they would be through with him, but darkness squeezed in around the edges of her vision.

She couldn't lift herself off the floor without her head spinning dizzily. What had hit her so hard? She never got sick, but when she heard the front door slam behind Scott, she decided it had to be stress. Too weak to stand, she turned to her hands and knees and crawled towards the wash basin, wanting desperately to rinse out her mouth.

"Holy Mackerel, Miss Elizabeth," Lucky screeched from the doorway and Ellie dropped the glass of water she had just managed to pour with shaking hands. Lucky scrambled over to where she sat in a heap. "Are you sick?"

If Ellie looked even one tenth as bad as she felt, Lucky didn't need to ask. He must have agreed when she lifted her face to peer bleary eyed at him, for he silently shook his head, dropping his hat to the chair and gently lifting her under the arms to help her to bed.

"Water," she whispered hoarsely.

After he fetched her a glass and took care of her chamber pot, Lucky stood by the bed, fidgeting with his hat.

"Go away." Ellie wanted to die in peace and didn't want witnesses to her dreadful state.

"I'd better get Zeke," Lucky contemplated out loud, "or maybe Jesse."

"No," Ellie tried to rear up in bed, but finding herself too weak, flopped back onto the pillow. "Please don't get Jesse," she cried softly. "I'm such a mess. I don't want him to see me this way. I'll be fine; I just need some rest." She reached for his arm, but he had become indistinct and Ellie wondered if he had turned into a ghost again. She tried to focus, but the room grew steadily dark, and she only hoped that if she was being transported back to her own time, she wouldn't arrive with the flu.

* * *

Ellie struggled against the fog in her brain. Arguing, though the exact words escaped her, slowly brought her back to consciousness, but with a sense of dread. Something had happened that she needed to remember. For whatever reason, she felt the urgency, but couldn't recall the message.

"What's we goin' to do if'n she don't get better?"

"Dang if I know. You sure you didn't feed her something upsetting to her innards?"

"You always blame me, Zeke. I ain't always at fault, you know."

Ellie groaned, figuring she had been transported to hell, the two crusty old miners with her. From the heat suffocating her and the feel of cotton in her mouth, she'd place even money on the devil's own back yard.

She tried to move her arms but couldn't; her legs didn't work either. Concentrating hard enough to give herself a headache, she forced scratchy eyes open to see two grisly faces peering down at her. Another groan escaped. Trying to raise an arm to block the bright sunshine from her eyes, she realized they had buried her under enough blankets to bake an Eskimo.

"Water," she croaked, then gagged when Lucky tilted the glass too rapidly against her mouth. It took every ounce of energy she could muster to get one arm out from beneath the pile of quilts. She made a grab at the glass, but a stinging pain shot up her arm and she cried out.

"You two get away before you kill her." The command came from the door. Lucky and Zeke immediately backed off.

Jesse marched over to the bed in a no nonsense fashion, a breakfast tray in his hands. He wore a soft blue chambray shirt tucked into snug breeches. His black hair glistened in the light; his blue eyes twinkled as he winked at her. To Ellie, he looked like an angel.

Here he came, all scrubbed and shiny and smelling of fresh air and male. Ellie could feel the sweat clinging to her skin; could tell from the way her head felt that her hair was tangled. Regardless of the heat from the wealth of covers piled on top her, she wanted to crawl under them so Jesse couldn't see her.

"Go away." Tears sprang to her eyes and she turned her head to the wall.

"Yes, you two skedaddle back up to the mine. Tell Carlos I won't get back today, and to let me know if he needs me." Jesse placed the tray on the table, reached over her for another pillow, and gently lifted her shoulders forward to prop her up to eat. He ignored her silent tears, and while Ellie wanted to die of embarrassment, he seemed not to notice her condition.

He settled the tray on her lap, gave her a dazzling smile, then turned to shoo the other two from the room like an old mother hen. Ellie could hear them talking in low voices, but decided to ignore them as the scent of bacon and eggs reached her. With her good arm, she reached for her coffee, savoring the rich dark brew, and was dipping her toast into the last of her egg when Jesse returned.

"What happened?" Though she felt better with a full stomach, she knew she had been very, very sick. The last

151

thing she recalled was retching when Clayton had come calling. That thought brought back the feeling of dread she had experienced earlier. She frowned in concentration.

Jesse sank into the chair beside her bed, stretching his long legs out before him, sipping his own coffee. For the moment, Ellie forgot her consternation as she took in the length of him, admiring the snug fit of his pants and the width of his shoulders.

"Somehow you got infection from that gunshot wound to your arm." Jesse shook his head slightly. "I cleaned it thoroughly, and it was only a crease. There was no cause for it to flare up like it did."

No wonder her arm still hurt, Ellie gingerly touched the bandage covering her upper arm. "I still feel woozy."

"You had a fever. It's a good thing Lucky found you when he did. Whatever kind of poison was on that bullet could have caused you to lose your arm." Even as fuzzy as Ellie's brain was, she could hear the anger in his voice.

"You went back up the trail, didn't you?" She didn't need his nod before she continued. "You never found anything?"

A shake of his head confirmed it. There appeared to be little way of investigating crimes in 1870. Ellie doubted fingerprinting had been discovered, at least not out west. Without the bullet that hit her, there was no way to get a fix on who had ambushed them.

"You need to get some rest." Jesse stood and removed the tray from her lap. "I'm staying here today and the boys will be back to watch over you tomorrow."

Ellie protested. "Jesse, we can't find out what Clayton's up to if you three are hovering around me all day. He told me to come see him when I got better."

"He was here?" Anger laced Jesse's curt question.

"Yes." Clayton's green pallor flashed before her eyes and she almost laughed. "He didn't quite take to my being sick."

"That's just fine and dandy. He'd better stay away or I'll sit on the porch with a shotgun."

152

A sense of panic Ellie couldn't understand rose in her chest. "No, you can't do that. We've got to know before--" she broke off when Jesse pinned her with a hard, calculating stare.

"Know what? By when?" He stood motionless with the breakfast tray in his hands.

Ellie groaned and fell back against the pillows. There were some things she just couldn't tell Jesse, and others she didn't understand herself. "Never mind, it must have been something I dreamed."

Jesse seemed to accept that. "Get some rest, El. I'll be here if you need me."

* * *

Jesse looked in on Ellie late in the afternoon to find her crawling back into bed. "What are you doing out of bed?"

A groan answered him as she hid her face in the pillow. He moved to adjust her covers when he heard her anguished words. "Just let me die in peace." A touch to her forehead and Jesse knew her fever was back.

"I've got to get you in a bath. You're burning up."

"Yeah, well it's summer and hotter than hell. What do you expect?" She immediately tossed aside the sheet he had pulled over her. He paused momentarily at the sight of her long legs, exposed past the knee where her gown had crept up. He gave a heartfelt sigh as he headed for the kitchen.

Under normal circumstances, Jesse would have enjoyed Ellie's attitude as he sponged her off in the tub of cool water. She kept trying to pull him into the water with her, curling her arms around his neck and lifting herself up so her wet breasts glistened in the lamplight.

However, every time her hot lips tried to capture his, he knew it was the fever making her act the way she did. And even as he chuckled at her antics, it was impossible for him to take advantage of the situation.

He grew more concerned as he lifted her out of the tub. Her legs seemed unable to support her, and he ended up with her on his lap as he rubbed her down with the soft towel.

Wrapped again in her robe, he tucked her into bed where she immediately curled onto her side and fell into a deep sleep. Jesse knew sleep would be the best thing for her, so he contented himself to sit by her side in the dark, listening to her breathing.

* * *

"Jesse!" Her scream tore through the black of night, raising the hair on Jesse's arms and shooting him straight out of the chair.

"Sh, it's all right." He sat on the side of her bed as she groped for his arm in the dark.

"Turn on the light. I hate the dark. You know I hate the dark!" She clung to him like a leech while he struggled to free one arm to strike a match to the lamp on the bedside table.

Once the low light chased away the darkest of the shadows, he turned only to realize that she really didn't see the room. Her eyes were glazed with fever. He rose from the bed to fetch some water.

"Don't leave me." This time it was a whimper and the sound of it tore at Jesse's heart more than her frightened screams had. He bent to kiss her hot cheek.

"Only for a moment, honey. I've got to cool you down."

"Alcohol."

He cocked a brow at her request. "I don't think you need a drink of anything but water."

"Alcohol...rub," she said on a sigh.

Jesse frowned over her words, but once he got to the kitchen, he paused at the pantry. Examining the containers, he found Dr. Melon's Wondrous Elixir among the bottles and tins. Knowing most of the so-called patented medicines were nothing more than flavored alcohol, he figured it might work just as well to rub her down with it as to let her drink it.

Thirty minutes later, Ellie rested easier, her fever abated, but Jesse's restlessness had grown. While he wouldn't entrust Ellie's health to anyone else, it had taken all his will power as he had rubbed the Elixir soaked cloth over her satiny body, leaving her uncovered and totally naked so the alcohol could evaporate and cool her body.

Earlier, he had controlled his lust because he kept telling himself she had a fever. Now, he repeated that lecture, but it didn't help considering he had seen her naked for the better part of the day. As if that weren't bad enough, she had moaned and wiggled under his ministrations until he thought he would burst into flames.

He could smell peppermint as he tucked the sheet under her chin and thought at least the Elixir wasn't licorice flavored. He hated licorice. "Lord, woman, what I don't sacrifice for you," he whispered. He had thought her asleep, but at his softly spoken words, she opened her eyes.

"I'm falling in love with you, Jesse Cole." Her words, husky and soft and passion laden, sounded more like a burden than a benediction.

He knelt on the floor beside her. "Is that so bad?" Truth of the matter was, he had fallen in love with her, too. Not the youthful lust he recalled from their early years. This was a deeper, more potent passion that she had just recently evoked in him. One that he knew would last a lifetime.

She had a passion for life that rubbed off on him. While he still worked the mine and searched for the motherlode, she had inspired him to truancy -- playing hooky, she called it. He thought of their recent trip to Steamboat Springs, where she had told him to "chill out." Her language was strange, her passion invigorating.

Jesse had tried to sort out his feelings on the train ride home. The rocking, clickety-clack of the train had lulled her to sleep, her head on his shoulder. He had thought at the time he would be content to spend the rest of his life with her tucked into the curve of his shoulder.

A sob interrupted his thoughts. "Now what?"

155

"I'm not really Elizabeth and I don't belong here. Zeke and Lucky dragged me back to Peavine to help. Clayton Scott is trying to take your mine and he's going to blow it up and you'll be killed." She cried in earnest now, and Jesse gathered her in his arms.

Jesse had to laugh, regardless of how sincere she sounded. Her story was just too preposterous to believe.

She weakly pounded his arm. "I'm telling the truth."

Trying to calm her, he asked, "All right, if you're not Elizabeth, who are you?"

"I'm Ellie; Ellie from New York and I work for a magazine." She tilted her head back to look him straight in the eye.

Jesse wondered if her fever had returned. Her beautiful brown eyes glistened with tears, and when he lightly kissed her forehead, he couldn't tell if it was her skin or his lips that felt so hot.

"I really am just Ellie. Does Jesse love Ellie?"

Jesse thought about the imp who kept disrupting his work; if not with her presence, then with his thoughts of her. He recalled her lush body beneath his; her cries of ecstasy as they plunged into the deepest passion he had ever thought to know.

"Oh, yes," he whispered, hugging her close, "Jesse definitely loves Ellie."

Chapter 12

Ellie felt much better the next day, but Jesse insisted on staying close at hand most of the morning. When he kept looking at her strangely, Ellie figured she must look a fright. Finally, when she promised not to overdo, he left her in peace, but sent Lucky by twice to check on her.

Ellie didn't want to spend her remaining time with Jesse by being sick, so she went to bed early that night to regain her strength. The second day, she sent a message to Clayton that although she had recovered from the flu, she was now femininely indisposed and figured that ailment could last up to a week.

Although Jesse continued to work long hours in the mine, he got word to her through Lucky or Zeke at least once a day, and they would spend a few hours together. That time became idyllic.

Even so, they still played a waiting game. She and Zeke and Lucky counted the days, hoping against hope that Elizabeth wouldn't show up before the Independence Day celebration. Zeke had convinced Jesse to close the mine for the celebration, even though they couldn't tell him the particulars. They had to play the game as close to the first happening as possible, but Ellie hadn't wanted the possibility of other men getting hurt. Since Zeke knew only Jesse had died in the first explosion, they didn't figure it would matter if they made sure the men were out of the mine this time. They did know charges would be set at the mine because that's what had happened before. And the educated guess was that Clayton would be involved.

Ellie just hoped the outcome would be different. Her heart ached at the possibility of Jesse being killed in the prime of his life. Regardless of the fact that she would no longer be here with him, she couldn't bear to have him sacrificed.

Now, she waded across the creek barefoot, stopping mid-stream to splash water on her bare arms. She laughed at herself, realizing she no longer missed the fast-paced craziness of her century and had even acclimated to the super-hot weather here on the slopes of the Sierra's.

She tried not to think of re-entering her own world; the world of microwave dinners, digital telecommunications and speedy transportation. One thing for sure, their plot to save Jesse wouldn't have worked in Ellie's world, for Elizabeth could have returned home in hours instead of days.

Ellie shrugged off the thought, knowing there was nothing she could do about any of it. Plans had been set in motion a hundred forty-five years ago and were beyond her control.

Jesse had asked her to meet him at the entrance to the mine. Ellie still refused to enter the Nightingale, even with Jesse, and she tried not to think about him being inside the dark pit.

As she left the tree lined path and entered a clearing in front of the mine, she could hear Jesse hollering at one of the men, but couldn't see him. Finally, she found him at the top of a wooden tower built like an oil derrick.

"Hey, I'll be down in a minute," he shouted as he waved from his perch.

Ellie waved back, then watched in amazement as he scrambled down rickety cross bars which formed ladder steps on the side of the framework.

"What is that?" She questioned when Jesse reached her, wiping the sweat from his forehead with a large red bandanna.

"What? Oh, that?" He frowned and Ellie figured she had goofed again. Since Elizabeth's father had once mined, she supposed she should already know the names of all this stuff.

"We started using headframes a few years ago when we tunneled under more level ground, instead of burrowing into the side of a mountain. The pulleys at the top are used to hoist ore from the mine shafts below. It saves alot of man-hours and hard work when we don't have to push ore carts up the slopes on rails through endless miles of tunnels to the main entrance."

Ellie looked at the apparatus with renewed interest. They knew Clayton would have to get into the mine to blow it, and Ellie now wondered how many different entrances they had to worry about. "Could a person go down into the mine from that?"

Jesse looked at her in surprise. "Why would you want to do that? I thought you didn't like dark places." He took a step closer and gave her a seductive smile. "Unless you were with me, that is, so I could keep your mind off it."

Her stomach immediately flip-flopped at his suggestive tone. His voice always did that to her. How was she to live without him? A shiver sliced through her. Dear Lord, why couldn't things be different?

"Jesse," his name escaped her lips on a sigh. Her eyes drifted closed as she leaned slightly forward to kiss him, only to be rudely interrupted when a shout came down the hill.

"Cole!" Carlos, Jesse's foreman, shouted. "You ready to put this timbering in?"

"Be right there." Jesse smile apologetically. "Sorry, but after I sent Lucky to get you, Carlos noticed the defective timbering in tunnel C. If we don't square set it, we won't be able to go any further. All indications are this is the place where we'll find the big vein, but I have to make sure it's safe for the men to be that far down."

"But is it safe for you?"

He shrugged. "After we get the timbering done, it will be. By building squares of framed timbers instead of the old cross beam method, we can work an ore vein of any width safely and alot quicker than before." He pointed to the headframe. "Tunnel C runs directly beneath that. Once we find the motherlode, it will be easy work hauling the ore to the surface and on to the stamp mill."

He winked. "That's the secret. Most of the mines are tunneling deeper and deeper into the mountain, and while they're finding small veins, nothing big has been found in years. All our assay reports indicate that this vein, running away from the slope, could yield three thousand to the ton."

"Dollars?" Ellie asked, incredulous.

"Yes, dollars," Jesse returned, his facing breaking into a grin.

"Cole, you coming?" Carlos yelled again.

"Sorry, sweetheart, I've got to go. I want this done right."

Ellie nodded numbly as Jesse hurried off. Suddenly Clayton's words came back to her. No wonder Clayton blew up Jesse's mine and killed him. Jesse had just told her, as Elizabeth, about the possible size of the strike. Elizabeth would have told Clayton, and together they would have plotted the end. Even though Ellie had no intention of telling Clayton anything, he still had mentioned "an accident." If he had any idea what could come from the Nightingale, Jesse wouldn't stand a chance.

Swinging around and heading back down the slope, Ellie was more determined than ever that it wouldn't happen again. Jesse and his men deserved to strike it rich, and she wouldn't allow Clayton or anyone else to rob them of it. She would save Jesse and the Nightingale, or die trying.

* * *

The next evening, Ellie watched as Jesse moved around his small cabin, gathering ingredients to make her supper. As he stretched to reach a top shelf, she admired the play of muscles across his bare back, and watched avidly as his trousers rode low on his hips with every movement. Her gaze continued down his long legs to his bare feet. Even his feet were sexy, she thought and giggled.

She had caught him unawares in a tub of water when she had arrived earlier than planned. Just moments after she had offered to wash his back, he had pulled her into the tub with him, leaving most of the bath water on the floor of the cabin. The rest had puddled beside the heap of wet clothes at the foot of the bed.

They had been so hungry for each other. No prelude; no foreplay as Jesse swept her into a whirlwind of passion, possessing her again and again. Ellie hadn't been a passive partner in what had transpired, because he had taught her well and she had become addicted to his loving.

By the time she lay sated across his bare chest, it had grown dark. As Jesse had said, she felt no fear, for his arms wrapped her in a cocoon of warmth and security.

His stomach had growled loud enough for Ellie to think a bear kept them company in the cabin, and with a sigh he had risen from bed to fix their supper. He had slipped his pants on but tossed his shirt to Ellie.

"Your clothes are wet," was all he said as he gathered the bundle and disappeared outside to hang them on a line.

Now, as she sat cross-legged on the bed, his cotton shirt rubbing against her bare breasts, she wanted him all over again. When she giggled, he glanced her way, winked, then resumed his biscuit making.

"You're poetry in motion, you know that?" she said. At his snort, she added, "No, I mean it. You're all fluid grace and it's like no action is wasted. Watching you move is like watching a ballerina."

Jesse cocked a brow as he scowled at her. "I hope you don't go around telling that to anyone. Sounds kinda sissified."

Ellie thought a moment. "Maybe what Robert Frost said will explain it. 'Love, the moon and murder have poetry in them by common consent. But it's in other places. It's in the axe-handle of a Canadian woodchopper, and it's in poultry-stricken ground.'"

She slowly rose from the bed and walked over to stand before him, her gaze never leaving his. Looping her arms around his neck, she added, "The most wondrous poetry isn't that of words on paper. Rather it is the beauty and movement of a man; majestically toiling, diligently seeking his dreams, tenderly loving."

"Does your Mr. Frost have a fondness for men?" Jesse asked sardonically.

Ellie laughed as he did, but slowly the humor faded from her voice as passion flared. "No; the last lines were mine."

"So sweet," he murmured as he lowered his head to meet her lips.

Ellie breathed in the scent of him as he kissed her, wondering if she could ever get enough of this man. With a groan, she surrendered her body to his lips, her heart to his safekeeping.

A pot bubbling over on the stove brought them back to awareness. With a light kiss on her nose, Jesse released her. "Dessert," he promised with a smile.

While Jesse finished the preparations for their meal, Ellie perused his book shelf. Pulling one slim volume off the shelf, she opened it to read the title. On the inside cover was the inscription, To Shelley J. Cole, I will love you always.

She slammed the book shut, spinning around to face Jesse. Who the hell was Shelley? Had Jesse written the inscription? A green haze swept across her vision and she forced her teeth together to keep from asking. She knew there was no one in his life right now, because in a town the size of Peavine, she would know of it. But had there been a love at one time? Perhaps he had found someone while Elizabeth was at school; someone he would never forget and who would always have his heart, regardless of what he kept saying to Ellie?

"Supper's done." He graciously held a chair out for her, and Ellie only hoped she could swallow around the lump in her throat.

Jesse's stories about the antics of Zeke and Lucky soon had Ellie forgetting everything except the cozy atmosphere in the cabin. After supper, she bent over the table to help clear away the dishes, and Jesse ran his hand up her bare leg. Dishes clattered everywhere.

"Jesse Cole." She lectured him, trying to keep a straight face. The dishes were tin and nothing broke, and

162

the look that accompanied his wandering hands instantly fanned the flames of passion left simmering from earlier in the evening.

"Why don't you read to me, while I do the dishes," she suggested.

Ironically Jesse pulled the very same volume off the shelf that she had seen earlier. The book seemed to naturally fall open and Jesse struck a pose, ridiculous in his half nakedness, but stunning enough that Ellie stopped in the middle of collecting plates to listen.

"'I arose, and for a space
The scene of woods and waters seemed to keep,
Though it was now broad day, a gentle trace
Of light diviner than the common sun
Sheds on the common earth, and all the place
Was filled with magic sounds woven into one
Oblivious melody, confusing sense
Amid the sliding waves and shadows dun...'"

He straightened with a frown and quietly closed the book.

"I haven't heard that passage since my mother used to read it to me as a child. I used to think it was written about my own special place in the woods." He shrugged, sliding the book back to the shelf and pulling out another.

"Mother loved that book, but I prefer Keats." He brought the book over and sat at the table as Ellie dumped the dishes in a pan and poured some hot water from the stove over them.

"'Ode To A Nightingale'. Is that where the name for the mine came from?" Ellie was no fan of the early romanticists, but she did know the titles of one or two of the more famous.

Jesse gave her a quizzical glance, then shrugged. "Who knows how our fathers came up with that name. Years ago in Cornwall it was said that birds were kept in cages in the coal mines as a way to tell whether there was enough air to breath. Maybe the birds were Nightingales and that's where they came up with the name."

163

"Boy, wouldn't the animal activists have a heyday with that," Ellie mumbled.

"What?"

"Ah, just that animals need activity, not a cage," Ellie improvised. Waving a hand towards the book, she commanded, "Read."

"'A thing of beauty is a joy forever:
Its loveliness increases; it will never
Pass into nothingness; but still will keep
A bower quiet for us, and a sleep
Full of sweet dreams, and health, and quiet breathing...
Therefore 't is with full happiness that I
Will trace the story of [Ellie}.'"

Ellie turned from the sink, gazing across the short expanse to where Jesse returned her gaze, his blue eyes stormy with passion.

He continued, not even glancing at the book, his gaze hypnotic, his voice seductive.

"'The very music of [her] name has gone
Into my being, and each pleasant scene
Is growing fresh before me as the green
Of our own valleys: so I will begin...'"

He stood, walked around the table, and held out his hand.

"...by saying that though I see poetry in the sway of the trees and in the bubbling creek, there are no words in any poet's song book to explain what happens to my heart when my fair lady graces me with a single smile."

Ellie placed her hand in his and he raised it to bestow a kiss so gentle, tears came to her eyes. He sketched her a bow like the knights of old.

"Would my lady honor me with this dance?"

Before she could gather her wits, he pulled her close and swept her into a waltz, circling the table and gliding gracefully around the chairs by the cold fireplace.

Even as he gazed at her in passion, Ellie couldn't help but remember the sadness that came to his eyes when he had read from the book with the loving inscription.

164

Curiosity and jealousy got the best of her. "Who is Shelley J. Cole?"

Jesse pulled her to a halt. "Where did you -- oh, the book." Even in the poor light from a single lamp on the table, Ellie could see a ruddiness in his cheeks. Was he embarrassed that she had found something so personal?

He racked a hand through his hair. "It has to do with my mother."

"Your mother's name was Shelley?"

"No." He hesitated so long, Ellie thought he wouldn't tell her more. "The book was from her, to me. She named me Shelley Jesse Cole. Shelley after her favorite poet."

His embarrassment was so acute, Ellie clapped a hand over her mouth to keep her laughter inside. Regardless, a giggle escaped and Jesse glared at her.

"It's not funny. You know how many fights I got into at school? I finally quit answering to my first name, so she had no choice but to call me Jesse. That's the only name I ever use."

With a sigh, Ellie glided back into his arms. Pulling his face down close to hers, she kissed the frown from his lips, the wrinkles from his brow. "You are full of surprises, Shelley Jesse Cole."

With a growl, he swung her up into his arms, blew out the lamp and tossed her onto the bed. As though his kisses weren't enough to drug her, his hands swept titillating forays up her legs to her bare hips, then slid beneath the shirt.

Jesse lay down beside her, pulling her back against him, and she could feel the evidence of his desire snug against her backside. The shirt she wore did nothing to prevent the heat of him from seeping through her skin and into her very soul. She groaned inwardly as his hand kneaded her belly. He whispered love words in her ear then nibbled on her earlobe.

Jesse had unleashed his passion in the hotel; that day when he had lost all control. For that, Ellie couldn't be sorry. But each day she was near him, even when she wasn't in bed with him, made her cry for the short amount of time they had left. It became worse when he did touch her, for he ignited sensations she didn't know she had and made her feel things she didn't want to live without. She knew she would never, ever find a man who could give her such tender passion; who understood her needs and desires, and could show her how to live, better than Jesse. Besides, she didn't want anyone but Jesse, so she'd live a very lonely life when this adventure was over.

Jesse's breath quickened at her throat; his hand a hot brand, sliding slowly downward. She could live without any of the modern conveniences, but she didn't want to live without Jesse's love. Still, she stopped his movements.

"Don't. If you keep doing that, I'll die from wanting you all the nights of my life."

"And would that be so bad? I will be right by your side all those nights for the rest of your life."

Silent tears ran down Ellie's cheeks, for he couldn't know that she wouldn't be here much longer. When she could speak, she whispered brokenly. "But I'll crave forever a love which I cannot keep."

He turned her to her back, kissing the hollow of her throat where her pulse beat rapidly. "Love isn't for keeping or taking. It is only in sharing love that it is returned to us in abundance."

"You sound like a poet, sir."

"Ah, but if I were, I would weave magical love words around you as though they were a golden bower, to keep you forever close to my heart."

He placed her hand against his pounding heart. Her gaze adored him.

"But alas, my words are mere whispers upon the wind when compared to the potency of the gaze you cast my way."

"Yes, a poet indeed." She touched his cheek, then pulled him down, her breath a caress against his lips. "Didn't I tell you how dearly I cherish poets?"

"Perhaps then, there is some of Shelley in me, after all." Jesse spoke in jest, trying to bring his passion under control as this incredible need for her careened through his

166

blood. However, all was lost when her lips opened in invitation, her tongue darting out to taste him. He knew pure ecstasy as only the great poets could describe. And yet, he doubted even Keats or Byron had known a love as sweet as this.

Much, much later, Ellie murmured, "I should get home."

"Stay." He nuzzled her neck. Having her curled into his side, naked skin to naked skin, felt so right.

"No, I don't want you seeing me in the morning. I'm not a morning person and am totally unbearable until I've had my coffee."

He propped himself up on an elbow, drawing lazy circles along her collarbone. "I didn't know that about you. You mean you're not always sweet and adorable?" He loved to bait her. Predictably, she swatted at his hand. "I'll make sure I have your coffee ready before I wake you with a kiss."

She apparently decided not to deny him, or herself, for she curled around him possessively, flinging an arm and leg over his body. Kissing his bare chest, she mumbled, "Definitely full of surprises," as she drifted off to sleep.

* * *

As promised, Jesse woke her before dawn, freshly brewed coffee in hand. Even so, she grumbled as she dressed, for although she thought it best if she were found in her own bed in the morning, she didn't want to leave the comfort of Jesse's arms.

They walked hand in hand along the creek to the crossing rocks. Once on the other side, Jesse stopped her for a quick kiss.

"You smell so sweet. How come I don't remember you ever smelling so sweet?"

"Are you hitting on me?" Ellie teased with a smile.

"What do you mean?" Jesse looked horrified. "Has that bastard, Scott, touched you again? I'll kill him, I swear."

167

Ellie quickly placed a palm on his chest, kneading softly until his expression gentled. "No, Jesse, please. It's just an expression; like flirting." She stood on tiptoe and lightly kissed his pursed lips. "Like this."

When he relaxed and drew a breath, she ran her tongue along the ridge of his teeth. His arms tightened around her.

After a kiss that went on forever and sapped her strength, Jesse raised his head, eyes twinkling. "Are you flirting with me?" He teased.

"Most definitely," she replied. And she did it again.

Chapter 13

Jesse had the mine operating around the clock and he stayed up there right in the thick of things. The problem was there weren't that many days left before the Independence Day celebration -- only seven, to be exact. That had to be why restlessness consumed Ellie, turning her nights sleepless and her days unsettled. It was a do-nothing, do-something kind of feeling that extended from the very depths of her outward. Where to go; what to do? In her current state of mind, nothing appealed to her.

Today was a perfect example. She paced from room to room. Regardless of the hot breeze through an open window, it felt like a cabin fever, mid-life crisis kind of day. The sun was shining now but the wind blew. The rain had quit, leaving the ground sloppy with puddles. On top of that her conscience nagged her to do something constructive, her ego dragged her through a quagmire of self-doubt, and her body craved both a cigarette and chocolate.

She had realized that morning it had been days since her last cigarette. So much had happened, she hadn't thought about it. She'd better not think about it now, or she'd race down to Murphy's for tobacco.

She scrubbed and rinsed out her clothes, carrying them outside to hang on the line. She dropped a blouse in the mud, then almost swallowed a clothespin when she sucked in a breath to swear.

How on earth had she ever allowed them to talk her into such a harebrained, stupid -- she hadn't. They had tricked her; kidnapped her and now here she was in a century she still didn't understand, living someone else's life and falling in love with a man she definitely had no business loving.

She knew it illogical; their lives were anything but similar. Regardless, nothing could stop the passion when Jesse held her; the need he created deep inside, and the restlessness she felt, like now, when she wasn't with him.

"You'd better not have tracked over my clean floor." She looked at Lucky's boots when she found him in the kitchen. She slapped her muddy blouse back in the sink.

"Well, here I come to see if'n you wanted fish for supper, but maybe I'll just go catch some for me and Zeke," Lucky said with a pout. While Ellie had learned some basic cooking skills during her tenure here, she still lived for the meals he cooked. And Lucky knew it.

"Wait," she shouted after him as he vacated the kitchen as fast as he had entered.

Ellie caught up with him at the edge of the trees. "Can't I go with you?" Anything was better than sitting around.

"What for?" Usually Lucky's attitude was buoyant, or at least he didn't pout for long. Perhaps he, too, was feeling pressure because of the short amount of time remaining.

Ellie thought furiously for an answer he would accept. "Well, I could catch a fish," she began, and then inspiration struck, "and cook supper. Ouch." A rock flipped into her shoe and she bent to slip both of them off, preferring to walk barefoot. When Lucky didn't answer, she looked up.

He stood, with his mouth open, arms slack at his side, staring at her. She picked up her shoes and tucked her long skirt into her waistband and still he hadn't said anything. She returned his stare in silence.

"You don't like my cooking no more?" He finally asked.

"Lucky, I love your cooking," she tried to soothe his ruffled feathers. "I just thought I could do something special for Jesse."

"You want to cook for Jesse." Lucky pushed his hat back to scratch his head in confusion. "You tryin' to kill him?"

Ellie sputtered in agitation, even though she knew he was probably right. "You could help."

Lucky started walking again and Ellie skipped to catch up.

"Please?" She smiled.

He scrunched up his face, but Ellie could already see a twinkle in his eyes. "All right, but you gotta do the work." They had reached the water and he dropped his poles on the riverbank.

"Like what?" Ellie had never been fishing in her life, and now felt leery of his tone.

Turning over a rock, Lucky pointed. "Like gettin' your own worm." Laughing, he grabbed one and turned towards the water.

Ellie puckered her lips and squatted down by the creatures that wiggled around in the moist dirt. Briefly, she thought back to the time she had refused a date with Paul, an outdoors writer for the travel magazine. He had once asked her to go trout fishing with him on the Colorado River. At the time she had declined, knowing Paul's reputation as a lecher. Now, she guessed she could have at least read his articles.

Sighing in frustration at the if onlys in her life, she gingerly reached down and picked up a worm. As she walked to the bank to get one of Lucky's poles, she tried to brush the dirt off the wiggly thing.

Lucky laughed. "You don't gotta scrub 'em. Some fish is goin' to chomp down on 'em anyhow, and the fish don't care if'n there's some grit to the squishy fellow."

"Lucky." Ellie grimaced in disgust. She wasn't a squeamish person, but he had a way of making the image very unappetizing.

Ellie baited her hook without problem, but she had trouble getting the worm and hook thrown out into the creek far enough to do any good. Besides, Lucky had chosen a point where the moving water cut the bank sharply away and the grass was slippery. She finally got the hang of it, swinging her fishing pole out over the water with one hand and holding a tree branch with the other.

Lucky had caught half a dozen before Ellie felt the tug of a single fish on her line. Excitedly, she jerked the pole back.

"I've got one," she yelled. Holding the pole with one hand, she stretched forward as far as she could to reach the other end where the pull of the fish bent the pole towards the water.

"Miss Eliz--" Lucky never got the words out.

Ellie's feet slipped out from under her and with a screech she pitched headlong into the water.

It took only seconds for her to come sputtering to the surface, for the water was only a few feet deep, but freezing cold from the mountain springs which fed it. Lucky was laughing so hard he couldn't even help her out of the water.

Shivering even in the heat of the summer day, Ellie waded downstream to where the bank wasn't as steep.

"I really wonder if any man is worth this much trouble." She muttered out loud as she sloshed back to where Lucky was gathering up the fishing gear.

Unsuccessful at hiding his smile, Lucky smirked. "I think we got enough for supper." Then with a chuckle, he added, "Course, you might have to go without, but we'll make sure Jesse's fed good."

Ellie tried to kick him, but ended up tangled in her wet skirts and flat on her fanny. Lucky left her sitting there, laughing all the way back to the house.

By the time Ellie had changed into dry clothes, her throat felt scratchy, her ears were clogged, and she had the sniffles. Regardless, she refused to let Lucky fix the meal they had planned. Besides, he didn't seem to mind telling her what to do and her throat hurt bad enough she didn't sass him back.

Confident that she knew when to take the pie out of the oven, and how long on each side the fish needed to fry in the big iron skillet, she sent Lucky after Jesse. The sun was setting behind the mountains, and regardless of the twenty-four hour operation of the mine, she knew Jesse took a break about the same time every night.

She put the last of the fish in the warming pan on the back of the stove and took the biscuits out and stacked them nicely on a clean plate. She went to the bedroom to give her hair a quick combing, only to realize she had flour on her skirt and face.

Knowing Jesse would arrive any minute, she quickly washed and changed to a new dress of red and white stripe, banded at the sleeves and cinched waist with red. As much as she had tried not to take advantage of having an unlimited bank account, she couldn't resist the dress when she saw it in Murphy's window. She figured she deserved at least that for giving up cigarettes.

She coughed several times, momentarily unable to catch her breath. "It's a good thing I did quit," she muttered, trying to clear her throat. It appeared the dunk in the stream had settled a cold in her throat. Shrugging, she decided it wasn't going to interfere with her surprise dinner for Jesse.

Speaking of, she wondered where he could be. She lit the lamps in the living room, then glanced out the door. The last of the daylight faded, which meant it had to be at least eight o'clock.

By nine o'clock, Ellie's throat bothered her enough she figured a glass of wine would help soothe the rough edges. Besides, waiting for a date to show up had never been her strong suit. She just hoped dinner would still taste good.

By eleven o'clock, Ellie didn't give a damn about dinner, or much of anything else. She had been stood up. Numbly, she set her wine glass down next to the near empty bottle, curled up on the couch and fell into a deep sleep.

* * *

Jesse knocked on Ellie's door bright and early. For too many days, he had been working long hours at the mine. They had to keep after it. Jesse felt in his bones they were within inches of the motherlode and he desperately wanted to clear his debt with Scott. He was just as weary as the rest of the men, but they were all hanging in there with him.

That must have been why, when Lucky told him Ellie wanted to see him and that he'd better be ready for a surprise, and that he'd better like the surprise, Jesse let the message run in one ear and out the other. Lucky was always muttering about something and Jesse had been too tired to listen.

He knocked again. It wasn't all that early, and Jesse thought to take Ellie out for breakfast. The door opened a crack as he raised his hand a third time.

"Whatcha want?" The voice, deep and scratchy, wasn't one Jesse recognized, and the gloom inside prevented him from seeing past the door.

"Ellie?" It had to be her, even though it didn't sound like it.

From what he could see through the widening crack, she was dressed in a pretty candy-cane-striped dress which accented her small waist, and for a moment Jesse was tempted to forego breakfast for a taste of her. When he glanced up, however, he noticed her hair was tangled about her face; her eyes were red and puffy. She looked worse than when she'd had the fever, but he knew better than to tell her that.

"Well, look whoz 'ere." She swung the door the rest of the way open as she spoke, but Jesse still wouldn't have recognized her voice.

"What happened to you?"

In response, she coughed. Jesse stepped forward to help, but she held up her hand.

"Stay right there, you...you varmint!"

Did she say varmint? "Ellie--"

"Don't you Ellie, me. I am so mad at you, I could--" coughing interrupted her outrage.

Jesse could tell from her stance he'd better not try getting any closer, so he used his voice to soothe her. "Calm down, darling."

Her hands went to her hips; a sure sign she was upset. Jesse just didn't have a clue why.

174

"I caught a cold 'cuz I fell in the creek. I fell in the creek fishin' for you. I cooked the damned fish, along with beans and biscuits and a cherry pie, and you weren't here to eat it." She drew in a deep breath. Jesse thought sure she'd start coughing again, but she was just stubborn enough to hold her breath and refuse to let even a little cough escape.

"I'm sorry, honey, I got busy." He offered the apology with a shrug. "I'll take you to breakfast instead."

"You...got...busy." She enunciated each word with an angry toss of her head. "So I'm suppose to just forget all the hard work I did; just suppose to toss it all to the dogs?"

Her attitude set Jesse's teeth on edge. He had worked all night in the mine, stopping near dawn to catch an hour's sleep before washing and coming to town. Didn't she know how close he was; didn't she care? Anger got the best of him.

"Be reasonable, Elizabeth. It never bothered you before if I worked late. Sometimes it never seemed to bother you if I came by at all."

"I'm tired of being reasonable." She shrieked at him. "Everyone tells me what to do. I can't say what I want, or do what I want." She stopped in the middle of her tirade to cough, her hand going to her throat. Jesse would have helped, but her posture prohibited him from getting close. Besides, at the moment he was just as mad.

Once she caught her breath, she poked a finger in his chest, sending him backwards across the porch. "I'm tired of this." She waved a hand that vaguely included him and the entire town. "I want hot running water, jazz on CD's, a cold beer and a hot pizza!" With a cry sounding close to despair, she whirled away from him and rushed back into the house.

The door slammed in his face.

* * *

It took a long walk up the mountain, a cold soak in the creek, and a few hours' sleep before Jesse's temper became manageable enough for him to think clearly. He went back to work but his mind remained on his troubles.

Lucky had told him to be in for a surprise, but Jesse could hardly warrant Ellie's fit of temper in that category. Well, come to think on it, the degree to which she had lambasted him was a surprise.

He grinned, then sighed in resignation. What was he to do with her? He loved her like crazy. He even recalled thinking how glorious she looked shrieking at him like some fishwife.

Obsessed -- that's what he was. He'd been around gold, silver and Elizabeth half his life and hadn't gotten "the fever" as the old-timers called it. But like reaching manhood, it must hit some later than others. At twenty-four years of age, he had an unquenchable thirst for one feisty, extraordinary woman who plagued his dreams and tormented his physical wellbeing.

With a manly sigh, Jesse knew what he had to do.

Later that day, he nervously stood on her doorstep, this time prepared, or so he hoped. She didn't immediately answer his knock, and he began to wonder if she would. He had turned to leave when he heard a tentative query.

"Now what?" At least she sounded better.

Before he lost his nerve, he thrust out his gifts. "I don't know what pizza is, but will daisies do?"

She looked from the handful of wildflowers and crock of beer up to his brooding gaze and with a cry, she flew into his outstretched arms. Hugging him close, she covered his face with kisses, regardless of the fact they stood on the porch in broad daylight.

That was Ellie for you.

"I'm sorry, Jesse, so sorry," she crooned as she tugged him inside and closed the door behind him. Before he could answer, she was in his arms again, hugging him tight enough to get inside his skin. He felt the same way.

"I don't care about the cold dinner; or the beer or pizza, or any of it. Really, I don't." Her cold lent her voice a deep, throaty quality Jesse found instantly appealing.

He kissed her deeply, breathing the scent that was her, all fresh air and sunshine. Finally lifting his head, he couldn't help but tease her. "Then you don't want my offerings; not even the cold beer?"

"Later," she breathed the single word close to his ear as she kissed his neck.

Jesse was fast forgetting everything except the feel of her, and regretted having his hands full so that he couldn't touch her. "Later the beer won't be cold." He threw back his head as her lips traveled along his shirt collar then down where he had the first couple of buttons undone.

"So?" Her question was a warm, fuzzy puff of air on his neck.

Reaching around her, he managed to set the crock of beer on a table without spilling, but the flowers dropped in a pile when her hands slid beneath his belt to massage his back. With a heartfelt sigh, he gave up the fight. "So, I can't remember." Laughing, he scooped her up in his arms and carried her to the bedroom.

With each piece of clothing he removed, Jesse's passion rose until he wondered how he could contain it long enough to make sure Ellie found her own pleasure.

"Jesse, now!" Her command brought a smile to his lips, and while her outstretched arms beckoned him, he lingered at her feet where he had tugged her stockings off and flung them across the room. Giving her a lecherous grin, he ignored her edict and began kissing the soles of her feet, her dainty ankles, her silken calves. With deliberate slowness, he worked his way up her legs, transferring his attend from one to the other.

"Do you know how desperately I love you?" He questioned huskily as he continued raining kisses on her hot skin. "I can't get enough of you; I want under your skin like you've gotten under mine."

Exotic kisses swept across Ellie and she thought she'd melt from the heat. "Oh," she moaned, rolling her head from side to side, panicking because of the intensity of feelings she experienced. This time was different; this time there was an aura of other worldliness about their lovemaking that scared her to death. Afraid that if she crested without him she would leave this world for another, she clutched his shoulders, tugging.

"Jesse, please," she begged, "I need you now; I can't wait." She breathed the words into the air, having lost her sense of direction and feeling as though he was everywhere around her at once.

Jesse relented, partially, and kissed the hollow of her belly, tongue swirling into her navel. She couldn't understand how he could be in such control; she sure wasn't. As he worked his way upwards, kissing the underside of her breast, she could finally reach him. The instant her hand circled his manhood, she knew he wasn't in control at all.

With a groan, he pulled her hand away, pinning both wrists above her head and with a yell of victory, took her with one swift stroke. Ellie's legs immediately circled his lean waist to hold him tight against her.

"More," her feverish whisper rasped and he obliged, sinking deep into her being and taking over her mind.

Just as she reached the brink of ecstasy, her body clutching around him, he stopped all movement. Ellie strained for fulfillment, pleading for what only Jesse could give her. She arched her hips; he didn't move. She lifted her head to nibble on his neck; still he didn't twitch. With a groan, she dropped her head back to the bed and lifted her eyes to his.

"Did you think it would be this easy? That I would let it end so quickly?" She hardly recognized his voice, so deep and husky and full of unspent passion. But even as he voiced his desire to extend their euphoria, she could tell the toll it took. His forehead creased in concentration, his sensuous mouth shut in a tight line.

Ellie couldn't stand it. She jerked her hips beneath his. "Please. We can always make love again later. I need you now."

An erotic smile touched his lips, spread to his eyes. With infinite slowness, he lowered to kiss her lips, his barely brushing hers; stopping to savor the corner of her mouth, sliding upward to lavish kisses on her eyes, her nose.

"Now; later. There is no time except infinity in which I will love you." He breathed the words against her skin. "No stopping for breath, no sunrises or sunsets to mark the days; no questions. Just forever."

And then Ellie clung to him as he took them both to the pinnacle of passion, where lovers can see to the ends of the earth and beyond, and know they will be together always.

* * *

Ellie watched Jesse sleep and tried to keep the desperation at bay a little longer. She gently brushed the hair back from his brow, memorizing the silky feel of it as she had already tucked away memories of his smile, his laughter, and his tender loving.

"How can I bare to leave you, sweet Jesse?" She whispered in the dark. "If I don't go to the mine in just a few days, I will not be sent back to my own time, but you will die." She bit her lips together to keep from crying out loud. There was no choice, and she knew it. She just couldn't stand the agony of it.

"I will love you forever," she murmured, bending forward to kiss his bare chest.

The arm which had been around her shoulders tightened. "Mmmm," he mumbled, but didn't wake up. Ellie guessed that would have to do for now.

* * *

Ellie wiggled closer to the warmth at her side, scooting a leg over the lean hips then sliding her foot up and down a hairy leg.

"Now that's a very nice way to wake up." Jesse murmured close to her ear, then kissed the corner of her mouth.

Ellie would have remained as is, but the clanking noise next to her ear roused her curiosity. She slowly raised her head. "What are you doing?" She licked the side of her mouth where he had kissed. "And why do I taste like cherry pie?"

"Because," Jesse smacked his lips, "I am having breakfast." He scooped the last forkful of pie into his mouth. "Delicious." He wiggled his eyebrows, and Ellie wasn't sure if he meant the pie at all.

Bemused, she brushed her hair out of her eyes as Jesse plunked the plate and fork on the side table then hung over the bed, mumbling as he dug through the clothes they had left piled on the floor.

Even though there was an enticing view of male buttocks as the sheet tugged lower with his movements, Ellie's attention was diverted. She smelled--

"Ah, here it is." Jesse straightened up just as Ellie scooted off the other side. "Hey, where are you going?"

"Coffee." Ellie thought by now he would remember she didn't do mornings well.

He grabbed her arm to stop her. "At your service, ma'am." A steaming mug was carefully waved under her nose.

She settled back against the headboard, content. "Ah, you're a good man, Jesse Cole." She smiled sideways at him.

"I like to think so."

For several minutes, they sat in silence, sipping their morning coffee, close but not touching, and yet Ellie felt him as though they were. She reached down to his free hand, entwining her fingers with his. He brought their hands up to his lips, kissing her knuckles one at a time.

As she watched, he set his coffee aside, then slid a ring onto the third finger of her right hand. It was a beautifully crafted solid gold band--like a wedding band. Ellie jerked her hand back, but he refused to release it.

"I want you to have this. It was my mother's, made from the first ounce of gold pa ever took from the

180

Nightingale." The ring felt like a burning brand against Ellie's skin.

"I can't," she whispered, not wanting to break the spell which held them, but fearing she had to say something; had to tell him the truth. Jesse didn't appear to notice her anguish.

"I know we're not married, yet. That's why I put it on your right hand."

"Oh, how can you want me when I shrieked at you and said such awful things?" The tears came, regardless of how hard Ellie fought against them.

"I won't run for cover, Ellie. I'm built to endure." He took her hand and placed it over his heart. "I won't desert you when things get tough...or when you wake up grumpy."

"It's not that--" her voice trailed off. She couldn't tell him; too much depended on everybody playing their roles, and if Jesse knew the original outcome, he'd try to change it around.

"What is it, El? You can tell me anything."

But she knew she couldn't. As his finger idly rubbed against the ring he had put on her finger, she cursed the day her editor had sent her to Reno; cursed Lucky and Zeke for finding her at Peavine and bringing her back through time. Then she realized she never would have met Jesse, so regardless of the bad surrounding them, she clung to the good; the love that was Jesse.

She laid across his chest, her forehead touching his. Ever so gently she kissed his lips, hungry for the taste of him. "I will wear your mother's ring, Jesse, with honor and with love, until the day you tell me you want it back." Or until I return to my own time and it will no longer matter to you, she thought mournfully.

"Never, El. You're mine for eternity, remember?" He returned her kiss.

"Oh, yes," she breathed. He just didn't know how close to the truth he really was.

Chapter 14

Sarah had returned to town and had invited Ellie to coffee. Glad for any excuse to keep her mind busy, Ellie hurried through her bath and dress. With only three days left before the celebration, it might be the last time she saw Sarah. Ellie refused to think of the fourth of July as being anything other than the celebration; she refused to voice any negative words.

"Welcome, Elizabeth." Sarah opened the door to a quaint little clapboard house not far from Ellie's own. Well, not far from Elizabeth's house. Sarah's use of that name reminded Ellie that she was just an impostor; borrowing someone else's name and life.

Determined not to allow melancholy to take over, she hugged Sarah then followed her into the sitting room. As the younger woman poured coffee, Ellie searched for a topic of conversation.

"So, how was your honeymoon?"

Sarah blushed. "Really, Elizabeth, how can you speak of such things?"

Ellie shrugged. "Speak of what?"

Sarah continued to stare at her coffee cup. "You know," she whispered. Then, her eyes widened. "Oh! I forgot you're not married."

Ellie had to laugh. It wouldn't matter in the long run whether Sarah knew how far she and Jesse had gone, but Ellie doubted the newlywed's sensibilities could handle it. She decided a confused smile was in order.

Sarah blushed. "Well, you will be getting married, won't you? Then you will--" Sarah didn't seem to know quite what to say, and Ellie couldn't think of a way to help.

In the twenty-first century, talking about sex was as open as asking what you had for dinner.

Ellie reached over and patted her hand. "Relax, Sarah. I won't tell anyone you actually enjoy being with your husband."

That brought the blush back to Sarah's cheeks, but she grinned along with it. "Am I terrible?"

Figuring this was probably the century where women endured lovemaking, Ellie could understand her thinking. She recalled Jesse's words from a few nights previous. "No, making love is the pathway to eternity." The minute she said the word, apprehension flooded her. Squaring her shoulders, she tried to shake off the feeling of doom.

"I have missed you, Sarah." Thinking of Jesse and even Lucky and Zeke, Ellie knew she would truly miss many of the residents of Peavine. Recalling the fast paced life she lived in New York, she wondered how she could prefer sedate Peavine to all that glitter, but she did. Without realizing it, she voiced her thoughts. "I don't miss my other life."

"What do you mean?"

Caught up in the daydream, Ellie mused, "You know. Country Clubs and playing golf and racquetball with friends; driving upstate to picnic and party at the lake."

"Playing what? You must have had an entirely different life back east because I've never heard of half the things you just said."

Ellie realized she had slipped, and took a sip of coffee to cover the pause as she furiously thought. Deciding to turn the talk away from herself, she asked, "Don't they have clubs or sororities here? I know there's not many women in Peavine, but don't they ever have get togethers?"

"Well, of course we do. We're not backward, you know. The Ladies' Auxiliary meets every Tuesday at the church--" Sarah's voice trailed off and in embarrassed silence.

"Sarah? Is it some secret I'm not suppose to know?"

"Not exactly, but..." she hesitated.

"Spill it, Sarah."

"Don't you remember? You made Amy Arnold and Suzy Miller so mad the last time you came to a meeting, they threatened to tar and feather you." At Ellie's apparent look of surprise, she hastened to add, "Of course, that was before you left for school, so it was a long time ago."

"I honestly don't recall. Did I say something terribly offensive?"

Sarah's mouth lifted in a grin. "Only the truth, but Amy didn't take kindly to being compared to a barn, nor Suzy to a laughing hyena."

It was no more than Ellie expected, coming to know Elizabeth as she did. "Oh, boy! It's no wonder I have no friends."

"Of course you have friends. Me and Henry; Zeke and Lucky, and your wonderfully handsome Jesse."

"Sarah Jefferson, you're a married woman." They laughed together. Still, with Sarah's insight into the people of Peavine, Ellie wondered-- "What about Clayton Scott? How do you classify him?"

Sarah pursed her lips. "I'd watch out for him if I were you. He's no huckleberry above my persimmon."

"He's what?" Ellie squeaked before bursting into laughter.

"He's not as good as my Henry, and that's a fact." Sarah's laughter joined hers.

As much as she enjoyed herself, Ellie knew it was time to leave. She hoped to see Jesse later that night and wanted a bath beforehand. "Sarah, I have really enjoyed your company this afternoon. You're a very good friend." Ellie wished she could express more, but knew better.

"Oh, do you have to leave so soon? I'm bored silly in this house by myself, but Henry insists no wife of his is going to work." She sighed. "Even in my own father's store."

"Well, perhaps he'll loosen up after awhile."

Sarah snorted. "I seriously doubt it. He's such a stickler for tradition. Did you know I wanted to see Lotta Crabtree in Virginia City, and he absolutely refused to even consider it."

Ellie shook her head. "Who's Lotta Crabtree?"

"Oh, Ellie, surely you must have heard of her. Why, she lives in New York City and travels all over the place, performing high comedy and stage extravaganzas." Sarah whispered the last two words.

Ellie figured this actress must be a striptease or something, but then why would Sarah want to see her? Doubtful it wasn't that risqué. "OK, so why wouldn't Henry, the love of your life who adores you, take you to see Lotta perform?"

"It wasn't anything so terrible. After all, I saw several women enter the establishment."

From the way she spoke, Ellie was getting a clearer picture of exactly what had gone on. Her admiration for Sarah grew as she recognized a kindred, liberated spirit. "Sarah?" She drew her name out.

"Well, all right. It was a Saloon and Dance Hall --but a very respectable one," she added quickly. "I really don't see why married women of our age aren't suppose to frequent such places. After all, we're not living in the dark ages."

Ellie laughed and hugged her friend tight. "Ah, Sarah, you are priceless. I suppose if you could, you'd just throw away your petticoats and purses and wear trousers around Peavine."

"Well, I wouldn't go that far." Sarah looked shocked. "Oh, my gosh, I almost forgot." Jumping up from the settee, Sarah headed out of the room. "Wait, I have something for you."

Returning quickly, she thrust a purse at her. Ellie turned it over in her hands, then shrugged. "I don't remember this. Whose is it?"

"Don't you recall; before Henry and I got married? You came into the mercantile one day quite agitated. Mr. Scott was with you. You shoved that into my hands and insisted it was mine. I didn't know what to do, but I figured you had a good reason for saying that, so I took it. In all the excitement of getting married, I plum forgot to give it back to you."

185

"Oh, my God," Ellie breathed the words so quietly she would have thought they only formed in her mind, but Sarah immediately took her hand.

"Are you all right? You've turned quite pale."

Ellie clutched the purse to her chest. "I'm...I'm fine, but I really have to go." Without much more of a good-bye than that, she hurriedly opened the door and stepped out into the dusty twilight.

"I'll see you at the Independence Day Celebration, won't I?" Sarah called after her.

Ellie didn't stop to answer. Picking her skirts up, she ran for home. Not until she got inside the house and locked the door behind her did she dare breathe any easier. With shaking hands she lit the lamps that kept the darkness away. She had a ring of them on the kitchen table before she quit. She just stood there staring, arms crossed over her waist, hugging herself against the chill that crept through her despite the summer heat.

In the center of the table, surrounded by light, was the purse Sarah had given her. The instant Sarah had said the bag was hers, she had recalled when last she had carried it and what it contained.

"God, I wish I had a cigarette." Her words escaped on a rush of breath. Rubbing sweaty palms down her thighs, she then reached out and opened the clasp of the bag. Carefully, she removed the wad of paper she had jammed in there when Clayton had surprised her in his office at the bank. It seemed so long ago, and yet it seemed like only yesterday. How could she have forgotten?

Her hands grew steadier as she smoothed the papers flat on the table. A smile even touched her lips as she studied the scribbly writing, faded with time. The first page had only a few lines of writing, stating that if the children married -- Ellie assumed he meant Jesse and Elizabeth -- there was no need for a business agreement since together they would own both the bank and the mine. If they did not marry, the attached codicil would insure each would be wealthy in their own right.

Ellie frowned and turned to the next page. She had to squint to make out the first couple of words, but then the faded print seemed to jump out at her.

"I, Wendall Calhoun, do hereby relinquish my one-quarter interest in the Nightingale Mine upon my death. Said one-quarter interest, which has been used to provide operating capital, will revert back to the owner, Warren Cole, or in the case of his death, to his heir, Jesse Cole, to become sole owner of said Nightingale Mine."

The evidence they had been looking for was right under their noses all the time. Ellie hadn't had time to read the pages when she had first taken them. In fact, she probably wouldn't have taken them at all if Clayton hadn't walked in on her. Boy, oh boy, was she glad she had.

While she thought Clayton had doctored bank records to provide a lien against the Nightingale Mine, he really hadn't had to do anything more than wait. The bank, through Wendall Calhoun, really did own an interest in the mine, and if no one knew of the codicil which canceled the mortgage, Scott could legitimately claim a portion of the mine proceeds on behalf of Elizabeth.

That was all the more reason for Clayton to want Elizabeth. Not only the bank, but one-fourth interest in the mine was hers; or would be if no one found out about the codicil.

She only wondered why Clayton kept the codicil. Anyone getting their hands on it would see that Jesse held the Nightingale free and clear. It would have been safer if he had destroyed it. Knowing what she did about Clayton Scott, though, she figured he kept the damn paper around just to take it out and gloat once in a while.

A knock on the front door interrupted her thought. She glanced from the papers to the entryway and back. The knock came again. Frustrated, she sighed and carefully folded the papers in a square and put them back in the handbag, then put the handbag as far back on the top shelf of the pantry as she could reach.

Taking a lamp from the kitchen table, she hurried through the house to the front door, hoping Jesse had quit early to spend time with her.

"Jess--" Her words stuck in her throat. Instead of Jesse, Clayton Scott stood on her porch in the dark. She tried to close the door, not knowing what excuse she would make for not seeing him. She just knew she could not.

"Now, Elizabeth." As slick as a whistle he planted his foot in the way, then shoved the door wide. The smile which curled his lips didn't reach his eyes, which were flinty cold in the lamplight. Not turning his back on her, he closed the door and slid the lock home.

The sound of it caused Ellie's stomach to drop.

Like a predator stalking his prey, he advanced on her. For each step he took, Ellie took two back, but she knew in a heartbeat she couldn't outrun him. She glanced wildly around for a weapon of some sort. Every time her gaze swung back to him, the look remained. Menacing, even evil, it told her without words that she was at his mercy.

She cleared her throat. "Clayton. I didn't expect you tonight."

"Apparently not," he drawled and she knew he referred to her slip when she first opened the door. As though talking to a slow-witted child, he lectured her. "You are spending far too much time with that miner. I told you before I didn't like it."

Ellie tried to bully her way through. "I thought that was the plan. I can't get any useful information if I never talk to the man." She spoke distinctly, as though Jesse meant nothing to her. She had to convince Clayton of that, if only to spare Jesse during the next day or two. Heaven forbid if Clayton decided to move up the timetable.

Clayton had moved directly in front of her, and unless she dropped the lamp she still held and ran, Ellie was stuck. She sucked in her breath when he ran a finger along the neckline of her dress, tugging slightly downward as his fingers slid across her breasts.

"Personally, I prefer not to talk while I'm in bed with a beautiful woman. I like action."

"What? I don't understand."

"Tsk, tsk. I never took you for a dumb woman, Elizabeth. Getting information from Cole was the plan, not screwing him. Is that the only way you could get him to tell you how close he is to that vein of gold?"

"No, it's not like that." Infuriated by the insult, she slapped his hand away and turned to put down the lamp.

It was a fatal mistake. Clayton grabbed her from behind, pulling her up against his lean body, his arms crossing her chest and hands roughly cupping her breasts. The more she struggled, the tighter he held her against his groin, breathing heavily in her ear.

"You want it this way tonight, huh? Well, I'll be happy to oblige. I told you I didn't mind sharing with Cole, but I do mind him getting what you won't give me anymore."

Ellie became deathly still, realizing that her movements only excited him. She silently prayed that Jesse would get here to save her from this humiliation, and just as quickly prayed he wouldn't. She couldn't bear the thought of him seeing her like this; not when it might be their last night together.

Her struggles had excited Scott; now her lack of resistance apparently meant acquiescence to the loathsome creature behind her. He bent her forward over the arm of the sofa, one hand on the back of her neck pushing her head down. The other hand bunched up her skirts until Ellie felt his cool hand on her naked thigh. As soon as she knew her foot was free of the petticoats she wore, she kicked upward, hitting his crotch with her heel.

With a grunt, Clayton released her and she quickly swiveled out of the way. Unfortunately, her kick hadn't disabled him. They stood facing each other, both breathing hard and she watched his gaze drop to her breasts. Glancing down, she discovered he had somehow gotten her buttons undone and her bodice sagged to reveal entirely too much skin.

She struggled for modesty. She berated herself for getting so deep into this situation over which she had lost control. She couldn't imagine giving in to this man, but they had come too far not to finish the game, and Ellie knew Elizabeth had taken him to her bed. While it would cause irreversible damage if she, acting as Elizabeth, didn't do the same, how could she live with herself after? How could she face Jesse? And, if she refused Clayton, would he kill her and somehow forge the documents necessary to take over the bank and the mine, thinking he had done away with Elizabeth?

"I don't believe you're telling me the truth," Clayton said as he took off his coat and threw it at a chair. Just as quickly, he jerked off his tie and began on the buttons of his shirt. "Maybe you don't want to be partners and share all that gold anymore."

Ellie tried to quell the panic clawing at her insides. Against her will, her gaze riveted to the movements of his hands. Belatedly, her mind registered his statements. To keep him talking instead of acting, she shook herself out of her stupor.

"I am; I do."

"You are what, Elizabeth? You're mine; or are you Cole's whore?"

"I'm yours," Ellie whispered, trying to steel her heart against the inevitable.

"Prove it." He jerked his shirt off, threw it after his coat, and stood before her, hands on hips. The feral grin was back in place. "Take off your clothes."

"Here?" The single word squeaked past dry lips. She swallowed convulsively. His reasons for seducing her -- assault would be a better word -- left a bitter taste in Ellie's mouth.

"Here. You never much cared before where we did it, as long as you got what you came for." He grinned at his choice of words. "Do it to me the way you did in Virginia City, and I might even tell you what I learned from--" he paused, and Ellie willed him to go on. Someone was feeding him information and he had confided in Elizabeth, just as Jesse had. Elizabeth was the only one who had known all the angles.

It occurred to Ellie that if she could keep from panicking, she could get more information out of Clayton. Information they desperately needed to help them prevent the accident from occurring again. As long as she stayed an arm's length away and facing him, she knew she could defend herself.

Coming to that conclusion eased the constriction in her chest. She once again felt in control and that brought a smile to her lips. She seductively swayed her hips and raised her hands to the buttons which had remained fastened.

"And what do I get if I do take it all off?" She undid one button, and though she felt her confidence flowing back, she still hoped she wouldn't have to do more.

Fatal mistake number two; not putting at least one piece of furniture between them. In the blink of an eye, Clayton came up against her, grabbing her upper arms in a hard grip.

"Tell me how I compare, Elizabeth," he rasped against her neck as he began nipping the sensitive skin along the top of her shoulder.

"Wha--what?"

He let loose one arm long enough to jerk her chemise down, baring her breasts. "I told you I didn't mind sharing, only because a few days from now it won't matter." His voice became harsher. "But I want to know -- does he set your blood on fire?"

"He couldn't do to me what you do," Ellie replied, trying again to keep the panic from building. "There's no comparison between the two of you." Why had she thought she could do this? What insane side of her brain made her think she was in control?

He shoved her up against the wall, pinning her there with his hips, freeing both hands. He raked his fingers through her hair, causing pins to fly everywhere and painfully pulling hard enough to bring tears to Ellie's eyes. Cruelly, his lips came down on hers, stealing her breath and curdling her stomach. There could be no doubt what

Clayton intended and she didn't have the strength to stop him.

Ellie tasted blood.

In those brief moments, time slowed and Ellie's whole life flashed before her eyes. Regrets tumbled about in her brain -- not marrying and having children; not telling her parents she loved them the last time she saw them alive.

Most precious were the all too brief glimpses of Jesse in her mind's eye. Smiling; laughing; eyes dark with passion, waltzing her around his cabin. In that instant, she knew she would sacrifice anything to keep Jesse safe; anything at all.

She loved Jesse with every fiber of her being, and if Clayton raped her, she would still love Jesse. If giving in to Clayton would get her the information she needed to save Jesse's life, then she would handle it; she would. And then she would find a way to kill him.

A sob escaped. Besides, on the fourth of July, none of this would matter. Regardless of how much she loved Jesse, she would save him and return to her own time -- alone, desolate, and heartbroken.

"Fire! Fire!" The alarm was shouted as someone pounded on the door. "Bank's on fire!"

Cursing, Clayton jerked away from Ellie and grabbed for his clothes. Buttoning his shirt as he went, he unbolted the door and raced off into the night without a backwards glance.

Ellie sank to the floor, arms crossed against her chest, tears streaming down her cheeks. Without realizing she had prayed beforehand, she now thanked the Lord for sparing her.

"You all right...Ellie?"

Startled, Ellie looked up to find Lucky crouched down at her side. She hadn't heard anyone enter the house. She thought about it for a minute and realized that she really was all right. While Clayton had definitely scared her; he really hadn't hurt her. She nodded, giving him a watery smile.

"Ouch." She touched a finger to her swollen lip.

Lucky scowled when he saw her puffy lips, but she shrugged before he could do anything more than growl.

"Never mind," she patted his arm, "this is a very minor incident in the scheme of things."

"Thought it right clever to yell the bank's on fire. Figured that'd be the only way to get him out of here."

"You mean it's really not?" Ellie glanced fearfully at the door, half expecting Clayton to come back and finish what he started.

"I locked the door. And he never even seen me when he teared out of here, so I 'spect he'll be awondering who was yelling."

"How did you know?" Ellie still couldn't believe her good fortune. Her panic and shame was being replaced by anger -- at herself for not being able to stand up against Clayton, but more so at him for his brutal attitude.

"I figured you was up at Jesse's tonight, so I never come by to make you supper. Then, when I did wander by, I seen a light on and figured if'n you was here, I'd better feed you some." He looked down at the floor, a blush clearly staining his cheeks. "I seen you through the window."

"Oh, God." Ellie put a hand over her eyes, embarrassed that Lucky would have seen what Clayton tried to do to her.

Lucky took her hand and pulled her to her feet. "I didn't see nothing Miss...Ellie, 'cept that Scott had you up against the wall."

"Why are you calling me Ellie?" She followed him to the kitchen, where she washed at the sink. She felt better after she got Scott's smell off her skin. She patted her face dry and peered at him over the top of the towel. "Well?"

Lucky put the tea pot on the stove, throwing a stick or two of wood below. He shrugged. "Guess I just figured you been here long enough. 'Sides, that's what Jesse calls you."

"Yes, but you always insisted on calling me Elizabeth to keep up the charade."

"Yeah, well, you ain't Elizabeth! You're nice and you're tryin' to keep Jesse from gettin' killed and you love him. She sure as heck don't."

Ellie had never seen Lucky so adamant. "Oh, Lucky, you mean to say after all this time, you like me?" Ellie gave him a big hug and a kiss on the cheek.

Scrubbing at his cheek, Lucky pushed her away. "Go on with you now. Get yourself fixed for bed and I'll bring you a cup of tea. Then I'm putting myself at the table with my shotgun the rest of the night in case that no good varmint comes back."

Ellie glanced around the shadowy kitchen. She couldn't stay there; not tonight.

"Lucky, take me to Jesse's. Please?"

Lucky glanced past her to the dark night. "You know Jesse'll be working. They're all working."

"I know, and I know you can protect me, but I'd just feel better at Jesse's."

With a sigh, he gave in, sliding the teakettle to the back of the stove and pushing a cover over the open flame. Ellie grabbed a few things from the bedroom, and in minutes they were weaving their way through the trees up the side of the mountain to Jesse' cabin.

Lucky wouldn't allow her to light a lantern, stating it would be too easy to see the light from town. Ellie clutched his hand and mumbled a litany about not being afraid of the dark.

Only when Ellie snuggled into Jesse's bed, by herself, did she feel safe. She breathed in his scent and hugged his pillow tight to her chest. Lucky had posted himself on the chair outside on Jesse's porch, although Ellie had made him swear he wouldn't tell Jesse about Clayton's attack. The letter and codicil were tucked safely in the canister where Jesse kept his cash. As Ellie drifted off to sleep, she hoped she dreamed of Jesse's loving and not of being blasted to kingdom come on the fourth of July.

Chapter 15

Jesse had returned to his cabin late in the night, only to fall exhausted into bed. If he hadn't absent-mindedly kissed her good-bye when he left again, she would have wondered if he had even realized she was there.

Knowing she couldn't go back to Elizabeth's house for fear of running into Clayton, she had paced the small cabin most of the day, alternately trying to read, then scrubbing the floors, table and stove until she couldn't scrub anymore. She washed everything in sight, including Jesse's long-johns which hung on a peg in the corner and which he wouldn't need again until winter.

The second night, Jesse hadn't returned at all, or so Ellie thought until she awoke the next morning to find a note and a glass full of daisies on the table. Now, she soaked in the brass tub in anticipation of Jesse's return that evening.

She held the note between damp fingers and read the hastily scribbled words for the hundredth time. "Shutting down at midnight. Wait for me. Jesse." The words were less than romantic, but Ellie kept re-reading the last sentence. Those three words had her alternating between disconsolate and euphoric. Ellie knew she couldn't leave this world without being with Jesse one more time. The thought of their lovemaking; of the touch of his hand caressing her skin raised the water temperature in her bath as her skin heated.

It was July 3, and the minute Ellie recalled the date, her heart sank. In just one more day -- only a little over twenty-four hours -- she would be gone from Peavine, Nevada. How would she ever know if their plan succeeded? She would never again see Jesse, or Zeke or even Lucky, unless she could somehow find a picture of them in an old history book.

Could they really change history? She was a gambler; that's how she had gotten in this trouble in the first place, but this was the biggest gamble of her life. Ellie closed her eyes, trying to recall all the pieces of their plan. Hoping everything was in place, she ticked off the elements on her fingers as she soaped herself.

Jesse would close the mine at midnight and through the next day so his miners could attend the Independence Day celebrations. She was to stick like glue to Jesse; Zeke and Lucky would keep an eye on Clayton. Late in the afternoon she would send word to Clayton to make him think Jesse had gone to the mine. She figured Clayton, or more likely someone he had hired, would already have the mine rigged, but this time the explosives would go off with no one getting hurt.

The only unclear part was where exactly she had to be. Being in the dark mine, waiting to be blown to smithereens was not a choice. Zeke and she had talked, and figured it would just happen. Since she wasn't suppose to be here in the first place, she would probably just fade away, or disappear in a flash.

She twisted Jesse's ring on her finger. How was she to leave him? Did he know how much she loved him? Would he love her forever instead of marrying Elizabeth? Would he even know?

The sound of heavy boots scrapping across the porch ended Ellie's string of rhetorical questions. Her heart flew to her throat, and she reached over the side of the tub for Jesse's revolver, which she had taken from the holster that hung by the door. Lucky had left earlier after thoughtfully bringing some stew and biscuits that Ellie had warming on the back of the stove. Who else could it be?

"You have this place lit up like the fourth of July," Jesse commented cheerfully as he entered the cabin, swinging the door closed behind him. "I thought the celebration wasn't until tomorrow."

"You know I don't like the dark." Ellie sagged in relief as she lowered the pistol to the chair by the tub. "Besides, you're early."

Ellie watched Jesse's eyes crinkle at the corners as he took in her nakedness. His lips turned up in a wolfish grin.

"If I'd known what was waiting for me, I would have been even earlier."

As he talked, he jerked off his boots, dropped them by the door and slowly walked towards her. She couldn't help but stare. When he stood directly in front of the tub, she slid upwards until the sudsy water just barely covered her nipples. She slid her tongue across her lips, then poked out her bottom lip in a pout. "You have way too many clothes on, woodsman."

The grin never left his face. "Yeah, well, what are you going to do about it, city girl?" He stood there, thumbs hooked in his trouser loops, and seemed perfectly content just to look at her. The heat in his eyes, though, set Ellie's blood to boiling, and she felt impatient for much more than he was offering.

She slid to the end of the tub, reaching up to unbuckle his wide leather belt. She threw her head back and her gaze fixed on his. She could feel the change in his desire as she undid his pants, one button at a time. Very male heat radiated from him as she slowly pulled his pants and drawers down past his knees. The instant she touched him, he jerked forward, groaned, and began rapidly shucking the rest of his clothes.

Though Jesse longed for Ellie's caresses to continue, he had no desire to end their lovemaking so quickly, and he knew without doubt his control was already gone.

Gently, he lifted her to her feet, then turned her around so her back was to him. He stepped into the tub and settled them both back into the tepid water, her on his lap. When she murmured a protest, he nibbled a path from her shoulder up her neck to her ear. One hand caressed her breast while the other slid unerringly down her belly to her womanhood, open and exposed to his touch.

Her protests turned to welcoming moans.

"Do you like that, Ellie? Do you want more?" He whispered, before his tongue dipped in and out of her ear, mimicking the motion of his hand, and soon she was writhing in his arms, gasping for breath. She arched her back, reaching over her head to grasp his shoulders.

"J-e-s-s-e!" Her cry echoed across the small cabin as she convulsed against his hand, the heat of her causing his manhood to throb against her bottom. He smiled at her complete and utter surrender to him. She held nothing back; there was no artifice to her response, and Jesse gloried in his ability to give her such pleasure.

Before he realized what she was doing, Ellie swiveled in the water and straddled him, laying her chest against his. "You don't play fair," she murmured just before she kissed him, and Jesse could have made the same point about her.

The kiss, bold and hot and lush, sent fire sweeping through him. No timid, maidenly brush of the lips from this gal, that's for sure. She took control, her tongue sweeping along the ridge of his teeth and wiggling inside when he parted his lips. Her hands started at his ears, circling then massaging down the side of his neck to his shoulders.

He hadn't realized how sore his muscles were, or how tense he had become until her gentle strokes persuaded him to relax. As his muscles loosened, she moved her hands to his chest. Jesse held his breath in anticipation of her touch, but she bypassed his sensitive nipples and slid her hands around to his back.

Breaking her kiss, she grinned -- saucy, sexy -- then kissed his chin. "Do you like being the teasee, instead of the teasor?" Her question stumped him, but before he could understand, she slid down and kissed his nipple, then licked it until it pebbled hard in her mouth. It was too much.

Jesse slid his hands along the back of her knees, pulling them toward him. When she transferred her attention to the other nipple, he made his move. Hands on her hips, he lifted her just enough to slide into her warm depths. The exquisite, tight length of her just about finished him right there.

"So, you want control, woodsman?" Ellie straightened, arching her back and in so doing took him even deeper into herself. Jesse's brows arched as he felt her clutch around him.

"Not if you're going to keep doing that," he moaned. Her breasts bounced enticingly in front of him, and he leaned forward to capture one with his lips. When she groaned, he sucked gently, hungry for her.

Ellie ground her hips against his, taking all of him and wanting more. Even when he sucked at her breast, she felt she couldn't get enough of him. When his hands moved to lift her, she instantly picked up the rhythm and repeatedly slid down his length. She had to grip the edges of the tub to steady herself for suddenly they were both out of control. Jesse bucked beneath her, his head thrown back, stormy blue eyes capturing her gaze and holding as he carried her ever upward.

Ellie could feel herself tightening, tingling sensations zipping up and down her legs. As the first wave hit, Jesse pushed hard, paused, then stroked her quickly again and again. Together, they climaxed, Jesse's hands firm on her hips to hold her tight against him as he throbbed his release into her body.

Ellie's own body squeezed again and again, and in her heart she hoped she took Jesse's seed into her womb to make a baby. If she couldn't have Jesse forever, maybe she could have his child.

"Hey, sweet lady, why the tears?" Jesse had released her and rubbed a callused thumb across her cheek.

Ellie hadn't realized she was crying and fought the urge to lay her burden at Jesse's feet. If he knew about the accident, he could prevent it from happening again, couldn't he? Or would his knowing somehow change history the wrong way? It was too complicated to think about.

With a sigh, she laid her head against Jesse's shoulder. "It's my prerogative to cry whenever I want to," she murmured against his throat.

"I thought maybe the shooting stars were just too bright for your eyes." He spoke softly into her hair.

"Stars?"

"Mmmm," was all the answer she got as he absently rubbed her back.

"Jesse?"

"I'm in love with you," Jesse said, the awe in his voice apparent.

"Of course you are," Ellie answered, her heart thudding, wondering if he meant her or Elizabeth.

He pushed her back by the shoulders. Dark brows came together over blue, blue eyes as he stared at her. "I'm serious. It's different now. You're different. I always felt we were friends, but I never thought about being passionately in love with you." He shrugged as though in apology. "I was comfortable with you because I'd known you half my life. I didn't think I needed stars and bells and lightning."

"And now?" Ellie held her breath in answer; an answer she hoped included her.

"This past couple of weeks, everything's changed."

"Is that bad?"

"Absolutely not." He punctuated his statement with a kiss. "In fact, I find I kinda like the shooting stars and flashing lightning."

Ellie laughed as he hauled her out of the tub and rubbed her dry. She clung to him as he carried her to bed, and she tried her damnedest to make sure he saw plenty of shooting stars throughout the night.

* * *

The Fourth of July, 1870, dawned rosy and clear. Ellie lay curled into Jesse, staring across the cabin at what she could see of the thin streams of pink clouds and blue sky. Her gaze surveyed the tiny cabin, memorizing all the nooks and crannies. Only when Jesse stirred in his sleep did she allow her thoughts to turn to him, knowing when she did that the tears would flow.

Would he forget her in a day? Had she given him enough love to last a lifetime? Even though she knew there was no choice, she wished for things to be different.

"Ellie, what's wrong?" Jesse whispered, nuzzling her neck and tightening his arm around her waist.

Ellie rolled to her back, turning her head to study his furrowed brow above those wonderful blue eyes. "How do you know anything's wrong?"

The furrows deepened. "There's not much about you I don't know." His hand slid from her bare midriff down to her hips to emphasize his point.

Ellie swallowed hard, fighting the tears that still threatened. "What if tomorrow never comes?"

Jesse gave a slight shake of his head. "That's not going to happen."

"But what if?"

"I'd hope to catch up with you in eternity. I have too much to say yet; too much love to still give you."

"You'd love me for eternity?"

He raised himself on his elbow and leaned forward, his lips a breath away from her own. "Ellie, I'll love you always and then some. Believe that if you believe nothing else in this world."

Ellie refused to let him out of bed until he proved his point. Which he did -- at great length and quite thoroughly.

* * *

If Peavine did anything well, it was celebrate, and the one celebration that year bigger than Sarah's wedding was Independence Day. By the time Jesse and Ellie had dressed and meandered into town, things were in full gear.

Red, white and blue banners hung from every building all up and down the street. Tables were set up in the grass beside the church for the picnic to be held later. People were everywhere.

Ellie had lived in Peavine a month, and she swore she had never encountered so many people, even at church on Sunday. Then again, she supposed the miners, working in shifts all week, didn't venture into town except on Saturdays, and she had learned early on not to wander far from home on that night.

Jesse amazed her throughout the day as he dragged her from event to event, laughing and joking with all the miners and townspeople, calling everyone by name. Since she didn't know them all, but was probably suppose to, she just nodded and smiled, hoping no one asked her any personal questions.

"C'mon, Jesse, you gotta enter the shootin' match. We want a chance to beat you from last year." Several hearty souls grabbed him by the arms and dragged him away. As he went, he threw her an apologetic smile over his shoulder and Ellie thought he really didn't look very sorry at all.

She helped the ladies put the food on the tables for the picnic, smiling shyly at Amy Arnold and Suzy Miller when she happened to overhear their names spoken by one of the older ladies. Recalling what Elizabeth had supposedly said about them, Ellie really wished she could meet Elizabeth. She would like to tell the woman a thing or two.

The shooting events had been set up to the north end of town, opposite the livery. Even so, the noise from the guns, not to mention the hooting and hollering, reached Ellie's ears. She grinned, recalling how carefree Jesse looked as he was being dragged off to join the fun. He reminded her of a little boy going out to play with his friends. The breeze had ruffled his hair; he had his shirt collar open and the sleeves rolled up, and the look of devilment in his eyes. Lordy, how she loved that man.

She didn't have long to reminisce before the troop of men, followed closely by every child in town, came roaring back up the street, Jesse perched high on the shoulders of two of the largest. Amongst cheers and good-natured bantering, they deposited him at her feet.

"Miss Elizabeth, he sure do beat all! Not a man around can whoop Jesse Cole with a pistol." Several men chorused in agreement.

Jesse stood before her, grinning like a banshee, with a blue ribbon pinned to his shirt. How little it took to bring joy to these people, Ellie thought, followed quickly by a feeling of contentment like she had never known. She could be just as happy here, with Jesse.

She stood on tiptoe and mimicked the men's words close to his ear. "Well, if you don't beat all." Then she flicked the blue ribbon, adding, "Are you the prize at the county fair?"

Quick as lightning, he grabbed her waist and swung her around in a circle, kissing her soundly in front of everyone. "I'll be your prize any time of year."

The church bell began to peel, announcing the start of the picnic. Jesse and Ellie were swept up in the crowd of men as they swarmed to the food tables. Since there weren't many wives in Peavine to bake and cook enough to feed all the hungry miners, the local eateries had also pitched in, setting up huge pots of chicken and dumplings, venison stew and cooked cinnamon apples.

Ellie was too nervous to eat much, and whenever she would bypass a dish, Jesse would scoop a spoonful onto her plate, anyway. "I can't eat all this," she protested.

"You're too skinny. I have to get some meat on your bones or you won't be able to keep me warm this winter." Jesse gave her a wolfish grin.

His comment didn't help Ellie's stomach at all. She offered him a weak smile before turning away from the food-laden tables. As the day wore on, she was becoming more and more tense, until she wondered if she could swallow a single bite. Earlier, she had spied Clayton moving among the spectators as the foot races used Main Street for their competition. She didn't recall seeing him at all for the past several hours. Lucky and Zeke had taken it upon themselves to keep him in their sights, so Ellie shouldn't worry. After all, they knew what would happen if things didn't go according to plan.

Jesse had steered her to the shade of a tree back behind the church. She recalled the last time they had been out here. The night of Sarah's wedding, she had basically thrown herself at the man! Her cheeks grew warm in remembrance and she cast Jesse a look from beneath her lashes to see if her need was visible.

Jesse sat cross-legged beside her, wolfing down his food, alternating with huge gulps of cold cider. Ellie just about got sick watching him and she wondered how he could eat so much. Of course, he didn't know there was anything wrong.

He had no idea that in a few hours, his life would hang by a thread and would totally depend on Lucky and Zeke and her. In a few short hours, it would all be over and Ellie would once again be stranded in the ghost town of Peavine, waiting to be rescued.

She laughed at the irony of it all. She had already been rescued when she came back to 1870. Zeke and Lucky had brought her, albeit unwilling at first, back to a time when her life actually meant something to someone. She realized that running from city to city, hurrying to make deadlines for the magazine, carousing around town at all hours with her high-stepping friends wasn't really living.

Having a good man smile at you; taking walks through the trees and picnicking beside a creek; making passionate love until you were exhausted and then snuggling close to another person -- that was living.

"Hey, sweetheart." Jesse tucked a stray strand of hair behind her ear. "Are you all right? You look like you've seen a ghost." He brushed a finger across her cheek.

Ellie shook herself out of her reverie. It would do no good to dwell on things she couldn't change. She offered Jesse a smile. "It's just hot, that's all." Then, she couldn't resist saying, "And I was just thinking about another event you could claim a blue ribbon in."

Jesse lifted a roguish eyebrow. "Oh, yeah? I didn't know there was a competition in that."

Ellie laughed, then leaned close to brush his lips with a kiss. "On second thought, maybe instead of a blue, I should give you best of show."

"You little minx." Jesse resettled his plate down on his lap. "I won't be able to stand, much less walk, if you keep talking like that." Ellie noticed the strategic placement of his plate and laughed all the harder.

Apparently, since Independence Day was one holiday a year when the entire town turned out and all the miners had the day off, no one was going to waste any of their time. Immediately after lunch, the ore cart races began.

Jesse, being a mine owner, couldn't compete, but his men were wearing bright blue bandannas on their arms to signify the Nightingale Mine. Other miners from the Northern Pride and the Golden Fleece had bands of green or yellow. Each team huddled close together on the side of the street.

"We didn't start these races until a few years ago, so you probably haven't seen them. Each mine has a team of five, and they have to take turns pulling one of those ore carts down the street, between the blacksmith's and Murphy's Mercantile." He pointed to the start and finish of the race. "If each man in turn gets to the end of the line without stopping, they add more ore and do it again."

"If they keep doing it, how do they know who wins?"

"Each round adds more ore. If a man can't pull to the end, he's eliminated and the next on his team pulls. They keep adding ore until only one man can pull his cart the length of the race."

A cheer went up from the crowd and Ellie turned her attention to the street where a man from each team scrambled to pick up a heavy rope, sling it over his shoulder and drag the ore cart down the road.

"You don't make them do that in your mine, do you?" Ellie indignantly asked Jesse.

"Of course not. We have our carts on wheels and rails. A pulley system makes it easy for a man to stand in one place and yet get the cart to the top of the tunnel."

It took two rounds before any of the men were eliminated, and several more rounds before it came down to two miners. Tom still held out for the Nightingale Mine, and Ellie had to laugh at how easy he made it look as he meandered down the street with the ore cart trailing him. The other miner was from the Golden Fleece, the mine Scott managed. Ellie hadn't seen Clayton anywhere around and though glad, she still worried about what he was up to.

The last of the ore was loaded into the carts, and each man hefted the rope used to pull it. Ellie scooted to the front of the boardwalk, hands clutching the wood rail. As the starter fired his pistol into the air and the men began pulling, Ellie found herself yelling at the top of her lungs, urging Tom faster and faster.

He crossed the finish line half a rope length in front, and Ellie squealed and spun around, bouncing up and down as she hugged Jesse. "He won! He won!" She gave him a quick kiss on the cheek then turned and joined the crowd in the street as they congratulated the huge miner.

There was a break in the festivities after the ore cart races so Jesse walked Ellie back to her house. As they walked, hand in hand, she couldn't get over how wonderful life was. The fact that she had gotten so excited over a simple foot race, as compared to the thoroughbred horses and NASCAR races she had observed, made her laugh with delight.

"What was that for?" Jesse asked.

She turned and hugged him. "Just because," she said, smiling.

He opened the door before he commented. "Am I part of that 'just because'?"

"Always, Jesse. Always."

Her smile disappeared when Jesse gave her a kiss good-bye, explaining he wanted to bathe and put some clean clothes on before the fireworks. Ellie panicked when he told her to wait for him at the house, but he promised to return within the hour. Besides, he'd said, there was plenty of time before the fireworks since it was several hours before dark. She still wanted to go with him, but she didn't need to make him suspicious. All she could do was wait as he disappeared into the trees.

* * *

The stage rattled into town, kicking up enough dust to chock a horse. If it weren't for the 5:15, Elmer thought, he'd be down at the ore cart races right now.

He put the wooden step in front of the stage door, hoping to hurry through this chore and still partake in the celebrations. "Don't know why the stage goes and runs on 'pendence day. Who'd be traveling, anyhow?" he grumbled.

The door slammed open against the stage. Before Elmer had time to step back, a bundle of petticoats and satin tumbled out. Elmer scrunched up his mouth as he looked at the newcomer to Peavine, then scratched his head in confusion.

"Well, ev'ning, Miss Elizabeth. How'd you get on this here stage? Din't I see you earlier today at the church picnic?"

Chapter 16

"What are you staring at, simpleton?" Dusty and hot, Elizabeth irritatedly flipped open her fan. She hadn't wanted to return to Peavine, not when Belmont had so much more to offer. But business was business.

She glanced around, not seeing anyone but hearing cheers echoing down the deserted street. The weasel-looking stage master shifted from foot to foot, apparently in a hurry to join whatever festivities the grand citizens of Peavine were having. Probably something gauche, like wrestling. Giving a tumultuous sigh, she rolled her eyes, hoping she could endure the next few days until she vacated this little hovel all together.

"Don't just stand there. Get my bags and take them up to my house."

"But, the races," the man whined. "I gots a bet on Tom from the Nightingale beating the Northern Pride and Judgment Day mines, along with ole' Scott's Golden Fleece. Why, I'll even bet--" he broke off when Elizabeth froze him with her stare.

Elizabeth snapped her fan shut, silently consigning the man to the devil, along with all the grumbly old men in this town. She narrowed her eyes, recalling the particular old man who had caused her such aggravation in the first place.

Lucky had practically dragged her to the stage, insisting the man at the telegraph office had sent him because her aunt was sick in Belmont. Her parents' relatives were an obscure lot in Elizabeth's mind, and she didn't even recall having an aunt, but she had allowed Lucky to put her on a coach. Any excuse was better than none to get out of this hick town, if only for a few weeks. Once she had arrived at Belmont and discovered its amenities, she had never even bothered to telegraph. It wouldn't hurt Clayton to stew a little.

In fact, if she and Clayton didn't have plans, she never would have returned at all. Belmont had a fine hotel with maid service and an opera house, and they had whiled away the afternoons playing lawn croquet. So, even though she discovered Lucky had tricked her, she had decided to stay for awhile.

Besides, in Belmont she had met William. She gave a little sigh. How she had hated to leave his arms, but she had assured him she would be back, right after she took care of business. And speaking of, her first piece of business happened to be walking toward her right at that moment.

Clayton Scott, suave even in the July heat, stirred her blood. So did William, but then Clay was here and William there, and a girl couldn't be expected not to enjoy the pleasures of whatever town she currently resided in. Now could she?

With no prelude, Clayton grabbed her arm and steered her around the corner and part way down the alley. Circling her waist, he pulled her to him. "I want to pick up where we left off," he whispered in her ear, grinding his hips suggestively.

Heat instantly pooled between Elizabeth's thighs. "Oh, I like it when you play rough."

"I'm glad you're finally seeing it my way."

Elizabeth pressed her breasts to his chest. "I've always seen it your way."

Clayton pulled back slightly, looking down his narrow nose at her. "It didn't appear so for the last month."

She gave a delicate shrug. "I can't help it if that old geezer sent me on a wild goose chase." Thinking again about William, she smiled. He had definitely been on the wild side. "I didn't plan to be out of town for a whole month."

Clayton shook her. Blonde brows came down over flinty eyes. "A whole month? What are you talking about. You only left town for two days with Cole."

"Jesse Cole?" Elizabeth laughed outright. That was one man she could do without. Though she had entertained a crush for him years ago, he didn't consider her the center of his universe. As far as Elizabeth was concerned, that relegated him to non-being status. Besides, he was a crummy miner and would probably die in that hole their fathers had dug without ever finding any gold. That was precisely why she had hooked up with Clayton.

Clayton scowled again and when Elizabeth tried to circle his neck for a kiss, he jerked her arms down, grabbed one forearm and practically dragged her down the street to his rooms. He never said a word until he slammed the door to his hotel suite and turned the key in the lock.

"Take it off." He glared at her.

"Mmmm, aren't we anxious," Elizabeth purred as she reached up to take the pin from her hat. She had barely placed her new confection on the dresser before Clayton spun her around, jerking on her jacket. Buttons flew everywhere.

Elizabeth shivered in delight at his brutal handling. She moaned as he cupped her breasts, pebbling the nipples between thumb and forefinger.

"Who are you?" He growled the words as his mouth came down on hers, crushing her lips before his tongue forced them to open. So caught up in his ferocious lovemaking she didn't understand his question, she tore at his clothes, wanting to feel hot, bare skin beneath her palms.

"Give it to me, baby," his coarse words rasped against her neck. He nipped her skin with his teeth and the ache in her intensified.

"Yes! Now!" She echoed his thoughts. She undid her skirt and shoved it down her hips. She watched as Clayton pulled off his shirt and vest as one piece, flinging them to the floor and then undoing his trousers. He didn't even give her time to remove her stockings, but pushed her roughly up against the wall. With one stroke, he impaled her with his length and she cried out.

Clayton handled her roughly and usually left love marks on her skin, but she loved the brutal strength of him and the forceful way he took her to the heights of ecstasy. Where William had been sweet and gentle and pandered to her every wish, Clayton saw to his own pleasure first. Elizabeth was just the type of girl who could hold her own and she always came right along with him. If she couldn't, he would have never seen her bed after that first time.

Clayton jerked one last time, sending her over the brink and straining for more. She cried out and offered her mouth to his kisses, drinking in the heat that was him. Gradually she became aware of the rough wall paper scratching her back, one stocking bunched down around her ankle, and a wetness slowly seeping down her leg.

Clayton released her and stepped back, his eyes still dark and stormy.

"Are you quite satisfied with yourself now?" She padded over to the washstand, rinsing a cloth and cleaning herself. She looked at him casually over her shoulder and found he hadn't moved. He still stared at her with questioning eyes. "That was a little fast. Don't tell me you haven't gotten any from Molly's girls for the last month?"

"Goddamnit! Why do you keep saying that? I've seen you practically every day for the last month, even if you haven't been putting out."

Elizabeth turned to face him squarely. "Clayton, I have been in Belmont for one month. If I had been here, rest assured I would have screwed you -- more than once a day if you wanted, just to keep from going out of my mind with boredom."

"I'll kill her." He began to swear as he picked up his clothes, jamming a bare leg into his trousers.

"Who?" Elizabeth stood directly in front of him, naked except for a delicate French lace camisole and silk stockings, re-tied above the knee with ribbon. She knew she looked good, and jealousy struck her that Clayton's mind was on another woman.

"Elizabeth. You...her." He stopped dead still, his gaze racked her form. Her nipples tightened automatically and the heat started all over again.

"Are you playing some kind of sick trick?" He jerked her to him. "I'm warning you, Elizabeth, I've taken enough off you this last month."

"It wasn't me, Clay, honest." She rubbed her hips suggestively against his.

"Prove it."

"How?"

"Do it like you did that time in Virginia City." He released her arms and stood there, hands on hips.

"Baby, you're all mine," Elizabeth purred as she slid her hands down his chest and circled the length of him.

* * *

"C'mon, Lucky, you can have just one drink," Carlos cajoled.

"Naw, I can't. I promised Zeke I wouldn't do it this time."

Carlos shook his head, not understanding. "What do you mean this time? Cole gave us the day off to have fun! Besides, nothing is going on now 'til the fireworks, and we'll be back long before that."

"Well, I guess one little drink won't hurt none. After all, you being Jesse's foreman and all, I can't see it coming to no harm."

"There you go," Carlos agreed, slapping him on the back and nudging him through the door of the smoky, dusky saloon. When Lucky looked across the room at one of the dance girls, Carlos slipped the powder into his drink.

"Here, drink up. Don't want to make you late getting to wherever you gotta go." Carlos forced a laugh, hoping he'd given Lucky enough sleeping draught to put him out. Mr. Scott had given him specific instructions to follow, and if he didn't get rid of Lucky and Zeke, he wouldn't get the charges set on time.

212

As soon as Lucky began to sway back and forth, Carlos hoisted him out of his chair, put an arm around his waist and walked him out of the saloon, joking with the bartender about Lucky having too much to drink. He stashed him under a mound of hay in the livery, then began the hike up to Jesse's cabin.

Earlier, he had watched as Jesse walked Miss Elizabeth home and then headed towards the tree line. It wouldn't take much to lure Jesse Cole to his mine. All the man thought about day and night was finding the damn motherlode. Well, the way he and Scott had it planned, Jesse never would find what he sought, unless it was in another world.

* * *

"Then it's someone who looks like you, damnit." Clayton exploded in anger at the thought that anyone, much less a female, had taken him for a fool over the past month.

Elizabeth's exact recreation of their night in Virginia City had sated his sexual appetite, and had convinced him that she was the real Elizabeth. Then who was the charlatan? Who had tied him in knots for thirty days?

Glancing out the window at the darkening sky, he knew it was time to set their plan in motion. He couldn't recall anything he had said to the other woman that would have leaked information, so he felt relatively safe.

He swung his legs over the bed, reaching back to swat Elizabeth on the butt. "Get dressed. It's time."

Elizabeth rolled over and stretched, the sheet sliding down past her hips to reveal the naked length of her. "She's not going anywhere, Clay. She thinks she's safe." Elizabeth secretly chuckled at the idea that someone, who apparently looked like her, had been living in Peavine for the last month and poor Clayton hadn't been able to get her into his bed.

"That doesn't matter. The plan has already been set in motion and it's time. Now get dressed."

Elizabeth gave a sigh as she began gathering her clothes. That was one thing about Clayton she didn't like. His ambitions were going to get him into trouble someday...soon.

She recalled the day she had found the codicil to her father's will, shortly after his death. She had realized that Jesse would never marry her, so according to her father's words, he would get the mine and she would get the bank. Which had been fine because she never thought he would find any gold anyway, and the cash of the bank was immediately gratifying -- just the way Elizabeth liked things.

But when she had shown the papers to Clayton, who was handling bank business, he had come up with a plan where, together, they could have the bank and the mine. He had explained that Jesse had given all the men stakes in the mine, so they had to take care of things before he found any rich veins. If Jesse were dead and no one knew about the codicil, a quarter of the mine would belong to Elizabeth, and they could use the bank's money to buy out the miner's shares.

A very clever plan, Elizabeth thought, as she dressed. She slid a look at Clayton, and wondered what he was thinking. He appeared quite anxious to see this thing through, and she wondered if he had changed the plan in her absence. Or perhaps had plans that didn't include her at all.

Well, she would just have to wait and see. She was sole trustee of the bank, even if Clayton managed it. She just might decide to buy the Nightingale shares herself and leave him out of it. Then she could go back to Belmont and William, or perhaps even tour Europe and find herself a Duke.

* * *

Ellie gave a last glance around the room she had occupied for most of the past month. She had nothing to take with her except memories, she thought as she laced up

214

her hiking boots and pulled her jeans down over the tops. Straightening, she tucked her shirt in and turned to leave Elizabeth's bedroom. A glint from the table at the window caught her attention and she scooped up her lighter. It was a dollar nineteen cent disposable and since she quit smoking, she didn't need it.

She started to lay it back down on the table, thought better of it and stuffed it into her pocket. Nobody knew exactly what would happen today. To preserve history as much as they were able, she'd better not leave any evidence of her presence.

A great weight pressed down on her shoulders and she felt a sadness beyond measure at leaving Peavine. She would even miss Zeke and Lucky. As she rounded the corner to the parlor, the front door opened, and thinking she must have conjured up the two, or that Jesse had returned, she pasted on a weak smile.

"Oh, my God," Ellie exclaimed. It was like looking in the mirror.

"Who the hell are you?" The woman screeched, taking a step back.

Ellie knew without doubt who stood before her. But she couldn't think of an answer to Elizabeth's question. The first words out of her mouth were, "Jesse doesn't think you swear."

"There's alot about me Jesse doesn't know, and thanks to my getting here in time, he never will."

Elizabeth started towards Ellie who spun on her heel and raced towards the kitchen.

The instance she crossed the threshold, strong arms grabbed her from behind, jerking her to a stop. Without hearing his curse as she kicked him in the shin with her hiking boots, Ellie knew Clayton held her. The evil scent of him was overpowering.

Elizabeth sauntered in, moving to stand right in front of Ellie. With a perfectly manicured forefinger, she tilted Ellie's chin up then very slowly moved her head from left to right. "She's really rather coarse, Clay. How in the world would you mistake her for me? And you say Jesse Cole is head over heels in love with her?"

Ellie struggled against his hold. Her heart beat frantically, knowing Jesse's life depended on the outcome of the next hour. Even if Clayton and Elizabeth held her hostage, Jesse would still be safe. Zeke and Lucky would see to that, or so she thought until Elizabeth spoke again, her voice catty. The woman knew exactly how to strike home.

"Maybe if he loves Elizabeth so much, I should go ahead and marry him. Then we could have the bank and the mine."

Ellie refused to believe her. She relied on bravado to keep her voice from quivering. "Jesse will never think you're me. Besides, he knows the plan and he's ready for you. Zeke and Lucky know, too. You'll both go to jail."

Clayton's arms tightened painfully, forcing her elbows closer together behind her back. Her shoulders burned and she tried to stand up straighter to ease the sharp pull. She only succeeded in causing Clayton to shift his hold, releasing one hand to bring it around in front to cup her breast.

Breath hot and vulgar close to her ear, he issued his ultimatum. "You owe me, bitch. Perhaps you want to pleasure me now to save your life."

From the front of the house, Ellie heard a faint shuffle of boots and a knock on the door. Just as she sucked in a breath to scream, Clayton clapped a hand over her mouth.

"It's that old coot, Zeke," Elizabeth hissed, dousing the kitchen lantern. "I thought you said Carlos would get rid of both of them. Silence her and get out front with me."

Oh, God, Ellie prayed, watching Elizabeth hurry from the kitchen to the front of the house. What chance did they have if Jesse's foreman, Carlos, was in on the scheme?

Before she could think about escaping, Clayton spun her around, still holding tightly to one arm. She saw his fist coming at her, but didn't react fast enough to keep him from punching her on the chin.

As lights blinked before her eyes and the darkness swirled around her, she couldn't react to Clayton's parting words.

"Since you like Jesse Cole so much, you might as well be blasted to hell with him."

Then all was black.

* * *

Zeke thought it odd that so many lights were lit and nobody answered the door at Miss Elizabeth's. He shuffled off the porch and around to the back of the house, just as the lantern there was doused. Figuring Miss Elizabeth must have heard him and was then on the way to the porch, he tried to hurry back 'round front afore he missed her.

"These old bones ain't working the way they used to," he grumbled to hisself as he rounded the corner of the porch. He grumbled, too, because he couldn't find Lucky, and the time was near when everything should be set to work right this go-round. Zeke's knee ached him like ne'er afore, and he couldn't help but worry.

"Well, hello, Zeke," the woman's voice came from the other side of the porch and as Zeke climbed the steps, he could see Miss Elizabeth sitting in the shadows with sneaky Clayton Scott.

He squinted at her; something sounded out of place. "Thought you was with--" he broke off, figuring he couldn't name Jesse since he knew their Elizabeth had been trying to keep up the pretense of liking Scott to get information. At least until two days ago when Lucky had rescued her and took her off to Jesse's.

"I merely came by to give my greetings to Elizabeth," Scott murmured in the dark, and something in his voice set Zeke's teeth on edge. "It seems like a month or more since I've seen her."

Zeke wished for a lantern. T'was too dark to figure out what was going on.

"Why don't you mosey on down to the saloon for a drink, Zeke. Elizabeth here has already told me Cole's escorting her to the fireworks, but if he doesn't get here in time, I'll be happy to offer my arm."

Zeke stepped off the porch into the dark, thinking he'd best find Lucky fast and get back up here. The hair on the back of his neck was standing straight up, he could feel it, and that meant somebody was up to no good.

* * *

"What are we going to do with her?" Clayton asked as he stood over Ellie's still form.

Elizabeth tilted her head and looked at him as he asked the question. "I thought you were the one with the plan." She was beginning to think Clayton rather inept, and her earlier idea took shape in her mind. Now that she had seen this impostor, she could pretend to be her, marry Jesse, and have it all. The bank would already be hers, and if Jesse did find gold, that would be hers as well.

As always, she would have to take matters into her own hands. But for a short time longer, she needed Clayton to see her plan through.

"Leave her. She's not going anywhere and by the time she comes to, it will be too late. Carlos should have Jesse at the mine by now, so that's where we go. If need be, we'll send Carlos back for her."

Expecting him to follow, Elizabeth left by the back door, hurrying along the path that lead to the trees. It had been a while since she had ventured up to the mine her father had once half owned, but she thought she could find her way. After all, she had a nose for money.

She explained her plan as they ascended the slight rise to the mine entrance. There, she waved Clayton off to the side. She could see a dim light deep in the mouth of the mine. Taking a fortifying breath, she grabbed the shoulder of her gown and jerked it down, the seam giving under pressure. She pulled a few pins from her hair, tossing them into the bushes then shook her head, causing ringlets to cascade down onto her shoulders.

Rushing forward into the mine, she screamed, forcing a breathlessness into her voice. "Jesse! Jesse! He's after me; you've got to save me."

"Who's after you?" Jesse wasn't as deep into the mine as she had thought, and at her outcry, he jerked his gun from its holster. Upon seeing it was her, he slid it back home. "Ellie, what the devil's the problem?"

Elizabeth smiled to herself. So, it wasn't just Clayton who thought she and the other woman looked alike. Her future was looking brighter by the minute. She took another faltering step, closed her eyes and dropped into a swoon. Predictably, Jesse rushed forward to catch her.

"Ellie, sweetheart. What--"

"Tsk, tsk. Isn't that just touching." Clayton stepped into the circle of light, catching Jesse by surprise and slipping his gun from the holster while his arms held Elizabeth. Clayton tucked it in the waist of his trousers then grabbed Elizabeth by the arm, shoving her towards the light.

"Get the lantern."

His lips curled into a nasty smile as he waved the gun towards the darkened mine shaft. "Let's go, dead man."

Chapter 17

Ellie groaned; rolled onto her back and drew a hand down over her face. She tried opening her eyes, saw nothing but stars and squeezed them shut again. Her chest hurt, as though a giant hand squeezed her heart. She swallowed past a throat burning with tears.

It was over.

She had landed back in her own time. From the feel of the hard wood floor beneath her, she probably laid on the broken down porch of the old hotel. The trip back to the present sure hurt a hell of a lot more than the one to 1870 Peavine.

Taking a fortifying breath, she turned to her stomach and pushed herself to her hands and knees, keeping her eyes shut so as not to get sick. That effort was futile, and she threw up what little food she had eaten at the picnic.

She refused to think of Jesse; couldn't allow herself to mourn for him right now. If she did, she'd curl up in a ball right here and never get up. She'd become part of the ghost town; a pile of bones with no heart and no future.

The only thought she let enter her head was getting back to Reno and recovering her photography equipment. She snorted. Wouldn't her publisher, Hartman, hit the roof if she tried to explain what happened. They'd all laugh, then send her off on a nice long assignment to the nearest sanitarium.

When she stuck her hand out, it hit something solid. She managed to crack open an eye to see the leg of the kitchen table. Using all her strength, she pulled herself upright and flopped across its smooth surface. Cracks and pops and distant light washed over her as she pried her other eye open. The fireworks must have started.

"Fireworks--" With a groan, she pushed herself upright, still leaning heavily against the table. She surveyed the darkened room, realizing she stood in Elizabeth's kitchen. With the next boom of a sky rocket, everything came back to her -- Clayton hitting her; Carlos turning traitor; Elizabeth being here.

"Damn!" She hadn't traveled back to her own time, which meant they hadn't blown up the mine yet and Jesse was still alive. He had to be.

Dizzily, Ellie stumbled out the back door and began the trek to the mine. There wasn't time to get help. She didn't even know if Lucky or Zeke were still alive. It was happening again! No matter what they had done, they apparently couldn't change history.

Still, she had to try to finish what they had started. At the creek, she used precious seconds to splash water on her face. Her vision cleared, although her jaw still throbbed painfully. If she had the chance, she was going to punch Clayton's lights out.

Ellie pushed herself beyond all limits as she stumbled and clawed her way up the hill to the mine. She focused only on putting one foot in front of the other, looking neither left nor right. She couldn't think about the dark; about Lucky and Zeke; about anything except rescuing Jesse. More than once, she had to slow down to catch her breath, but she refused to stop until she stood at the mine entrance.

Deep within the dark interior, she could hear faint voices. She peered into the gloom, heart pounding and palms sweating. A lantern lay knocked over on its side and Ellie righted it, looking around for a match. Remembering her lighter, she pulled it from her pocket and tried to use it to light the lantern. She couldn't get even a spark.

She glanced again into the darkness, seeing a faint glimmer of light. She looked back at the lantern. If she lit it to take away the darkness, whoever was in there would know she was coming. The dark could be the only thing between her and death.

Ellie took a deep breath, closed her eyes and prayed. "Please, dear God, help me through this for Jesse's sake." She took a dozen tentative steps into the mine before she stopped, barely breathing as her eyes grew accustomed to the gloom.

Slowly she moved forward, putting one hand out against the cool mine wall, using it to guide her. She shuffled along, using her booted foot like a blind man's cane -- tapping back and forth in front of her before she took a step. The illumination from the entrance faded. She swallowed, thinking only of Jesse somewhere up ahead; keeping her eyes on the pinpoint of light which flickered in the distance. She had no idea what she would do when she caught up with whoever was ahead, but instinctively knew she had to get there.

Ellie couldn't hear any voices as she quietly approached. When the mine shaft formed a tee, she turned towards the brighter shaft, too late realizing her mistake. The lantern sat on the ground, its wavering light casting shadows on the damp walls of the mine and sending shivers up and down her spine. Standing just at the far edge of the brightness was Jesse, hands tied behind his back.

"Jesse." She took a step toward him before she heard the voice.

"Well, well, well. It seems we can't get rid of the Ice Lady, now can we?" Clayton's drawl came from behind her, through the dark. A second later, he grabbed a handful of her hair and jerked. "How about a kiss, now, Ice Lady? It's too late to save yourself for him." Clayton laughed harshly, but when Ellie feared he would kiss her, he shoved her across the small space instead.

She stumbled against Jesse, grabbing his shirt front to steady herself. What she saw in his eyes when she looked up frightened her more than anything Clayton had done. How could she let him know she hadn't betrayed him?

"Jesse, I--"

"Keep her quiet," Clayton yelled as he pulled his pocket watch out of his vest. "What the devil's keeping

Carlos? He was supposed to meet us when he got the charges set."

"Sonofabitch." Jesse swore under his breath, just now realizing his foreman had betrayed him. As she stood so close in front of him, she could feel him twitching, and it took a minute or two for her to realize that he was trying to untie his hands. She had to find a way to help or they'd never get out alive.

"Keep an eye on those two." Clayton pulled a pistol from his waistband and shoved it into Elizabeth's hands. "I'm going to find Carlos."

The instant he faded into the darkness, Ellie slid her hands around Jesse's waist, finding the rope and blindly searching for the knot. To cover her actions, she pretended to cuddle close. When she caught his gaze, she pleaded with her eyes, keeping her voice pitched too low for Elizabeth to hear. "Jesse, you have to understand. I didn't know--"

"Who the hell are you two?" He hissed at her, even as his fingers worked with hers to loosen the knots. His gaze darted from her to Elizabeth and back, clearly unable to understand the likeness.

Ellie glanced over to where Elizabeth paced nervously by the opening where Clayton had disappeared. A pensive frown marred her features as she observed how Ellie crowded next to Jesse, as though locked in a lover's embrace. Ellie couldn't begin to imagine what she thought. Right now, she could care less. She had to save Jesse and give him a reason not to think she had betrayed him.

"You said you loved me," Ellie whispered, her fingers brushing his as she felt the knot loosen.

Jesse barked a laugh, not trying to conceal his words. "I don't think I even know you. A week ago, I couldn't force you -- one of you--" his gaze flickered between the two women, "into the mouth of a cave, even after you'd been shot. Now, you come right into a mine shaft without even a lantern to guide you?" He shook his head, and Ellie couldn't think of a way to make him understand.

Evidently Elizabeth decided that whatever game she and Clayton played needed some excitement. Ellie watched her come their way, and presumably thinking Jesse's hands were tied and he was harmless, she shoved Ellie out of the way. Keeping the gun trained on her, Elizabeth circled Jesse's neck with her other arm.

"Remember my sixteenth birthday, Jesse," she crooned next to his ear, but loud enough for Ellie to overhear.

Jesse stiffened at her touch, but didn't pull away. "I remember," he mumbled.

Ellie's heart broke. She didn't know the secrets of their pasts.

"Do you remember how I let you steal a kiss under that old tree behind the church?" As though to prove her point, Elizabeth proceeded to steal a kiss from Jesse, slanting her lips across his, letting her hips slide suggestively back and forth against him.

Ellie let out a cry and stepped forward, but just as quick Elizabeth jerked back, raising the gun to point right at Ellie's heart.

Elizabeth captured Ellie's gaze, her eyes glowing with evil light as she proceeded to lie to Jesse. "She's the impostor, Jesse. She and Clayton are in this together. I've just been waiting for the chance to free you; to get us both out of here."

If Ellie didn't know better, she would swear Elizabeth told the truth. Her words rang sincere because Ellie knew she was an impostor. But not when it came to loving Jesse.

Before she could protest Elizabeth's bold move, Clayton roared back into the circle of light, grabbing Elizabeth by the shoulder and jerking her away from Jesse. "You whore! You two-timing, back stabbing--"

He never finished the sentence because Jesse, freed from the ropes, barreled into him and together the two men fell to the ground in a death grip. Fists connected with flesh; one leg kicked out and overturned the lantern.

Ellie screamed as immediate darkness enveloped her, freezing her against the wall. The struggle continued and she thought she heard Elizabeth's harsh breathing somewhere close by, but she couldn't focus. She knew her eyes were open, but she saw nothing. She felt on the edge of an abyss, petrified to move even a fraction of an inch, for fear she would fall into the pit and die.

A gunshot echoed up and down the mine walls, reverberating again and again inside Ellie's head. Then, all was silent. She held her breath as a match scrapped against rock.

The sulfur flame appeared extra bright after the total darkness and Ellie couldn't make out who held the match aloft. It flared briefly then went out. The mild curse that followed, as though he held on too long and scorched his fingers, made her smile.

Jesse was alive.

Another match flared and Ellie saw that Clayton lay not two feet from her, Elizabeth sobbing over his lifeless body. Ellie scooted back against the wall, tucking her legs close to her chest.

That was when she felt the ground vibrate beneath her. A deep rumbling began, as though a giant animal had been awakened.

"Oh, dear God, it's started," she choked out the words.

Again the match snuffed out; again the agonizing seconds in pitch black, the earth quaking beneath her.

When Jesse lit a third match, Ellie felt panic tightening the muscles in her chest, knowing the final moments were at hand. Elizabeth must have sensed the danger also, because at the exact same instant, she and Ellie both held a hand out to Jesse. Silently, they each begged him to choose her; to save her from the destruction they all realized was only moments away.

Ellie couldn't fight anymore; didn't have any ammunition to use against Elizabeth, who had known Jesse most of her life. But no matter what happened, she couldn't leave without saying the words one last time.

"I love you, Jesse Cole. Always remember that, even when I'm not here to tell you."

His gaze found hers in the last flair of the match, but Ellie could swear his hand reached toward Elizabeth.

"No, I won't lose you."

Ellie was yanked roughly to her feet as the trembling increased. She stumbled blindly along behind Jesse, heart pounding.

They didn't go far before Jesse propped her against the mine wall. "Stay here," he shouted above the increasingly loud roar. "I can't leave Elizabeth."

He turned to go back to the intersection and Ellie realized she could see him through a blue haze. As he took a step away from her, a strange blue streak appeared to shoot straight down the other shaft, the light of it almost blinding.

Immediately it was gone. Jesse stepped around the corner, but was back within seconds, his face white as a ghost.

"They're gone," he whispered, "disappeared; both of them." As though to emphasize his point, a deep bellowing came to them from further down the mine shaft. The earth began shaking beneath them again.

Ellie reached for his hand, more scared than she had ever been in her life.

The physical contact seemed to bring Jesse out of his shock. He glanced back down the shaft where Elizabeth and Clayton had been only seconds before. Then, with a squeeze of her hand, Jesse took off running, pulling Ellie behind. Unerringly, he raced up one shaft and down another, all the while the ground shook beneath their feet.

Ellie didn't have time to be frightened of the dark. She put complete faith in Jesse and hung on for dear life. A pain shot across her ribs and she grabbed her midsection.

"Wait," she gasped.

Jesse turned, but never really stopped. He slid his arm around her waist and hugged her close to his side. "Come on, sweetheart. I don't know what the hell's down here, but we can't stop now." As if to emphasize his point, the ground swelled under their feet, the rumblings sending vibrations clear through Ellie's body.

When they did stop, it was so abrupt Ellie almost flipped head over heels. She couldn't fathom how Jesse could see in the dark, but he propped her against the wall, then gave her a quick kiss and didn't even miss her lips. "Wait here just a second."

Ellie heard gears squeak and wheels grind, but couldn't discern what it was until Jesse grabbed her again, lifting her into some sort of large bucket. The container jiggled when he hopped in with her, and Ellie grabbed the sides.

"Hold on tight, honey, and let's hope this headframe holds." Ellie felt Jesse moving beside her; could almost visualize him pulling, hand over hand, slowly raising the ore bucket up through the narrow shaft.

"They must have set the charges in tunnel A. It's a good thing we put this headframe above tunnel C. We couldn't have made it back to the mine entrance without getting caught in the blast." Jesse grunted in exertion and Ellie held her breath as the contraption swayed back and forth.

"I don't know what the devil happened down there, but I hope there's still plenty of solid rock between us and shaft A to keep the explosion contained until we get out."

Ellie cried with delight when she saw stars above them. By the time Jesse had tied off the pulley rope, they could see dozens of lanterns bobbing up the hillside as townspeople apparently came to the rescue.

Jesse jumped out of the ore bucket and reached for her, but in her anxiety over getting out of the dark mine, she already had one leg out, and they managed to tangle in each other's arms and go rolling down the side of the hill. Laughing and crying at the same time, Ellie let Jesse pull her to her feet and again they took off running, Jesse waving an arm and yelling for the miners to get back.

"She's going to blow!" He shouted as an incredible roar shook the heavens. Everyone hit the ground. Jesse pulled Ellie down, covering her with his body, until the last of the rumbling died and the dust settled over them. Slowly, he let her up, and they turned toward the front of the mine.

The same eerie- blue light glowed from the mouth of the Nightingale Mine, shrank in on itself, then burgeoned out again.

227

"It's happening all over," Lucky's awed whisper sounded directly behind Ellie. She turned and could tell by their expressions neither he nor Zeke knew if she was Elizabeth or plain Eleanor Weaver.

Thinking of only one way to convince them, she grinned as she spoke. "Damned if we didn't do it, you old coots! We really did it!" She raised both hands in the air, palms towards them. With a hoot and a holler, Zeke and Lucky each gave her a high five.

* * *

In the aftermath of the explosion, the townspeople all said it was better than the fireworks. Then someone noticed Carlos and Clayton didn't appear to have come to the rescue with the rest of the miners.

"Carlos is the one who set the charges in the mine, by Clayton Scott's instructions." Jesse told the Sheriff as questions began. "I don't know where they are, but I will definitely press charges when you bring them to justice." He gave Ellie's hand a squeeze as he spoke, and she returned the gesture, for neither of them cared to explain anybody's disappearance, nor what they had witnessed below.

The sheriff seemed satisfied with his answers, and a few at a time, the people from town drifted back down the hill, lanterns bobbing in the night.

Ellie had finally caught her breath, calmed her racing heart, and grinned mightily, knowing she had rooked history and remained in 1870 with Jesse. Her hands still shook, no doubt the result of the trauma she had endured. And now that she thought about it, a trauma which could be laid directly at the feet of one man -- the man who couldn't follow the simplest directions and stay out of the mine for one day.

She stormed over to where Jesse now stood by Zeke and Lucky, who were congratulating themselves for a job well done. It brought back memories of her transport to Peavine.

"Damn your hide, Jesse Cole!" She screeched at him across the space. "You scared the hell out of me down there."

"Elizabeth! You're a lady. You shouldn't swear." He tossed the comment right back, but she could tell by the twinkle in his eyes he could hardly contain his laughter. That was the last straw.

Toe to toe, her pert nose lifted in righteous indignation, she gave him the truth that would take the wind out of his sails. "I've had it. I'm not Elizabeth, I don't even belong here and--"

"I know." His voice was a whisper against her temple as he settled his hands gently on her hips, pulling her closer.

"You know? How?" Ellie was really confused now. He shouldn't have known anything; they weren't allowed to tell him.

"It's your smell," Jesse said, nuzzling her neck and kissing the sensitive skin behind her ear. "I couldn't believe two woman could look so alike, and in the dimness of the mine, at first I couldn't tell the difference. But when you stood close to me, I knew. You're all fresh air and sunshine."

Ellie wasn't convinced. "But why did you save me? I'm not your fiancée."

"Yes, you are. I never loved Elizabeth. In that instant when I saw both of you, I realized you were the one I loved, Ellie. From the moment you dropped into my life, I felt more alive than I ever had. I wanted more, I needed more. Elizabeth never sparked the fires in me that you did." He smiled at her, that shy, seductive smile that sent her heart racing.

He lowered his voice so only she could hear. "Besides, in those tight jeans, I'd know your cute little backside anywhere." For a moment, he scowled. "What didn't make sense is that you came right into the mine. I thought you were terrified of dark places."

Ellie kissed him deeply, snuggling as close to him as she could get, wanting to make sure he understood how

229

much he meant to her. "I'd travel to the darkest pits of hell for you, Jesse Cole. I need you in my life that much."

"Oh, bother," Zeke snorted. "Me and Lucky's going down to the saloon. Won't be back for a long spell."

"We won't?" Lucky asked.

Zeke smacked him with his felt hat before settling it on his head and giving his brother a shove towards town, muttering all the way. "For being 'round as long as we have, you sure are slow some days."

Ellie laughed before turning back to Jesse, wondering how she would make him understand what Zeke had said. Before she could form a thought, he shook his head, placing a finger over her lips.

"I don't understand, and someday you can explain." He paused and stared deep into her eyes, touching her very soul. "When we're old and gray and all I can do is sit on the porch and hold your hand. But that's an eternity away; an eternity in which I want to share your life and your dreams and give you my love every hour of every day."

"Really? For how long?" She teased him.

"For always and forever."

Epilogue

"Uncle Lucky, I wanna see my papa"

"Well, up you go then, Peapod." Lucky hoisted the dark-haired, little girl to his shoulder so she could see over the platform.

She giggled. "That's not my name."

"Nope, you're right, but you was born in Peavine, so you'll jest have to be my peapod. 'Sides, you and your brother look jest like two peas in a pod."

In answer, Lilly curled a chubby arm around his neck, squeezing, trusting him to keep her safe so high in the air.

Lucky felt they had done good in the last four years. He and Zeke might be too old to work the mines, but they sure knew how to take care of babies -- especially Jesse and Miss Ellie's two younguns'.

Zeke put a hand on Josh's shoulder as the boy stared at his papa who was just about to finish his speech. Their mama stood beside him all gussied up in ruffles and a huge hat with feathers in it. Sure didn't look like that cussing, smoking lady they dragged back to Peavine four years ago.

"Makes a fine Senator, don't he, Zeke?" Lucky asked.

Zeke nodded. "Guess that voice was right. Jesse had things left to do on this here earth."

Lucky reached up to steady Lilly, who was bouncing around and trying to clap her little hands along with the crowd. "Maybe now as he's got those mining laws passed, he can sit back and enjoy all that gold." He chuckled, thinking back to one particular Independence Day. After all the dust had settled, come to find out the explosion in the Nightingale had opened one of the richest veins of gold in the state.

"I don't think Jesse'll have a chance to relax if she's got any say." Zeke nodded and Lucky saw Miss Ellie hug her husband and wave at the crowd. "I heared her yakking the other day 'bout en-viron-ment or some such thing, and how Jesse had to go and make sure there was laws 'bout that, too." Zeke shook his head and Lucky understood perfectly.

Miss Ellie made a fine wife for Jesse, and together they made beautiful babies, but she sure enough had some strange ideas about what should be done with this ol' world they lived in.

If you *loved* this book
(or even just liked it)

Please leave a review ...
Authors need reviews! Keep this author writing.

Barbara Baldwin books also published by Books We Love

Lost Knight of Arabia
Spinning Through Time

Barbara was born in California and now resides in the midwest. She loves to travel and explore new places, which usually means each of her novels is set in a different locale. She has been published in formats from poetry and short stories to full-length fiction. She wrote and co-produced a documentary on state history which won state and national awards, but she really loves writing romance, whether it be contemporary, historical or time travel. Just for fun, each year she writes a Christmas short story for family and friends—some heartfelt and others whimsical — but always a gift from her heart. She has an MA in Communication, has taught at the college level and has made over 100 presentations at state and national conferences. She also loves to create art through pottery and fused glass, candles, baskets and quilts. Visit her website at http://www.authorsden.com/barbarajbaldwin.